The LAWS of GRAVITY

The LAWS of GRAVITY

liz rosenberg

amazonpublishing

Published by Amazon Publishing
PO Box 400818
Las Vegas, NV 89140

ISBN-13: 9781611099546
ISBN-10: 1611099544
Library of Congress Control Number: 2012922282

AS PROMISED, TO MY MOTHER.

What thou lovest well remains.

Acknowledgments

I want to thank my wonderful agent, Jenny Bent, for performing miracles every day. My brilliant and indefatigable editor, Kelli Martin, a cheerleader and wise advisor—every writer deserves an editor like her, but not everyone is so lucky. To the Dream Team at Amazon Publishing, working their magic. Deep gratitude to the late Justice John Flaherty of Pennsylvania, who took an early interest in this book, and whose support and generosity were unflagging. I quote from his legal opinions here, but any mistakes or missteps are my own. Thanks to the staff at the Supreme Courts of New York at Mineola and Riverhead for patiently answering so many questions. A long-overdue thanks to my late great friends and soul mates, the fiction writer Sheila Schwartz and the poet Jason Shinder. To Lucie Brock-Broido and Marie Howe, from whom I have here shamelessly borrowed stories about Jason. Thanks to Carrie Feron, for my start in adult fiction, and to Denise Silvestri, who believed in this book and promised to keep it by her bedside. Thanks to family and friends who stood by me and made all the difference. Long-standing thanks to Binghamton University, and the students who inspire me. To the Kates cousins, who are nothing like Ari. To my sister Ellen, always. Above all, above everything, I want to thank my children, Eli and Lily, and my beloved husband, David. You make getting up in the morning worthwhile; you make life whole. And finally, to all who struggle and lose and all who struggle and win—my heart is with you.

MAY 1982
The Cousins

The two cousins sat in the sunlight of a May afternoon, overlooking the edge of a suburban backyard. Ari Wiesenthal was seven, a sturdy-looking boy who wore a distracted look and seemed to have a permanent frown line between his eyes. His hair was dark brown, but moppy—somewhere between wavy and curly. Nicole was only four. She was as slight and airy as he was solid, with a pair of long, thin dancer's legs. For a child so young, she was eerily beautiful; red haired, her eyes deep brown and level. She was barefoot, wearing a sweatshirt over a pair of flowered shorts.

Their two chairs were angled toward each other. They were child-size versions of Adirondack chairs, and the dew still gleamed on the forest-green wood. The chairs had broad curving arms, and on each arm sat a highball glass with a straw sticking out of it, so the children looked like adults having miniature cocktails. The two sisters, their mothers, joked about it, looking out the kitchen window. Salt and pepper. The Inseparables. Their children sat with their legs crossed, mirroring each other. They could sit like this and talk for an hour at least, calmly and quietly.

The cousins had been this close from the time they were toddlers: Ari and Nikki. One brown head; one dark red with threads of strawberry blonde and gold and blood red running through it. Ari's toy poodles, the older dog, London, and Florence the puppy, lay sleeping at their feet.

Ari's mother was telling her younger sister a funny story. She was short, stocky, dark-haired, and dramatic. Suburbia bored her. Telling outrageous stories—at least half of them lies—was how she kept herself sane.

"It was a dinky little diner," she said. "And they were already asking people to make their early reservations for Thanksgiving. In *May*, for Pete's sake! They had up a little sign by the cash register. So on my way out I announced, *I* would like to make a reservation for Thanksgiving dinner."

"You didn't," said her sister, shaking her head disapprovingly. She was as fair and thin as her sister was dark and voluptuous.

"Yes, I did. The cashier asked, How large is your party? —Oh, I said. Just one. Party of one. But I like to plan ahead!"

The two sisters burst out laughing.

As if on cue, a large brown-and-black mongrel charged around the corner, growling and snapping his jaws. Forever after Ari, the boy cousin, would associate the sound of women laughing together with danger.

The strange dog lunged straight for the toy poodles, as if he'd heard them trash-talking him down the hill, and had come to kill both. His eyes were a bright yellowish color, closer to a bird of prey's than a dog's. He sprang at them, snarling, jaw flecked with foam. He lowered his head, fur bristling like a military crew cut. The poodles woke, hysterically yapping. The strange dog floated forward, sank his teeth into the smaller one's neck, then her foreleg, and there was a sudden flurry, a terrifying storm of sharp pained yelps and flying blood and leaping fur.

Nikki looked to Ari for direction, as she always did. Ari was paralyzed. He could not move, his hands frozen to the sides of the wooden chair. Nicole jumped to her feet, screaming shrilly, but she dashed straight for the strange dog, hauling him off the two barking poodles. Ari stared at Nicole's thin bare feet, planted apart on the wood deck. Her red hair was glowing, her mouth was trembling; he had never seen anyone look so *alive.* The mongrel abruptly changed his objective and sank his teeth into Nicole's wrist. The dog's tail went as rigid as if it had been made of stone. Nikki was shrieking but stood guard over the two smaller dogs.

At the same instant three things happened. The sliding door from the kitchen to the deck rolled open like thunder; Nikki's mother yanked a dish towel from the kitchen drawer and ran out to wrap up her sobbing daughter's hand. The mongrel changed direction again and began to gallop back down the hill, his tail flat. And Ari scooped Nikki into his arms and carried her into the house, her blood running in a line down his arm, like a wavy red ribbon heading toward an uncertain future. His face was as white as paper.

Later that night Ari's father, Charlie Wiesenthal, drove up and down the streets of Little Neck in his old Chevy hunting for the dog. If he saw it, he told anyone who would listen, he would kill it on sight. He would run it over with his car. His intentions were murderous. But no one ever saw the strange animal again. Florence, the puppy, walked with a limp after that, though she long outlived the other poodle, London, and never ceased to mourn him—not even after they brought home a cat to keep her company. And four-year-old Nicole was left with a scar shining on her right wrist like a thin white zipper, small and elegant.

OCTOBER 2010
Halloween: I Told You I Was Sick

The Huntington School District had decided to hold its registration in the fall, instead of spring—so Nicole found herself registering her daughter, Daisy, for kindergarten on Halloween. As she signed the form, her coat sleeve slid back and the childhood scar on the inside of her wrist revealed itself.

The neighborhood was a riot of witches, goblins, and ghosts hanging from doorways. Front yards were converted to graveyards with cardboard headstones that read "Now I'll finally have some peace and quiet," "I told you I was sick."

"I want our pumpkin to look friendly," Daisy had said. "I *want* people to come to our door." Not many trick-or-treaters would show up, although Nicole had strung orange lanterns over the house and put out a smiling jack-o'-lantern and would keep the porch lights burning till nine. Potter's Lane was a narrow street up a small steep hill from town, and most kids would skip the incline.

Daisy would be one of the older kindergartners next fall. Nicole and her husband, Jay, had debated about whether it was best to push her forward or hold her back. She was a September baby—typical Virgo, the eternal caretaker, order-loving, neat as a pin.

"Think about it this way," Nicole's best friend, Mimi, said. "Do you want Daisy going off to college when she's only seventeen?"

"No," Nicole said. "I don't want her going off to college ever."

"You'll change your mind when she's fifteen and steals all your makeup," Mimi said. Mimi was the wife of Nicole's cousin, Ari, which made the two friends feel related. "Blood is thicker than water, but I never understood why that was a good thing," Mimi would say. They spoke on the phone every day, sometimes more. It might be just Mimi testing out a new joke, but Nicole was a bad test audience, she said—she always laughed. Mimi was a comedy writer. Occasionally she performed stand-up, though she suffered from stage fright. She taught comedy writing at Nassau Community College; she lectured about it at elder hostels; she ghostwrote for famous comics; she took being funny seriously.

Nicole stood alone in the main corridor in her wool coat among a gaggle of other women, most of them ten years younger than she. All of these young women seemed to know each other and stood chatting in a close knot of five or six. Nicole wished Mimi were there to keep her company, crack some jokes. A few of the younger mothers rocked baby carriages back and forth, perpetual motion machines. Nicole felt lonely, like an outsider. She hoped this didn't mean that Daisy would be, too. The parents—nearly all of them mothers, with one or two fathers skulking around—lined up and filled out the kindergarten registration forms. They listened to a woman trying to enlist them in future PTA fund-raising events. Finally they were all congratulated, then dismissed like schoolchildren themselves.

Nicole clutched her registration form as she made her way blindly down the hall. She was shocked by the desolation she felt at the prospect of leaving her daughter in public school all day. The tiled walls were painted a pale institutional blue that no sprucing-up or Halloween decorations could disguise. Daisy now went to a Montessori preschool program three mornings a week. What would it be like dropping her off at eight every morning, not getting her back till almost three in the afternoon? The hours apart seemed to stretch ahead endlessly. They had begun a long, steady process of separation from which there was no return.

A large boy came racing by, probably a fifth-grader. His hair fell over his eyes, his belly bounced as he ran. He was as tall as a grown man. Nicole felt tempted to holler at him, *Pay attention!* Daisy was still petite, almost Lilliputian, the lower fifth percentile in both height and weight.

The first-graders had crayoned huge-eyed owls for Halloween. They were taped in rows to the walls. The owls all looked alike, with large cylindrical bodies and immense glowing yellow eyes the size of platters. Nicole couldn't see them clearly; her own eyes were filled with tears. She spotted another woman about her age, one of the few black women she'd seen on line, also studying the owls. When the woman finally turned her head toward Nicole, tears glittered on her chocolate-colored skin and ran toward her jawline.

"Look at me," the strange woman said. "I'm acting like a damned fool. Darnell is my baby. He's my last one home."

Nicole dug a clean tissue out of her purse and offered it to the woman. "Daisy is our only," she said. "We've been trying to have another, but it hasn't happened yet." She didn't normally confide in strangers like this.

"I'm Ruby," the woman said, accepting the tissue and blowing her nose. "Aren't we a pair?"

Nicole gestured toward the other parents gliding out of the building, chatting and laughing. "I don't know how they do it."

"Hard-hearted," the woman named Ruby said. She half smiled through her tears. "You'd be surprised how many women get pregnant once they got a child in kindergarten. I seen it happen time and again. Could happen for you."

"That would be nice," said Nicole.

"We should count ourselves lucky," Ruby said. "I know one woman, she registered her daughter for kindergarten last year. *Same afternoon,* she finds out she has a brain tumor. Incurable cancer. Dead before that child hit the third grade."

"Oh, God. That's awful." Nicole shivered, though she was sweating inside her wool coat. She suddenly felt sick. The story filled her with dread—as if some fortune-teller had wandered over, read her palm, and foreseen something terrible. Halloween was getting to her, all those fake ghouls and gravestones.

She wanted to cry to this woman, Take it back! Untell me that story! She wondered if the dead woman had lived there in Huntington, but didn't ask. Besides, what difference could it possibly make?

"Trust me, this is a nice school," Ruby said. "Your little girl gonna love it here."

"I'm sure your son will, too."

Ruby's face relaxed into a split grin. All trace of tears was gone, except the crumpled tissue still held in one large fist. She was a tall woman, athletic. "Darnell loves everything," she said. "He's a big kidder. Class clown type—I just hope he gets a teacher with some sense of humor."

All the way back home Nicole brooded about the woman who'd died. She couldn't stop thinking about it. That daughter left motherless—*dead before that child hit the third grade*, the grade she would soon be teaching again. She knew what little girls were like at that age; she remembered one motherless child in her class who had shown up at school still wearing her pajamas, egg smeared on her face. All that Halloween morning, the woman's words swooped in and settled crowlike in the back of her mind.

And there was that lump at the side of her neck—a swollen gland, her doctor said. But it would not go away, like the thought of this dying woman. When she'd mentioned it to Jay months earlier, he'd told her to go to a specialist, adding, "I'm sure it's nothing," his eyes bright blue. There was something about his confidence that irked her. Did he think people couldn't die? Did he think he could bat it all away, like an easy home run? She found her fingers returning to the swollen place on her neck again and again. Yet she refused to speak about it, as if ignoring it would help it disappear. And here it was Halloween, a holiday. Soon would come Thanksgiving, then the winter holidays. Time enough to deal with it in the new year.

Nicole and Mimi had arranged for their children Daisy and Julian to go trick-or-treating in Mimi's posh Glen Cove neighborhood. Later they'd come back to Huntington and answer Nikki's doorbell in their costumes. Julian's neighborhood was richer, safer, and gave out better candy. Whole candy bars, free movie tickets, packs instead of sticks of gum. Nicole's cousin Ari had bought individually wrapped Lindt dark chocolate truffles and organic dried fruit rolls. He insisted on giving each trick-or-treater one of each.

"Chocolate is high in antioxidants, and organic is organic," he said. "There's no excuse for giving kids junk."

Nicole decided not to mention that they had Snickers bars and red Twizzlers back at her house. In the old days, he would have known exactly what was in her cupboard. In the old days, as children, they would have had the same junk food and they'd have eaten it in secret together, up in the attic, playing board games.

Daisy and Julian dressed up as vampires that year. Second cousins, three years apart, they looked nothing alike, and were an unlikely pair. Yet they'd been inseparable almost from the moment of Daisy's birth, closer even than Nikki and Ari had been decades earlier. Each child seemed to feel safer in the other's company. Perhaps it was because they were each, in their own way, a little bit odd. For Halloween Daisy wore a long black silky dress with tiers of uneven layers and a hooded cloak trimmed in velvet, from a secondhand store. Julian kept drawing his vampire cloak partway across his face, showing off his plastic fangs, gargling "Nyah! Ha! Ha!" and pretending to bite Daisy.

Nicole took out the baby blanket she was knitting for Mimi's baby-on-the-way. The work was almost halfway done. Ari and Mimi already knew it was going to be a girl, so the blanket was yellow cable stitching with a new pink stripe. Mimi had taken every prenatal test available, under orders from the ever-vigilant Ari.

"The only test this baby hasn't taken yet is the SAT," Mimi said. "But Ari's already got her enrolled at Kaplan's." The mothers sent the children upstairs to nap for half an hour or so before the trick-or-treating began.

Mimi sank into a chair with a groan. She had just gotten past the first rough trimester a few weeks earlier. Till then she had been existing on crackers and peppermints. "Julian won't sleep, but Daisy might. We should let them rest, or they'll be basket cases by tonight," Mimi said. "You'll see next year, when Daisy goes to school all day. Hundred Book Challenge. Learning her colors and shapes. She'll come home with bags under her eyes, looking like death on a cracker."

Nicole's hands felt clammy, just hearing the word *death*. Trying to sound casual, she mentioned the woman she'd heard about that day, the one who had died so young of a brain tumor. She knit faster, as if she could push the story away with the clicking speed of the needles. "That mother died before her daughter even reached third grade."

"There's nothing scarier than having kids," Mimi said, her dark eyes wide. "Halloween can't touch it."

"I know. But just think—" Nicole began.

"I can't," Mimi said. "I won't. And you shouldn't, either. Everything to do with having children is terrifying. You can't afford to sweat the details—and it's all details," she added. "Now talk about something else, or I'm going to start telling knock-knock jokes."

Nicole knew there was no point in pushing. And anyway, Mimi was usually right about these things. "Are we dressing up for Halloween?" Nicole had brought along a large pink witch's hat with a broad brim. Some of the trick-or-treating grown-ups went the whole nine yards, bought expensive costumes, wore masks, cloaks—the works. Others just went disguised as suburban parents, trailing behind their kids.

"Maybe I'll go as a pumpkin," Mimi said, patting her stomach. She already had a high, small round tummy. She pulled her T-shirt tighter, to demonstrate. "See? I can paint the bump orange, with a little stem on top."

"Suit yourself," Nicole said. She unraveled and started over at the beginning of the row.

"It's not fair," Mimi said. "If I went a year from now, I'd have this cute little baby, and no matter how I dressed her, people would coo and say, Aw, how adorable."

"*I* think you're adorable right now," Nicole said.

"Well, you're in the minority," said Mimi. "Julian thinks I'm gross. Ari tactfully avoids the subject, and Dr. Kassis thinks this baby is going to come early. She wants me on bed rest by the time I hit six months."

"You're kidding," Nicole said.

"Nope. The baby's head is pressed too far down. My muscles aren't tight enough down there. That's what the doctor said. It's my own fault. I should have done more exercises."

"I don't believe this," Nicole said. "You're blaming yourself. Seriously. You are, aren't you?"

Mimi blushed. "I am not."

"You are." Nicole set down her knitting in her lap and looked sternly at her friend. She pointed one needle at Mimi. "Repeat after me: There is nothing wrong with my vagina."

"Okay," Mimi said. "I'm sure you're right."

"Repeat after me!" Nicole waved the knitting needle like a baton. "There is nothing wrong with my vagina! —Say it with me."

They chanted it together. "Again!" Nicole called.

"We're going to scare the kids," Mimi said. They chanted again, this time more softly.

"Thank you." Nicole picked up the needles and resumed knitting. She frowned, counting her stitches.

"You are completely insane," Mimi said. "I hope you know that. You *seem* normal, but really, you're not."

"Quiet, or I'll make you chant again," Nicole said.

———·—·———

Later, when Mimi went upstairs to check on Julian—Daisy was curled up against his side, asleep, wrapped in his vampire cloak—her son put down his chapter book and asked, "What were you and Aunt Nicole singing about?"

"We weren't singing, sweetie."

"It sounded like cheerleading."

"It was nothing."

He nodded and stretched. He reached for the vampire fangs and put them in his mouth. Then, when she nearly reached the door he said, "Mom? Who is China?"

"China is a what, not a who. It's a big country in Asia. Or it can be a kind of dishware, too."

"Then why were you singing, 'There is nothing wrong with my friend China'?"

"Oh!" Mimi said.

"Mom?" Julian said. "What's so funny?"

"Nothing," she said. "There *is* nothing wrong with my friend China."

———·—·———

Nicole posed the two costumed cousins outside Mimi's sprawling house and took photos. The sun was beginning its slow early descent; it was still light, but the peak of the day had turned. Now the colors shone out preternaturally bright and clear, crisp at the edges. This part of Glen Cove was so lushly wooded, it felt like stepping back in time. Inching along the expressway, you could easily forget that Long Island still had peaceful deep green corners like this, full of trees and meadows. Ari had created a full-length stretch of decorated pumpkins, alternating orange and white, a natural gate that ran the width of the property. He'd bagged his fall leaves inside orange plastic bags that looked like soft-sided pumpkins. The lawn was perfectly clean of loose leaves.

Daisy sat cross-legged and skinny next to one of the bags. Julian loomed over her, one cloaked arm around her, grinning fiercely, as if about to suck her blood. It was that time of day that Nicole's father—an amateur photographer—used to call "magic hour." The horizontal light touched every surface and made it gleam, fired up the colors in their costumes and in the changing leaves behind them. Even the black of Daisy's dress glowed under her autumn-colored hair.

Walking in the streets, a few of the first trick-or-treaters were meandering back and forth across Glen Cove Estates like dressed-up drunks, weaving from door to door. A few went in flocks or couples, but many of the children walked alone.

"We're so lucky," Nicole said to Mimi, standing close by her side. Their shoulders touched.

Mimi followed her gaze. "That our kids have each other, you mean?"

"Not just them," Nicole said. "We *all* do."

Then she snapped the shutter. It seemed, in retrospect, like the last perfectly happy day on earth. That photo of the two young vampires hung brightly in the Greenes' kitchen for years.

JANUARY 1, 2011
The Future

Justice Sol Richter lay awake beside his wife, Sarah, near dawn, his chin pointing at the ceiling, contemplating the year ahead. Looming up was his seventieth birthday, the age of mandatory retirement from the Supreme Court of New York State. He could picture himself lying there in the glimmering winter dark, arms crossed across his chest like one of the Egyptian mummies in the Metropolitan Museum. He'd taken Tylenol for his headache, and when that didn't work he had opened Sarah's side of the medicine cabinet and selected one of the small, flat pale-yellow tablets she took on nights when she could not sleep.

The judge had been frightened of the dark as a child. Often he'd crept into bed with Arthur, his youngest and gentlest brother. Sol's older siblings had passed away long ago, and slept peacefully now with his parents in Woodlawn Cemetery, that vast granite city of the dead at the outskirts of the Bronx. There lay Otto Preminger and Oscar Hammerstein, Miles Davis, Irving Berlin, Duke Ellington, and Herman Melville. His siblings' plots settled modestly beside "Our Beloved Bessie, Yiddishe Mama" and the imposing white stone belonging to Max Richter, Solomon's stepfather.

He pictured Woodlawn, a peaceful place, inhabited by marble angels. One stone couple lay entangled in each other's arms. It was especially beautiful in the autumn, when the granite glimmered beneath crimson leaves.

———·———

Now retirement was around the corner, less than twelve months away and the clock ticking. A lifetime gone in the blink of an eye. A few steps farther along lay Woodlawn and the plots that waited there. A man's working life defined him. Which meant he was—what? He still wasn't sure.

His wife Sarah slept soundly beside him, the overhead light turned down very low so you could just see a faint glow through the floral swirls of the milk-white lamp. Outside it had begun to snow lightly on the new decade. He wrapped his arms around her. She did not move. Her feet were icy cold, and he tried to warm them with his own—a small kindness given too late, and one she slept through unaware. She no longer looked like the young woman he had married; her skin at the chest was loose under her flannel nightgown. Yet she was still beautiful to him, still mysterious. She slept with her mouth slightly open, as if she had swallowed a disk of darkness.

"Happy New Year," the judge told the darkness, hugging her tighter, pressing himself against the familiar length of her body, and finally he, too, slept.

JANUARY 2011
Waiting

Nicole and Jay sat in the waiting room of the radiology department. He was reading *Sports Illustrated*, turning the pages with one hand, frowning in concentration, while the other hand clasped one of hers. Nicole did not read. She tried to ignore the soap opera blaring in a corner of the room. In an hour they had to pick Daisy up from school. They'd already been waiting forty-five minutes. Her heart was fluttering in her chest, fluid and ice cold.

"Maybe we should go," she said. "It's getting late."

Jay looked up from the magazine and smiled reassuringly. He inched his chair toward her, and strengthened his hold on her hand. "They said it would only be another five or ten minutes."

"Okay, but then we should go."

He shook his head. "Relax," he said. "Everything is going to be fine."

When someone walked into the room, her head jerked up. It was not the radiologist, but someone else she knew. At first she could not place him, his round, pleasant face, the navy-blue watch cap—it was the crossing guard at Daisy's elementary school, a man she knew simply as Angelo. He recognized her, too. His face broke into a wide grin, one gold tooth gleaming.

"Little Daisy, right?" He held out one hand to demonstrate the little girl's height.

"Right," Nicole said. "Jay, this is Angelo. Angelo—my husband Jay."

He sat right across from her, dropping heavily into the chair. He rubbed one of his knees. She had noticed whenever he helped them cross the street that he walked with a slightly rocking gait.

Jay looked up, friendly but cautious. "How you doing," he said.

"Angelo is the best crossing guard in the world. I once saw him charm a little runaway back into the school."

Angelo laughed. "Happens all the time. What are you in for?" he asked. He gestured around the room.

"Oh!" she said. "Tests."

"You okay?"

"I don't know," she said. "I hope so. We'll know better in about ten minutes." Jay had gone back to reading his *Sports Illustrated*. They had dropped hands, but Jay kept one palm protectively over Nicole's blue-jeaned knee.

"Doctors," Angelo said. "Doctors and their tests. You can't believe everything they tell you."

"I suppose not," she said.

"That's what I keep telling her," Jay said, looking up. He licked one finger and turned a page.

"I've got a bum knee," Angelo said. "Two bum knees, in fact. One I hurt on the job six years ago, mowing that steep hill behind the school. Smashed my leg to pieces. The school didn't want to pay. Made me go to court over it, but the judge was a true gentleman. He told them where to go. He says to me, Mr. Lucca, I understand you spent eight hours in the hospital waiting for the X-ray results. Can you tell the court why it took so long? I says, that's because to save money they sent the X-rays to Australia. Australia? he says. That's right, Your Honor. The continent of Australia. You may have heard of it."

Nicole laughed.

"Daisy is a real nice little girl," he said. "Some of the kids, they were poking fun at me on account of my swarthy complexion. Hurt my feelings. You know what she says? She says, I think Angie is beautiful just the way he is. She stood right up for me. Bee-yootiful. I told my wife about it."

"Sounds just like her mother," Jay said, at the exact same instant that Nicole said, "She takes after her father." They gazed at one another and laughed.

Angie looked from one parent to the other. "My wife says we should get your little girl a present. Wanted to bake her a batch of cookies. Trust me, you and your little girl, you're both going to be A-okay."

There was a burst of gunfire from the TV set. Nicole and Jay both flinched and turned to look at the same time. On the TV the music swelled. Angelo shrugged and laughed.

"If I'm going to find out I'm dying, I don't want to do it to organ music," Nicole said.

"Aw, now—" Angelo began.

"Mrs. Greene?" The radiologist was standing in the doorway, wearing pale blue scrubs. He blinked, as if surprised to find himself standing in the light. He wasn't smiling, and he didn't look directly at her. Instead he kept his eyes on Jay, who jumped to his feet, as if he were in the backcourt and could dart in front of her and shield her. She forgot sometimes how tall her husband was. There was a sudden roaring in her head as of rushing waters. When she stood, she tottered for an instant. Jay put out one hand; it closed protectively around her wrist.

"Good luck," Angelo said.

"Mrs. Greene? This way, please." There was a touch of impatience in the radiologist's voice, though he tried to disguise it by smiling in her general direction. Still he had not met her eyes. Then he turned and disappeared back through the doorway. Jay was looking at her pleadingly. She would have kissed him good-bye, as they always kissed at every parting, no matter how brief, but the radiologist had already gone inside. She would have stopped time for Jay's sake. She wanted to say something reassuring, but could think of no words. There was nothing for her to do but follow.

April 2011
A Moment

By spring of 2011, Nicole had been sick long enough that she barely remembered how it felt to be well. How to behave like a nonsick person, how to function in that world. It was like trying to stand on two land masses slowly drifting apart. Whoever had invented the phrase "in sickness and in health" had no idea how hard it was to keep the two together. The rules of each sphere, the measures, the people, the vocabulary—all were different. She could rattle off the names of every medication they had tried, but couldn't conjure up the names of her daughter's classmates. What was it like to wake in the morning with enough energy to meet the day—how to get through a night without pain, nausea, or panic—she no longer knew. The diagnosis of leukemia and lymphoma seemed to have come a century ago, falling like a hammer.

Jay and Daisy had learned to tiptoe around her. They planned morning expeditions on the weekends to Dunkin' Donuts so that Nicole could sleep a little longer. They went to parent/child swim classes at the Huntington Y. For the first time since her daughter's birth, Nikki was not the primary caregiver, not the center of her daughter's universe. After a particularly ghastly round of chemo, she'd missed one of Daisy's dance recitals. She vowed never to let that happen again, not while there was a breath left in her body. She got angry, and the anger carried her. From that day forward, she would schedule her medical life around Daisy, not the other way around. But the energy came at a price. Every month, every week, she was losing ground.

Nikki was in her midthirties, but she looked older these days; cords stood out on either side of her neck. Her eyes, a dark brown, gleamed with unearthly intensity, and her skin, still porcelain and glowing under the faintest dusting of freckles, had the bluish-white translucence of a teacup's rim. As a teenager she had been cast in a few bit parts in movies, and she had worked as a print model for Macy's in her twenties. Now, ill as she was, she was still beautiful enough to turn heads on the street.

Her cousin Ari rested his cheek on one hand and considered this, without wanting to seem as if he were staring. When they were children, he was mesmerized by Nicole's beauty, and often teased about it. He had learned how to sneak glances at his red-haired cousin, when to look away. It was not some silly romantic feeling that had moved him but something deeper. It was, he thought, the way some people felt about a sunset or a mountain view—the fascination you had with something so beautiful because of the sheer wonder of it. It was hard to believe they were related by blood. No one else in his family looked quite like her. His own parents were downright funny looking. Yet there Nikki was. She was the closest he came to having a baby sister. Ari had learned about loving by the way he practiced loving Nicole. And he hadn't always been all that good at it. He remembered the feel of her sharp flannel-pajamaed ribs when they used to play Tickle Torture, a game he had enjoyed far more than she did, with an almost guilty pleasure, and the thought that he may have actually tormented her still made him blush.

At the moment he appeared to be gazing just past Nicole into the depths of his long, sloping backyard. It was as smooth and green as a golf course, interrupted only by the turquoise cover of the pool. He could see his tennis court beyond a scrim of trees. Daisy and Julian were upstairs, playing a board game. Now and again he could hear shouts of laughter. The baby, Arianna, napped in her nursery on the third floor. The intercom to the nursery lay on the kitchen table, emitting nothing but steady, quiet static. His wife Mimi was still in the shower. The sound of rushing water overhead made a ringing background noise against the silence between the cousins. Here was a chance to talk. He never knew what to say. Once upon a time they had talked for hours, without awkwardness or reservation. When had that stopped? They were seldom alone together anymore, Nicole and Ari.

Nicole sat at her cousin's kitchen table, leaning her face on her hand. It was an expensive table that matched the long countertops, with the sheen of mother of pearl, but deeper, the shimmering electric blue of a twilight sky. Ammonites, millions of years old, were embedded in it as well. The table and counters, custom-made, had cost thirty thousand dollars.

They sat like mirror images, Nicole and Ari, head in hand. But it was really Mimi that Nikki was great friends with now; everyone knew that. In college she had introduced Mimi to Ari Wiesenthal, and then—as it seemed to Ari—his cousin had forgotten all about him. She grew up, she moved on. Suddenly he no longer knew all her tastes, her secrets. He remembered how, when she was a newlywed, he had bought her an expensive angora sweater for her birthday. Nikki had looked with him almost in pity and said, "Oh, Ari."

"What's the matter?" he'd asked. "You don't like it? Wrong color?"

"No, no, it's beautiful," she said, chuckling. "But I'm allergic to angora. If I wore this I'd stop breathing in an hour."

It was Mimi she went out to lunch with, and shopping, and to the movies; Mimi she asked for when she phoned late at night. Mimi drove her to the chemo appointments when Jay was working, chauffeured her back home, tucked her in bed, comforted her, cheered her on. Ari tried not to resent any of it. But it was hard. He had been robbed of one of the few intimate friends he had ever had. Now he felt clumsy around her, blundering.

"Your hair looks nice," he said. "Different hairstyle." Actually, he thought her hair had lost some of its usual luster.

"Oh, this." She rubbed the top of her head, and to his horror, the red hair moved at the scalp. "It's a wig," she said. She smiled ruefully. "How's business?" she asked in her soft voice.

"Awesome," Ari said automatically. Then, realizing he was speaking to his blood relative and not to a prospective customer, he said, "Slow as hell. Mortgages are tight right now—people keep waiting for the rates to go down, and the banks are acting crazy. Of course, I deal with commercial clients, so I'm protected from most of that. Can't complain."

"You still traveling a lot?"

"Constantly," Ari said. "I'm exhausted. I feel like I live in my car." Upstairs, the shower water abruptly shut off. "How are *you* feeling?" The words sounded too loud, as if he had shouted the question at her, but Nicole smiled.

"Exhausted. The latest chemo makes me sick as a dog. I feel like I live at the doctor's office."

"I'll bet," he said. "If there's anything I can ever do—"

"I'll let you know," she said. "Thank you."

"I mean it," he persisted. "I already saved your life once when we were kids, you know. I'd do it again."

"So you say," she answered, but the smile lingered at the corners of her lips. Her lips were full, almost pouty. She wore lipstick the color of cranberries.

"I did save you," he said. "You were drowning."

"Why don't I remember it?" she said. "Was this Cape Cod or Montauk?"

"Montauk Point," he said. "The Atlantic Ocean."

"Figures."

"What does that mean?" Ari said.

"Nothing, just—didn't I always get sick when we went to Montauk?"

"You got sick wherever we went. You were always getting stomach bugs. This time you almost drowned. You swam out too far. I dragged you all the way back to shore."

"Funny how I don't remember. I must have blocked it out." She moved her glass of lemonade around on the kitchen table. One wet ring blurred into another. The ammonites glimmered bluish black, with flashes of rainbow coloration like an opal. Nearly everything in the house was extraordinary in some way, and custom-made. It struck Nikki as funny because her cousin had always been such an ordinary kid. Not anymore. Even his suits and shirts were bespoke. Ari was a wine aficionado with a temperature-controlled wine cellar. He cooked large, lavish meals. He redecorated the house every few years, each time more extravagantly than the last.

He doesn't know what to do with his money, so he spends it, Mimi had told her. I think we should just stuff a few pillows with thousand-dollar bills and be done with it.

"I do remember you hanging my doll," Nicole said to Ari now.

"Oh, my God. One time. One bad thing."

"It's a vivid memory," she said, teasing him. "You made a noose and everything."

"Al put me up to it," Ari protested. Big Al, the eldest cousin, Ari's older brother, had been rough and sometimes mean. He'd been killed in a boating accident ten years earlier.

"Easy to blame everything on Big Al now," she said. "Better not let that happen when I'm gone." The scar on the inside of her wrist glimmered like a streak of light.

"You're not going anywhere," Ari said. "The doctors say the leukemia and lymphoma are chronic, not terminal. Remember?"

"I'm not responding to any of the treatments," she said. "That's why they switched from Tasigna to the chemo."

"I never found you unresponsive," he said. It sounded suggestive. He flushed and backpedaled. "I mean—you will," he said. "I'm sure you will." He heard his wife open the closet door, rolling it in its long track, then slide it closed again. Soon he would hear her light footsteps on the stairs, her easy laughter. He both longed for and dreaded her interruption of this rare moment of conversation alone.

"Listen, Nikki," he said, leaning forward. He was looking straight at Nicole now, directly into her dark brown eyes, which were as wide open as a child's, and seemed almost frightened, certainly startled. She reminded him of a deer, he realized. Any second she might unfreeze, change direction, and bound away.

He put his hand over her hand, pinning it down. "If there's anything I can ever do to help, I want you to tell me," he said. "I'm serious. We're family. Nothing will ever change that."

His hand was brown and square and muscular. It made her uneasy, the way he was holding her, staring intensely into her eyes. She stood it as long as she could—just a couple of seconds—then slid her own thin hand away.

The expression on his face shifted. He seemed at that moment actually ugly, his face heavy and resentful. Ari was not yet forty, but his hair, she suddenly noticed, was strongly threaded with silver. His chin sagged, he was starting to get jowls. "Right," he said. He looked exactly like his father, her uncle Charlie, a squat bullfrog's look on his normally handsome face. He squinted, as if he were in the throes of one of his headaches. Nicole would look back at this moment in Ari's kitchen and replay it again and again, as the seed of so much that would follow.

"Thank you, Ari," she added quickly. She reached out to touch him. He sat back and folded his arms. "You've always been so generous." It was true. Ari had bought Daisy an elaborate swing set for her fifth birthday, with swings and slides and fancy red cedar climbing equipment, something far nicer than they could have afforded on Jay's salary. Ari had picked up more restaurant tabs than Nikki could count, treated them to plays and concerts, pretending a client had given him the tickets, pretending they'd cost nothing.

But Ari was already looking out the back window again, picking at his upper lip, the spitting image of his father. Silence dropped down between them like a curtain. It was not the comfortable silence of old friends and relations, but a dull wordlessness. The thing held suspended between them, delicate as a spider's web, whatever it was, in that moment, whatever assurance he had wanted, whatever he had hoped for—now hung broken, too tiny to detect or mend.

MAY 2011
Flying

Daisy and Julian were playing at Daisy's house, which was always less fun than his own house. There was no swimming pool, for one thing. No video games, no large-screen TV, no basement movie theater, no rec room, and Daisy always wanted to play Barbies. If any of Julian's friends had known he sometimes still played Barbies with his little girl cousin, he might as well have packed up and moved to a new school. Luckily he went to Glen Cove, Daisy lived in Huntington.

Julian was turning eleven that June. He was one of the tallest kids in the fifth grade. He had a face that looked at one instant like an grown-up's, and the next like he was still a little kid—there was an openness about his features, a purity of expression, and he still dressed like an elementary school kid in elastic-banded sweat pants and Velcro shoes: "to save time," he said.

He wanted to be an efficiency expert when he grew up. He went to school with his pajamas on under his clothes for this reason. "Why waste time changing clothes twice?" he asked. He was fascinated by the whole idea of saving time, minute by minute. He liked to time himself in the shower. His best time so far was two minutes and forty-eight seconds. His favorite possession was a waterproof stopwatch with a built-in compass, calendar, and calculator. Julian laughed like an adult, in short, surprised barks. The sharpness of his profile—he already had a long, beaked nose like his father's—made him sometimes look like a teenager, sometimes like a wise old man. Around his friends he said little, but he was the leader of most groups, from school to sports to Hebrew school. He had won the leadership award in his fifth-grade class.

"Are you sure you want to invite Daisy to your birthday party?" Ari had asked Julian earlier that week. "She'll be so much younger and smaller than everyone else. How much fun is she going to have?"

"I'm sure," Julian said.

"Maybe we could have a separate family get-together, go out to dinner someplace fancy. Someplace elegant. Daisy might like that better." Ari was smiling his wide salesman smile, doing his best to convince.

"I'm super sure, Dad. We can still do that, too. She's invited to my party, I'm not going to hurt her feelings."

"But—"

Julian held up one small broad hand, palm out, like a traffic cop. "Drop it."

Now Julian watched Daisy lay out all her dolls. He pushed his black-rimmed spectacles back up—they were always sliding down, giving him a professorial air. Eleven Barbie dolls and one lone Ken doll, a token male in a sea of overdressed females.

This moment was just the opposite of his upcoming paintball birthday party, which was going to be a testosterone fest in June in the woods in Great Neck. Daisy would just sit on a bench and watch, he was pretty sure.

She might decide to play for a little while. He'd slaughter anyone who tried to nail her with a paintball. That paint stuff could sting. It wasn't his idea of fun. Julian would rather have herded everyone into the basement for a Charlie Chaplin film festival, with gourmet popcorn and movie-themed party favors, but his father had researched all the Long Island paintball venues and come up with the best one, with state-of-the-art equipment, the one that had been written up in *New York* magazine. So—paintball it was.

Julian tried to shove the Ken doll's feet into a pair of loafers, hoping they were the right size. They were not. Everything else was a narrow high heel in silver or hot pink.

"This is the mommy doll," Daisy said, choosing her red-haired Stacey doll, the hair in a 1950s-style flip, wearing a blue-flowered housecoat. "She's lying down because she doesn't feel good." She placed her carefully down on a pink-and-yellow-striped toiletry case, which Daisy pretended was a sofa.

Julian laughed. "Mommies don't lie down. They stand up and tell jokes."

"Yes, they do. Mine does." Her dark eyes, fixed on his, looked worried and deep, deep, almost fathomless. Daisy's skin was tawny; her hair had grown past her shoulders and halfway down her back. He was fascinated by her red hair. It was as if it were made up of hundreds of silky threads, each one a slightly different color—russet and gold, apricot and cherry red, all cascading in a coppery waterfall. She was going to be gorgeous, he thought, feeling almost angry about it. He would have to protect her—her whole life, creeps were going to be chasing after her.

As if she had read his mind, she grabbed his hand and hung on to it, squeezing it so hard it actually hurt him, made him say, "Hey!" before he realized she was not doing it to be tough.

"I'm scared," she said.

"What are you scared about?" he said, like he didn't know. "Don't be scared. Your mom's going to be fine. Everyone says so."

"But what if they're wrong?" she said. "What if she isn't fine? Sometimes I think they're all wrong, and she's going to die. Who will take care of me?"

Julian laid the Ken doll down on the make-believe sofa. "Your dad will. My family. All of us. Look, Daisy, look at me."

But she wouldn't look at him. She had picked up the tiny brown toy loafers and was working the Ken doll's feet into them toe first, then stretching the brown plastic over the heels. Her hair glimmered in the light.

Julian scootched forward and put his arm around his cousin. She didn't exactly lean into him, but she didn't pull away, either. The only time she ever really showed affection was when you were saying good-bye, or when she was about to go to sleep. Then she would cling to you like a monkey.

"I will always take care of you," he told her. "You don't ever have to worry. Ever."

"Okay." She raised the Ken doll up in the air like a trophy. "See?" she said. "The shoes fit fine. You just have to know how to do it. You have to pay close attention."

Later, they went into her backyard and Daisy made Julian push her on the old tire swing. It always made him nervous; he wished the thing had a seatbelt or something.

"Make it go super-fast!" she said.

"Right," he said, giving it a slight push.

"Not like that." She jumped off the tire and hung on to two of the ropes that held it suspended from the maple tree. She raced around and around in a circle, leaning back, hanging onto the ropes. It made him dizzy and sick to his stomach to watch. Then, suddenly, both feet left the ground and she was whirling around like a dervish on top of the tire, legs curved, head thrown back, her red hair whipping across her face, in a blur of motion.

"Don't," he pleaded. "Daisy, slow down."

But she was too busy flying.

—— · ——

"So Sam runs into his old friend Irving on the street and says, 'Irving, I got a new hobby.'" Mimi pronounced it with a guttural wet Yiddish *ch* sound— "chobby." She was trying to feed Arianna, who kept twisting her round little head away, lips tight.

"'What kind of hobby?' Irving asks.

"'I keep bees,' Sam says.

"'Bees? That's a hobby? You keep them in the house—don't they sting you?'

"'Nah,' says Sam. 'I keep them in the bedroom.'

"'In the bedroom? They don't fly around and sting you?'

"'Nah,' says Sam. 'I keep them in the closet.'

"'In the closet?' Irving says. 'Don't they get into your clothes?'

"'I keep them in a sealed box.'

"'Don't they die?' Irving asks.

"'Fock 'em,' Sam says. 'It's just a hobby.'"

As if on cue, Arianna seized the bowl of rice cereal and dumped it on the kitchen floor.

"Everybody's a critic," Mimi said.

Nicole laughed, that lovely contagious laugh of hers, and the baby laughed, too. Her laugh sounded like heh-heh-heh. It startled the two women and made them laugh all over again.

But there was a darker something behind Nicole's eyes, Mimi thought. Something akin to desperation, a look that Mimi had never seen in her best friend before, not in all the years they'd known each other, not even these last few hard months after the diagnosis. Mimi felt a heaviness in the pit of her own stomach. Nicole kept toying with the salt and pepper shakers on the table, swapping them around, back and forth. She seemed on the verge of asking for something. What could she possibly want that Mimi would not instantly give?

Still, Mimi was scared. Her instinct, normally so loving, was to run and hide. "I wish you'd come with me to the elder hostel," Mimi said to cover over the silence. "Daisy would love it there. They have a huge swimming pool, full of old Jews bobbing around. Enough chlorine to kill any germ within a hundred-mile radius. Nineteen-fifties-style elegance. But a tough crowd. Very tough. You know the joke: Three cranky old Jewish women are eating lunch. Constant complaining. The waiter comes by at the end and says, 'Well, ladies, was *anything* all right?' I need you there with me. We can hang out by the pool and breathe chlorine fumes."

"Tempting," Nicole said. "Let me think about it, okay?"

"You're done with treatments for now, aren't you?" Mimi asked.

"For now," Nicole said. "But it makes me nervous to be far away from the hospitals I know." She made a wry face. "I'll fit right in at an elder hostel. Hobbling around. Afraid to leave my doctors." She drummed her fingers on the tabletop. The baby tried to imitate her.

"This baby will not eat," Mimi said. "Seriously. Not a bite. She seems offended by the sight of a spoon." To demonstrate, she lifted a spoon and brought it close to her daughter's little lips. Arianna looked like she was about to cry, swatted it away.

"Hey," Nicole said, interested. She sat up a little straighter.

"All she does is drink from a bottle."

"You're not breast-feeding her anymore?"

"Can't," Mimi said. "She bites."

Nicole chuckled and shook her head.

"The kid's got teeth, and she's not afraid to use them. Top and bottom. I've got the scars to prove it," Mimi said.

"But she really won't eat?"

Mimi lifted the spoon again. The baby tightened her lips.

"How old is she now?"

They both bent close to the baby, as if examining an interesting specimen. Her hair was dark, like her father's, and springy.

"Almost fourteen months. I'm going nuts. She's chugging eight bottles a day. She's still waking up every four hours during the night. She's exhausted, I'm exhausted, Ari's acting like a son of a bitch. He hates it when he can't fix everything. Does she look underweight? I'm honestly afraid she's starving."

"Have you tried finger foods? Maybe she just doesn't like silverware." Nicole put one hand under the baby's face and tilted it up. "Is that right, Rianna? Are you a little savage like your auntie Nicole?"

Arianna was named after her father, in defiance of Jewish custom never to name a child after a living parent—but no one ever called her anything but Rianna, or sometimes, Ana.

"We've tried finger foods," Mimi said gloomily. "Cheerios, noodles, cooked baby carrots. I think she looks a little pale. Does she seem unhealthy to you?"

"Well, I'd be the wrong one to ask," Nicole said, "but no." She lifted one little forearm and held it between two fingers. "She looks skinny, though. We have to fatten you up so we can eat you," she told the baby, who reached for her bottle and drank greedily.

"Maybe she's a budding alcoholic," Mimi said. "All she does is drink."

"Maybe." Nicole appeared to study the baby for a few minutes. Mimi again had the distinct impression she was about to ask for something, something urgent. Instead Nicole turned her head and said, "Have you thought of dipping the end of the bottle into food?"

"What?" Mimi said.

"Get me a jar of baby food," Nicole said. "Please."

Mimi handed her some baby carrots. "Organic, of course. Ari wants me to grind my own. He bought a three-hundred-dollar food mill. It just sits there. You want it?" She stood by the counter.

"No, thanks," Nicole said. "I'm still eating solids. So far. You know, Ari grew up on a lot of TV dinners. His mom was not exactly the domestic type." She unscrewed the jar, plucked the bottle out of Rianna's small hand. "I'll get that back to you in just a minute," she said. The baby looked more interested than worried.

"Ba ba," Rianna said.

"Coming right up." Nicole dipped the nipple of the bottle into the baby food and handed it back to the baby. Rianna looked at it for maybe half a second before plopping it into her mouth. Her eyes widened. She sucked more vigorously. Stopped, held it out to Nicole.

"Mo'," she said.

Mimi fell back into her seat, her jean-clad legs splayed out in front of her. She dressed more like a teenage boy than a grown woman, and kept her dark curly hair short. "You are a genius, my friend," she said. "A serious, freaking genius."

Nicole dipped the bottle nipple into the jar of food again and handed it back to Rianna, who grabbed for it.

Mimi was half laughing, half crying. "Oh, my God. Nicole! It's amazing. *You* are amazing. See, she was hungry. You saved us. The poor little kid was starving." They both watched Rianna sucking at the bottle. She held it out for a refill.

"You try it," Nicole said.

Mimi did so, dipping the end of the bottle slowly and seriously, as if this were some kind of elaborate science experiment.

"Mo!" Rianna cried. "Mo!"

"Pick up the pace, girl," Nicole said.

Mimi's hand was shaking when she fed her daughter.

"I bet once she gets the idea, you can sneak it to her on a spoon, too," Nicole said.

"How can I ever thank you enough for this?" Mimi said. "I'm serious."

"Are you?" Nicole turned her deep gaze on her best friend.

"No problem," Mimi said. "What can I give you? Half my kingdom. Just name it."

Nicole waved it away, but her face looked thoughtful. The dark, fathomless something, whatever it was, shadowed her eyes again. She was keeping something secret. "I don't know—a free vacation to an elder hostel in the Catskills. Don't worry. I'll think of something."

And for no reason at all Mimi felt frightened again.

Midsummer 2011
Your Sister Rose

The friends sat on the balcony of their hotel suite in the balmy summer night of the Catskills. The balcony railing was old black wrought iron, rickety, attached to the white stucco of the hotel. Inside, the air conditioner worked fitfully and noisily. The baby slept in Mimi's room. Julian slept on the twin bed that matched Nicole's and sat beside it, like a bed in a sitcom from the 1950s, divided by a single night table and a single table lamp. All of the furniture, and the hotel itself, looked like some outcast from another era.

Daisy, small enough to sleep in a junior bed at home, lay curled up on the rollaway cot, her red hair fanned out around her and her rump in the air, covered by a flowered summer nightgown. The lamp still burned over Julian's head—he had fallen asleep reading, and the book now lay open on his chest. *To Kill a Mockingbird.* One hand lay over the book, spread out over his chest, as if he were pledging allegiance to it in his sleep.

Cicadas whirred noisily in the green trees, drowning out even the noisy air conditioner.

"I'll never eat again." Mimi groaned. They had finished an enormous dinner an hour before, in the yawning expanse of the hotel dining room, with its glittering old chandeliers, ornate as old ladies' dangling diamond earrings.

"You said that last night," Nicole reminded her. "And the night before." She was reading a novel, or trying to, under the dim balcony light. She wore reading glasses with lime-green rims; Daisy had picked them out. Nicole's eyes had gotten worse since the chemo.

"I mean it. No matter how much they beg me tomorrow—no matter how many knishes they offer, how much *derma*, how many plates of chopped liver... Never mind. I'm getting hungry again, just thinking about it." Mimi's face was plump, making her look heavier than she was; she was pear-shaped. She was always on one kind of diet or another. She consulted a pad of paper in her lap.

"So there's a Jewish talking doll," Mimi said. "You pull the string at the back, and it says, Again with the string?" She sat with a pile of notebooks, papers, and books next to her chair. "That's the quintessential Jewish joke."

"No," said Nicole. "The singing telegram one."

"Oh. —Right," Mimi said. "That's a good one, too."

"Tell it," Nicole said.

"You've heard me tell it fifty times."

"Tell it fifty-one."

Mimi sighed, but it was a patient, contented sigh, the sigh of an expert. "Okay, there's a knock on the apartment door, and Gertie sees a man with a telegram standing there. 'A singing telegram!' she cries. 'I've all my life wanted a singing telegram!'

"'Lady,' the man says. 'This ain't no singing telegram. That costs extra.'

"'Can't you sing it?' Gertie begs. 'I've always wanted a singing telegram. Please, mister, please.'

"The man shrugs inside his uniform. He hums a little intro, vaudeville style, strikes a pose—'*Ba* da, da dum dum *dum*…Your sister Rose is dead!'"

"That's it," Nicole said. "That's the perfect Jewish joke."

"Well, of course," Mimi said. "It's about family and death."

"And money," Nicole said. "The holy trinity."

"I'm an antique in the comedy world," said Mimi. "Nobody tells jokes anymore, that's why old people like me. The new comics all tell heartbreaking stories. Or long political rants. Nobody actually tells jokes, they're considered corny."

"I like corny," Nicole said. "The cornier, the better."

"I can't tell them that keeping-bees joke," Mimi says. "Such a shame."

"Why not? Is someone allergic to bees?"

"I can't say *fock*. 'Fock em, it's just a chobby.'"

"Can't you substitute something else?"

Mimi shakes her head. "I've tried. Screw 'em. The hell with 'em. —It has to be *fock*. It's like trying to substitute a Yiddish word with English. Some words are irreplaceable."

"*Fock* is one of them," Nicole said.

"Definitely," Mimi said. "Speaking of which—"

Nicole tilted her head. "Are you about to tell me something about your sex life that I really don't want to know?"

"We hardly do it anymore," Mimi said. "Not since the baby arrived. Is that normal?"

Nicole closed her eyes. She tilted back her head, revealing her long, beautiful throat. "I don't know anymore. I can't remember. This is the new normal."

Mimi touched the back of her friend's hand. "I'm sorry," she said.

"Mimi," said Nicole.

Mimi's heart lurched. She experienced what people feel during a car accident. Time slowed down. Each leaf hanging black on the trees in the Catskill darkness became suddenly visible and distinct to her. She heard the cicadas and the noisy hotel air conditioner, she felt the breeze stir on her face. Down in the parking lot, a car door slammed. Later, much later, she believed she could trace everything else that would happen in her life to this one instant.

Nikki leaned forward on her chair, laying her book facedown on her lap. "I need to ask you something, and I know it's going to be hard. Try not to make a joke for a few minutes. Okay?"

"Okay," said Mimi.

"My doctor said that I might be helped by cord blood," said Nicole.

"Cord blood?" Mimi echoed.

"You know—Julian's cord blood."

"Oh," Mimi said.

"I know," Nicole said. "I know it's a tricky subject."

"Ari is—Ari is nuts about it," Mimi said. "Because of what happened with the baby." They had banked Julian's cord blood—an expensive procedure in those early days when it was still so new and experimental—and kept it stored at great cost, because Ari was fussy about the conditions. He had found just one private hospital in California that he trusted, but it cost five times what everyone else charged. When the baby came along, Ari insisted they preserve and store her umbilical cord as well. But Rianna was an emergency C-section, things happened fast, and by the time the surgery was over, someone had accidentally disposed of the cord. Ari had raged about it for weeks. He had threatened to sue the hospital. Even now, it was not a safe subject. That was our safety net! he had fumed.

That was our children's life insurance policy. And some *moron* just threw it away. He had hounded the hospital administrators till the woman in charge of labor and delivery was moved down to another ward.

"Let me talk to Ari," Mimi said. "You know if it's up to me the answer is yes. Whatever you need. Whatever might help. Ari controls all that stuff."

"I'm not responding to the chemo well enough to get a bone marrow transplant," Nicole said. The words started tumbling out. "Cord blood is much more straightforward than bone marrow. They've had some amazing results. With family members, it's more likely to work. And it's effective for both leukemia and lymphoma. But we might not even be a match." Then she added. "We should probably have a little blood drawn first...It's funny—I hate the idea of Julian having to give blood because of me. And yet here I am, asking for this enormous thing."

"It's not so enormous," Mimi said. "You know how we feel. We would do anything to help."

"Well, Julian might not even be a good match," Nicole said again, this time appearing to talk directly to the darkness. "He's a second cousin."

"No, he might not be." Mimi felt a sudden tug of hope, like the tug of a kite string going up. Then she hated herself for hoping against hope.

"Fock it," Nicole said. "Let's just see what happens."

"Fock it," Mimi agreed.

———·———

In fact, it was much easier than Mimi had imagined. Ari rubbed his forehead—a characteristic gesture for him, he was prone to migraines—but then he nodded.

The LAWS of GRAVITY

"Okay," he said.

"Okay, really?" Mimi asked.

"She's my cousin," Ari said. "Blood is blood."

"This might save her life," Mimi said.

Ari didn't smile. "It might not," he said. "And we'd be using up the one thing that could protect our children. Both of our children."

"By the time they need it, they'll have found something else," she said. "Our kids will have kids of their own. I promise, we can bank the cord blood of every single grandchild."

Then he did grin. "I'd like a dozen grandchildren," he said. "I want a tribe!"

"Run that by Julian and Arianna," she said. "It's a tad early."

"You know what Julian told me the other day?" he said. "He told me he plans to marry Daisy. He wanted to make sure it would be legal."

"Is it?"

Ari wrapped one hand over his other fist and studied both hands on the table. "Second cousins," he said. "It's not illegal but hardly the best gene pool. He'll forget about it the first time some little teenybopper sashays past in a short skirt. Trust me, I felt the same way about Nicole when I was a kid."

"You did?" Mimi was amazed. Ari had never mentioned anything about it.

"Oh sure," he said. "She was gorgeous. Brave. Gentle." Then in a more casual voice he added, "She was also the only girl I was ever around."

———

They all went out to dinner to celebrate, Jay's treat. They ate at a Greek place in downtown Huntington. Three old men stood in front, singing Greek songs, and one of them played a stringed instrument that looked like a short round guitar. Their songs all sounded sad. An upturned hat sat nearby. A few people dropped in coins, or dollars. Jay dropped in a twenty-dollar bill; he was grateful for everything. He could not let go of Nicole, he had to be touching her every minute, as if he'd just gotten her back from an infinitely far and foreign country.

Daisy and Julian were fascinated by the toothless Greek singers. It was a warm Friday night in midsummer, and knots of people strolled up and down New York Avenue, creating a party atmosphere, even when it meant just standing in front of closed clothing stores and staring into the lit storefront windows. A small crowd gathered around the musicians. Daisy and Julian planted themselves on a nearby bench. They refused to come inside and eat. Julian kept dashing inside for more spare change from Ari's pocket, then rushing back out front again. Ari finally got up himself and went outside to see what all the fuss was about.

He came back in, shaking his head. "Three toothless old men singing off-tune," he said. "In Greek. I don't get it."

"Tell them their spinach pie is getting cold," Mimi said. She was busy feeding Arianna, who was gnawing wetly on a piece of pita bread.

"Daisy won't care," Nicole said. "All she eats is cereal, anyway."

"I'll go," Jay said. He squeezed Nicole's arm once before he went.

They all watched through the window while Jay gathered up the children. The singers were taking a short break. Jay was a former athlete. He was tall and skinny now, but his shoulders were still broad. He had been a state champion basketball player in college, and then played for a year in a European league. Then he came home and became a high school athletic director. He put one long leg up on the park bench, between Julian and Daisy. He and the musicians began holding a lively conversation, talking with their hands. Ari laughed. "Now we'll have to send someone out to drag Jay inside."

"He's happy," Nicole said. "He's so grateful. We all are." She put one hand on Ari's sleeve, and felt the soft touch of his cashmere jacket under her fingers. He always dressed elegantly, even for a casual night out. Ari turned his head and smiled at her.

"Hey. Thank you," Nicole said. "For this chance."

"You're family," he said. "We grew up together." But he wasn't looking at her; for some reason he was watching the crowd outside the restaurant.

"I know," Nicole said. She ducked her head to hide the tears that had sprung into her eyes. She, too, looked out the window, at the kids and at Jay.

"You got the letter of intent I sent, right? My lawyer put it together. It should give you access to as much of the cord blood as you'll need."

"I hope I won't need it all," she said.

"There's not that much in the first place," Ari said. "Come on, come *on.*" He rapped impatiently on the window glass and gestured at Julian, whom Jay was now pulling to his feet. Daisy kept trying to tug him back down on the bench beside her. "The year Julian was born was the second year they used gravity extraction at this collection center. They just kept sixty milligrams. Now they usually keep between seventy-five and a hundred. But it doesn't matter. It's yours."

"I'm going to be really embarrassed if I die anyway."

"Yeah, that's what we're all worried about," Mimi said, looking with love from one cousin to the other.

"I might die of shame if I waste this," Nicole said.

"Or you might live," Mimi said.

———

Usually the family spent their time together at the Wiesenthals' sprawling colonial in Glen Cove. That night they gathered at the Greenes' house in Huntington. It was a small Cape Cod. Nothing special about it, except its purple-gray color.

Jay was allergic to anything with fur. So poor animal-loving Daisy was stuck with a tank of two goldfish and one aging turtle named Speedy Gonzales who crawled around and around his terrarium like a depression case in a lunatic asylum.

This was the first summer since Daisy was born that the two families had not planned a weeklong trip to the beach together. Nicole hadn't felt up to it, and now there would be the cord blood transplants to work around. Julian and Daisy were so disappointed about the missing vacation that the parents had finally agreed to let them go to the same expensive summer camp, though it meant a longer bus ride for Julian. Ari paid for both children's camp tuitions.

The camp was located in an old mansion in Cold Spring Harbor; it was an arts camp chiefly, which meant Julian could polish his skills on the saxophone and Daisy could spend all day bouncing back and forth between art and dancing. Ari had thoroughly investigated, checked the reviews online, called and personally interviewed the camp director. "I could carve a better man from a banana," he finally declared, "but the place is all right."

The camp had two swimming pools and served organic lunches and snacks. It might even be good for their health, Ari decided. Daisy was still thin and frail looking. Julian had a perpetual squint. At eleven, he already got migraines and sometimes had to lie down in a dark room with a washcloth over his face. Daisy would tiptoe into the room and rub his hands and feet, which helped. She, too, got what they called "sick headaches" because they usually made her sick to her stomach; she would not begin getting true migraines till after she hit puberty. The family took to calling them "the sick twins." Whenever they went away on vacation—as they had gone every summer, to the Hamptons or Cape Cod—either Julian or Daisy would end up in some urgent care clinic, or the emergency room in Hyannis.

Julian preferred the Hamptons because he got carsick on the long drives to New England. But Daisy loved the Provincetown dunes. She said when she grew up she was going to become a New Englander, and read *Yankee Magazine* and *Vermont Life* and pronounce *car* as "caaah." One time Julian got sun poisoning. Another time Daisy sliced her foot open on a clamshell. Still, they looked forward to those brief summer vacations as if to a return to Eden. Summer camp, everyone knew, was no substitute for paradise. But at least they could be together.

The Greenes' house was filled with Daisy's toys or animal drawings or art materials. The outside of the Cape Cod was painted a shade of purple halfway between lavender and lilac-gray, with darker gray shutters—but that was the color it had been when they bought it, and Nicole felt that they shouldn't change it, as if it would insult the house to imply that anything was wrong. Even the inside walls were painted lilac. Ari wondered how Jay could stand it, living in a pale purple house with a wife and daughter. But he didn't seem to mind, or even, for that matter, to notice. Some of the furniture was downright shabby; Jay's study was little more than a closet stuffed with playbooks and soccer films, old basketball trophies, and his worn leather briefcase—yet he seemed content with all of that, too. "Cows are contented," Ari's mother used to say. "People are either happy or miserable."

The secret, Ari thought, was that Jay adored his wife. Head over heels in love. He didn't just admire her, or believe they formed a good team—which was how Ari felt in his marriage to Mimi. Jay practically worshipped the ground Nicole walked on. He had spotted her when they were both taking education classes in graduate school, and said he knew the moment he laid eyes on her that she was the one he'd always wanted. She was wearing high-waisted gray pants and a burgundy cashmere cardigan that almost matched the color of her hair.

But it wasn't her beauty that first knocked him out—it was her voice. Soft and clear, a few notes lower than you expected. Like a song on the radio; her voice went on playing in his head long after she had stopped speaking. And she was quiet, so he had to pay close attention to make sure he didn't miss a word. They'd only had the one class together—he was headed toward becoming a gym teacher or coach, she was about to start teaching third grade—so Jay had to act fast. And he did. He asked her out after the second class, and he asked her to marry him after their third date. Ari could imagine what it might feel like to be that dizzily in love with someone, especially somebody like Nicole. But as far as his own life went, it just didn't apply.

Julian and Daisy went upstairs to see what Speedy Gonzales the turtle was up to—which would be nothing, as usual, but Julian liked feeding him from his round pink rubber dish; the turtle chewed his lettuce slowly, thoughtfully, like an old man bent over a salad.

Nicole rummaged around in the kitchen cupboard looking for cookies, wishing she had something fancier to offer than Oreos, and finally came up with a box of assorted Pepperidge Farm cookies. She saw the slight wince on Ari's face, but Mimi said, "Oh, I love these!" and went straight for the Milanos. Nikki brewed some imported coffee she'd gotten as a gift.

The night had grown steadily cooler, despite the heat of the day, and the house felt chilly. Nicole asked, "Is anyone cold? I can turn up the heat. We have plenty of extra sweatshirts."

Ari said, "Hey—that reminds me!" and left the house. They all heard the beep the BMW made every time he locked or unlocked it. He came back inside carrying an old Bendel's shopping bag with something inside.

The kids wandered back into the kitchen. Like all children, Nicole thought, they had a preternatural sense of when a box of cookies was being opened. They sat happily on the kitchen stools, browsing through the assortment. Julian liked anything with chocolate. Daisy could take forever choosing between one cookie and another of the exact same kind, her small hand hovering back and forth over the box, as if she were making a life-and-death decision. Was one slightly rounder? One slightly larger?

"Hurry up and pick," Julian moaned, his mouth full of cookie crumbs. Nicole set a bottle of cider and two plastic tumblers down in front of them. Daisy was still young enough that she dropped a glass at least once or twice a week.

When Ari came in holding the bag, looking strangely excited, Daisy said, "Is that a present for me?"

"Is it your birthday?" Ari asked her.

"No," she said, disappointed.

"Is it Christmas?"

"Hanukkah," she corrected him.

"Is it either one?"

"No," Daisy said.

"Actually," Ari said. "I just thought of it because your mother happened to mention sweatshirts. I've had this around forever, and wasn't sure what to do with it."

He drew something out of the shopping bag. Only Julian seemed to know what it was. "Gross!" he yelled. "Get rid of it!"

"What is it?" Mimi asked, puzzled. She reached with one hand as if to touch the vintage child-size sweatshirt, then paused, with her hand in midair.

"It's that gross sweatshirt from when the dog attacked Aunt Nicole. It's got her old blood all over it. Dad once showed it to me like it was a treasure or something."

"Is that my mom's blood?" Daisy asked, interested. "Can I see it?"

Ari kept it close to his side, one fist around the small sweatshirt. "I just wasn't sure what to do with it," he said.

"Get rid of it," Mimi said.

"I don't want to look at it," Julian said. He swung around in a half circle, and deliberately kept his back turned.

Only Nicole's voice was gentle. "It's sort of a piece of family history," she said.

"Yes! That's exactly what it is!" Ari said. "I knew you'd understand. You saved our dogs' lives that day."

"Dude," said Jay. "Why would you keep such a weird artifact? Just throw it in the trash can around back."

Ari smiled, but the smile was twisted sideways. "I can dispose of it properly," he said. "I just wanted to make sure no one objected."

"No, I don't," Nicole said. "I don't need to keep it."

"I want to see my mother's blood!" Daisy insisted.

"No," Jay said, stepping in front of her. "Jeez."

"Why would you keep a weird thing like that?" Julian demanded, his back still turned, his arms folded.

Ari folded his arms, too, one hand still clutching the sweatshirt. "I kept it," Ari said, "to remind myself. That was a key moment in my childhood, and I vowed that if I ever had the chance I would never be a coward again."

"Well, you aren't one," Nicole said, smiling. "I don't think you ever were."

"Just get rid of it," Mimi said, shaking her head.

"Please," Julian added. "Before I throw up." Everyone laughed.

But Ari had already turned back to the door, carrying the shopping bag, into which he had hastily stuffed the old bloodstained sweatshirt. "I'm going," he said. Watching him go, his shoulders slumped, Nicole thought he looked like an old man. He shuffled out the door. Again they heard the beep of the BMW as the door unlocked and relocked.

"I wish we could shut that thing off," Mimi said, "It's impossible to sneak up on someone."

"Is that why my mom has that scar on her wrist?" Daisy said. "Because of the bad dog?"

"Yes," said Julian. "She was totally brave. My dad was a wuss."

"He carried me inside," Nicole reminded him.

Julian snorted. "Big deal."

"It's *my* family's blood," Daisy said. "I think I should get to keep the shirt."

"Shh," Nicole said, stroking her daughter's long hair. "Let's not talk about this anymore." Daisy's hair felt like strands of silk, the way it would get tangled up under your fingers. If you sat with Daisy in your lap at the movies—and she almost always ended up in your lap, something scary was bound to happen at some point—it was like sitting there with a mouthful of thread. "Hey, Julian, what are you planning to be for Halloween this year?"

"I'm choosing between the Tramp and Wolverine," Julian said.

"Who's the Tramp?" Daisy said. "I'm going to be Captain Hook."

"Captain Hook is a guy, dummy," said Julian.

So by the time Ari came back from the car without the bag, they had changed the subject and moved on to lighter things.

Nicole always hugged Mimi good-bye, and she never let Julian go home without a good-night kiss, but she was shy when it came to embracing other men—even her cousin. This night, though, she walked straight up to Ari and wrapped her arms around his waist. He smelled like her childhood, of pine and salt water. She tilted back her head to look at him—he was a good five inches taller than she was. "I've always looked up to you," she said quietly, only half kidding. She tried standing on her tiptoes, to demonstrate.

He returned the hug but quickly stepped back, his hands at his sides. "I don't see why," he said. "There's not that much to admire."

"Oh, yes there is," she said.

He shrugged but half smiled back at her, and gave her a little salute—an old childhood gesture she had forgotten. "Keep your nose clean," he said—something his father used to say.

"Don't go out with a wet head," she said, echoing her mother. They both laughed.

"What's so funny?" Mimi called over.

"Nothing," Ari said. "It's an inside joke."

"Why is everybody leaving?" Daisy said plaintively. "Look. It's still light out." There was the faintest glimmer of blue still left shimmering in the night sky.

"It's way past your bedtime," Jay said, scooping her up and walking back into the house.

Nicole stood in the driveway and waved while Ari put his BMW in reverse and honked lightly, two times, as he pulled away—an old, old farewell signal, as familiar and far away as the whistle of the Long Island Railroad.

———·——

Nicole went for a walk after the company had gone home. For the first time in a long time, something in her chest felt lighter, looser—she realized it was the absence of panic, the beginning of hope. It gave her more energy, and instead of creeping into bed like a wounded animal, she felt well enough to stroll around the neighborhood. She headed downhill to be closer to Huntington Bay, close enough to smell the brine in the air.

Summer evenings were louder than any other time of year. People played music with their windows open. Teenagers stayed up late, talking in packs near their cars. Cars seemed to pass more noisily. And always, there was the sound of laughter in summer, brighter and sharper. Did people just have more to laugh about when the weather turned sweet? Nicole wondered. Maybe it was just that all the kids were out of school, playing Manhunt after dark. Teenagers who laughed raucously the way that peacocks spread their tail feathers—who laughed the most easily. Who laughed the longest.

Summer roses bloomed luxuriantly, climbing up neighbors' front gates, shining under streetlights. The air smelled fresh and sweet—a mixture of honeysuckle and the faint salty smell of the sea that pervades the edges of Long Island. Nicole stopped for a moment, with one hand on her chest. It was a smell of childhood. Yes, she was breathing more easily. She heard glass chimes clinking together on a porch. Thank you, God, she thought. Thank you for this second chance.

August 2011
A Change of Plan

Julian woke in the middle of the hot summer night, calling hoarsely for a glass of water. He had not done this for years, and when Mimi touched his forehead, it felt burning to the touch, his skin dry and sandy.

He drank the water, wincing. "My throat hurts, Mom."

Mimi hurried to the bathroom and rummaged around in the cupboard, looking for the thermometer. Why were the simplest things impossible to find when you needed them most? —Bactine, Band-Aids, hydrogen peroxide. In front of the cupboard sat eight different kinds of moisturizing cream, suntan lotion, at least a dozen different shampoos and conditioners. If she were a good mother, prepared, she'd have a first-aid kit ready for moments like these. She'd be the kind of woman who memorized the contents of her medicine cabinet—or at least organized them. She called, "One minute, sweetie!" Julian coughed in response.

Two bottles of mouthwash fell off the shelves, waking Ari, who came out of the bedroom like a rumpled lion, in plaid Brooks Brothers pajamas. His hair stuck out wildly in all directions. He put his hands on the thermometer in ten seconds, and shooed Mimi back to bed. He reappeared in the doorway five minutes later, clutching the glass thermometer, waving it as if conducting some terrifying phrase of music. "His fever's over a hundred and four," he announced. "I'm calling Dr. Martin. Meanwhile, I gave him Tylenol and adjusted the air conditioning. How does the baby seem?"

"Rianna? Rianna's fine." It had not yet occurred to Mimi to check on the baby. But Ari was already off into the nursery. He came back, smiling grimly. "She seems all right for now," he said. "Her forehead was cool to the touch. I didn't want to wake her. Whatever it is, I hope she doesn't catch it."

"Should we take him to the emergency room?" Mimi asked. In these family situations, she often felt like a spectator rather than someone involved. It was as if she were watching television, asking herself, I wonder if they'll go to the ER now? She could guess, she might even have an opinion, but Ari ran the show. Always.

"They have nothing but quacks in the ER," he said. "Most of the doctors don't even speak English. I wouldn't trust my kid to any of them. Let's see if I can reach Dr. Martin. Then if Julian takes a turn for the worse, we can go to urgent care as a last resort."

"That sounds good," Mimi said, but Ari had already turned and plunged downstairs to the living room. His heavy footsteps pounded on the wooden stairs. Mimi heard Ari's low voice below, making one call, then another.

Mimi called into Julian's room, "Sweetie? You okay?" but there was no answer, so she assumed he had fallen asleep again, and the next thing she knew it was early morning and Ari was dressed for work, nudging her awake. Normally he dropped Julian off at camp on his way to the real estate office. But there was no Julian poking his owlish face behind Ari's to say good-bye or to ask her a question. Ari spoke softly.

"Dr. Martin wasn't on call last night," he said. "I didn't want to deal with an unknown. We have an appointment at one o'clock—Julian can miss a day of camp. It's not like he's missing school."

"I'll take him," Mimi said. "One o'clock, right?"

"No," said Ari. "I'll take him myself. That's why I'm heading in early this morning. I'll cancel my afternoon appointments."

"That's silly," Mimi said. "I can take care of this."

Ari didn't smile; he didn't even look at her. "No," he said. "I'm doing this. He's my son."

"He's my son, too," she said quietly.

Ari just ran his hand through his hair. He frowned. Ari, the lion. Then he tried to soften his tone. "I'll feel better hearing everything from Dr. Martin myself." He leaned down and brushed her forehead with his lips. "Try to keep a close eye on Arianna today, right? Keep checking on her."

"I will," she said. She felt an accusation in his request, but it was too slippery or deep for her to grasp. "So I'll see you around one?" she said.

"I'll be here by noon," Ari said. He put one broad hand up as if stopping her next question. "You always have to allow for the goddamn traffic around here. Nothing is as easy as it seems."

"No," she agreed. "Nothing ever is."

———·———

Ari sat beside his son in Dr. Martin's waiting room again a few days after he woke with his throat hurting. Julian felt better now, just the remnants of a sore throat, and the swollen glands that hadn't entirely gone away for some reason.

Ari wished he could sit Julian on his lap the way he had when his son was a little boy during pediatrics appointments, but Julian had his head down, rereading one of his Harry Potter books, and he would have been horrified had Ari done so much as touch his hand. Ari settled for resting his palm on the back of his boy's neck. It no longer felt hot to the touch. Julian shifted a little in his chair, but didn't shake the hand off. In fact, he looked up and smiled through those beautiful myopic brown eyes, at the same instant that Ari's name was called.

Ari stood at once, laying down the magazine he'd been halfheartedly skimming. "Me and Julian, or—" He pointed to himself, and the nurse nodded.

"Just you this time," she said cheerily.

"Be right back," Ari told Julian.

"Mm-hmm." Julian's attention was refocused on the book in his lap.

"What's going on?" Ari asked the nurse, but she led him quickly into Dr. Martin's office, the one with the swivel chairs and the desk, not an examining room. "Dr. Martin will be with you shortly," she said. She flashed him a smile and was off, shutting the door, and his questions in with him.

Dr. Martin was not smiling when he came in. He was holding Julian's folder in one hand, and X-rays in the other.

"I'm not sure how to say this," said Dr. Martin. "And I don't want you to overreact. I know you."

Ari was already on his feet. Whatever the news, he was not going to take it sitting down. "Tell me," he demanded.

"There's a very slight chance Julian may have Hodgkin's disease," said the doctor. "I want to rule it out, I'm just being conservative. His blood count is off. And there's this. You remember we took some X-rays." He slapped them up against a white screen, and flipped on a light. He pointed at something in the neck area. Julian's neck. "I don't like the look of this lump, I'd like to biopsy it."

"When?" said Ari. He felt as if someone had socked him hard in the stomach. He needed time to prepare himself, time to marshal his forces.

"Right away. Today, if you're willing." The doctor took the X-ray off the white screen and laid it back down on his desk. "I'm in surgery this afternoon, and this is strictly an outpatient procedure. Won't even leave a scar."

Ari moaned at this. It was an animal sound. He shook his head, like a bull sinking to its knees, shaking off the first stick of a sword. "All right," he said. "We'll do it today."

"You want to call your wife?" Dr. Martin pushed the office phone toward him.

Ari waved it away. "No." There would be time for phone calls later. His stomach was churning. He needed to be completely focused now. He couldn't be sure Mimi would react the right way, and he didn't want to chance it. And he couldn't risk upsetting Julian. For now, it would be something secret between them, father and son.

He felt the preciousness of that bond, which he'd never had with his own father, and also felt, like a sudden blow, what a howling wilderness the world was when you did not believe in any power from anywhere else to rescue you. He wished he could believe. He would pray if there had been anything to pray to.

"I'd like to sit here for two minutes if that's all right," Ari said. He feared he was going to throw up. Ari was a generous donor to the hospital.

His name was on one of those brass plaques in the lobby. He and his son would be treated well. He'd made sure of that. Beyond that—nothing. Despite all his precautions. All his care, all his money and connections and success. No guarantees.

"Take all the time you need," the doctor said. "And don't go assuming the worst. Please. That's *my* job. Chances are it's nothing but a summer cold."

"A summer cold. God, I hope so." That was as close as Ari could get to a prayer. He nodded, his eyes swimming.

Before he went out to the waiting room he splashed his face with cold water. He squared his shoulders and walked out with a big smile. "All right, boy-o," he told Julian. "They just want to run a couple more pain-in-the-ass tests."

"Aww jeez," Julian groaned. Then, fearfully, the child in him coming out: "The tests won't hurt, will they?"

"I won't let anyone hurt you," Ari said, his voice thick with emotion. "I swear it."

Julian looked up, startled.

"And after, I'll take you out for deli sandwiches. You pick the deli. Anything you want." His voice returned to normal.

"Deli on the Green," Julian answered promptly, flashing him a grin. "Guess it's not all bad, getting sick."

"You are going to be fine," Ari said, closing his fingers around his son's shoulder. "Just fine."

Mimi barely waited for Nicole to say hello before she blurted it out. "Ari changed his mind. I'm so sorry."

The phone was slick in Nicole's hand. She sank into the kitchen chair. "About the cord blood? He changed his mind?" It felt like a wave had rolled over her, knocking her off her feet. She thought how cowardly Mimi was to tell her this over the phone. She forced herself to take a breath. "Why?" she said. "When did this happen?"

"Can I come over?" Mimi said. "I wasn't sure you'd want to see me."

"I'll always want to see you," Nicole said. "Come. —It'll be all right," she forced herself to say, though she did not believe it. Outside she heard the sound of children playing kickball in the street. An ordinary late summer's day. She felt the room slipping out from underneath her—as if she might slide off the chair and end up on the linoleum floor.

"I'll be right over," Mimi said.

"You want coffee?" Nicole said. "I can make some."

"I think I'd rather have a whiskey," Mimi said. "Nikki—I love you."

"I love you, too," Nicole said. She felt embarrassed saying the words out loud. Mimi had always been the more demonstrative one.

Forty minutes later Mimi rang her doorbell. She held little Rianna in her arms, all bundled up though the day was sultry. Only the girl's small face stuck out like a baby Eskimo's.

"Does Rianna want a whiskey, too?" Nicole asked, after she'd helped unwrap the baby from her cotton blanket. Her small face looked flushed and furious. Her pink booties were removed and set in front of the closet. Rianna rocked slightly on the kitchen floor, inside her flowered infant seat, which doubled as a car seat.

"She would, if she knew what's going on," Mimi said. "Julian came down with something about a week and a half ago. He had swollen glands, a high fever. We took him to our GP, who thought it might be Hodgkin's disease."

"Oh, Mimi," Nicole said. Her hand went out instinctively to touch her friend's arm. "Why didn't you call me? Is Julian all right?"

"He's fine," Mimi said. "Don't worry. It was just swollen glands—a summer cold, maybe a touch of flu. They drew blood, they ran all the tests. He's fine. He's playing soccer, he's playing Guitar Hero—he's absolutely fine."

"I don't understand," Nicole said. "Then what's the problem?"

Mimi twisted her thin gold wedding band around and around on her finger. Ari had given her a large pear-shaped diamond ring for their tenth anniversary, but she hardly ever wore it. Now and again she'd sport some piece of costume jewelry that Julian had bought her for Mother's Day. Mimi wore a black T-shirt and jeans. Her hair looked as if she'd forgotten to brush it.

"Ari is scared," she finally said. "He's just scared to death. 'What if it really *had* been Hodgkin's?' he keeps asking me. 'What if Arianna gets sick? We might need this cord blood.' Julian's blood is a better protection for Rianna than it is for Julian. Did you know that? They have a six/six match. It's perfect. That's practically unheard of."

Nicole said nothing. She stared at her own hands, lying in her lap. They looked unfamiliar. She put them on top of the counter, but that only made it worse.

Mimi said, "I told Ari that's a risk I'm willing to take. Chances are we can use this cord blood more than once. *You* are sick right now. You need this now."

"Thank you," Nicole said. She hated the quiver in her voice. She hated the pathetic gratitude she felt. She hated being sick, like being stuck alone, lost in a country where you didn't know the rules or the language. She was sick and tired of it, and she knew it was all just beginning.

"Don't thank me," Mimi said. She looked grim. "It didn't do any good. Ari just went ballistic, shouting that I'm a terrible mother. Maybe I am."

"You're a great mother," Nicole said.

"I don't know what I am," Mimi said. "Ari thinks I'm some kind of monster."

"You are not," Nicole said, "any kind of a monster."

"It was the worst fight we've ever had," Mimi said. "We said things neither of us will ever forget."

Nicole wondered if she should ask about those things, but she wasn't sure she could stand to hear them. Jay was always so gentle with her, so loving. The worst fight they'd ever had was over some ice cream he'd eaten when she was pregnant. Jay had finished the last of it and put the empty carton back in the freezer—like a little kid. She'd thrown the carton at him. He'd gone out and bought some more. End of story.

"If you feel like talking about any of it, I'm here," Nicole said. "You know that."

"Thanks, sweetie," Mimi said. "It was bad enough hearing it once." She leaned down and did something to the back of Rianna's infant seat that made it bounce lightly back and forth. The baby looked more startled than pleased. Her arms and legs went straight out in the air. "Rianna woke up in the middle of the night and couldn't get back to sleep," she added. "I ended up sleeping on the nursery floor. None of us got much rest except Julian. He could sleep through an earthquake."

Nicole looked more closely. Rianna had bags under her baby eyes, like a little old lady. Her cheeks sagged. Her head was nodding, but she was fighting to stay awake. Mimi didn't look much better.

"You want that whiskey now?" Nicole asked. She went over to the liquor cabinet to see what was inside. Not much. A few bottles of wine that Ari had given them, a dusty bottle of rum she used for baking, and a quarter of a bottle of brandy.

"I have to work today. I owe a new comedy routine to that guy out in Hollywood. The least funny man on earth. At least he's living in the right place. —I'll take a glass of cold water, though."

Nicole went to the fridge and poured some into a blue glass.

"Don't give up on us," Mimi said. "That's what I really came to say. —Ari might change his mind back. You know how he is. He just got scared when Julian was so sick. He went nuts. But he loves you. Your cousin is not a bad guy."

"Of course he's not," Nicole said. She gazed down into the glass of water, as if it were a cup of tea leaves, as if she could read her fortune there.

Mimi smiled wearily. "I may be trying to convince myself," she said. "I don't know for sure *what* kind of a guy he is anymore. But I'm so sorry, Nikki, about the delay. I know you need to move forward."

"I had set up the TBI consult appointment for next week," Nicole admitted. Now she wished she'd made the appointment the minute Ari had handed her that letter. She had to fight against a rising tide of panic.

"Can you push it back a couple of weeks?" Mimi asked. "I hate to ask…"

"Of course I can," Nicole said. She put one hand on Mimi's back. The solid touch was comforting, it steadied her for a second. "Stop worrying so much."

"Yeah. Good luck to that." Mimi fiddled with the buckles on the infant seat and lifted Rianna with a groan. "I'm too old to be the mother of a little baby," she said. "What was I thinking?"

Nicole fought down her own jealousy. She had always wanted two children. A pair. She worried about Daisy being lonely for the rest of her life. Especially now. So much more now. "You probably weren't. Thinking," she said.

"Well, help me get her into those pink booties," Mimi said. "It's a two-person operation."

Once Rianna was strapped and wrapped again, Mimi hesitated at the door. "I'll move him along as fast as I can," Mimi said. "But you know Ari. If you push too hard, he digs his heels in. And everything medical is in his name."

"He was like that even as a kid," Nicole said, fighting to keep her voice steady. "Divine stubbornness. In spades."

"I'm not sure about the divine part," Mimi said. "Stubborn, yes. — Okay. Wave bye-bye to Auntie Nicole." She maneuvered Rianna's little hand. "And listen," she added. "I don't want to put too much pressure on you or anything, but this cord thing has to work. If you died, I'd have to die. I wouldn't want to go on living. Plus I'd have no one to practice my lousy comedy material on. So please don't think I'm doing this for purely altruistic reasons."

"Oh, no," Nicole said. Her eyes were wet. "I know you're a selfish pig."

When Nicole closed the door behind Mimi and Rianna, she saw through the glass a few early red leaves falling to the ground like drops of blood. The house suddenly felt terrifyingly claustrophobic. She had been dreading the total body irradiation, "day zero"—the nickname for the cord blood transplant itself—the side effects, headaches, body sores, the long dragging recovery period. But now she had something much worse to dread: no hope at all.

Outside, the trees were green- and rust-colored scribbles. Nothing else in sight. No one out on the streets. It was too hot to go for a walk. She had let so much of her life slide, first staying home to raise Daisy, then suddenly getting sick. *Leukemia, lymphoma.* The words sounded unreal inside her head; they could not possibly apply to her. Almost the only places she went any-more were to doctors' offices, cancer clinics, infusion rooms, and hospitals. What could she do, this minute, to keep from screaming? She looked around her as if the answer might be hanging on the walls, among the bric-a-brac. Daisy would not be home for another three and a half hours.

She could clean the kitchen floor, she thought. She could do another load of laundry. A wave of panic was coming toward her like a truck. She put up one hand against it. "No," she said out loud. She was not sure why she was continuing in what felt like a futile and ghastly struggle against the inevitable. Why not just crawl into bed, pull up the covers, and let death come? Daisy and Jay, she reminded herself. For them. She steeled herself with this thought.

She walked to the window. She took hold of the curtains and with a sudden, ferocious movement, tore them down. Everything came toppling over with a crash—the billowing material, the metal rod; even the hinges that held the curtain rod pulled loose from their nails and hung tilting crazily forward. Now there was one more broken thing she had to mend.

A flock of brown birds flew away to the feeder outside the dining room window, raising a racket she could hear even through the glass. Their small wings beat furiously. Their throats bobbed up and down as if they were arguing.

Ari, she knew, was not going to change his mind.

SEPTEMBER 2011
The Matriarch of the Family

Phone calls flew back and forth between Nikki's house and Ari's. Ari called and said, "I'm sorry, but that's the way it is. Rip up the letter."

Mimi called Nicole from her cell phone and said, "I need a little more time to work on him. Please don't give up on us."

Jay called Ari and the two men shouted at each other. Jay threatened to pound Ari into dust, and Ari hung up.

Nicole called Mimi's house because she longed for the comforting sound of her best friend's voice, but Mimi got off the phone in under a minute, sounding like someone who had been caught consorting with the enemy.

A week later Mimi called back, apologized, and said, "This may take more time than I thought."

Nicole said, "I may have less time than we thought."

"I'm sorry. I don't know what to say or do. I'm so sorry." Mimi was crying, sobbing into the phone. The sound was harrowing. Nicole's mothering instinct overrode her own instinct for survival.

"Shh…Don't cry," Nicole said. "I know you tried." She heard the baby's voice in the background. "You're going to upset Rianna."

"I don't know who I married anymore," Mimi sobbed. "Sometimes I think I hate him. I don't know what else to do or say."

"You don't have to say anything. —We'll get together soon, okay?"

They swore to each other they would. Nothing could come between them.

Nicole spent a few days just trying to think clearly. Every muscle in her body ached from the exertion of trying to get through to something like a clear idea, a way out. At the end of each day she'd find her jaw ached because she'd been clenching her teeth, hanging on, barely. She felt like someone looking at a blank wall of ice. It towered above them all, threatening to crush them. Somehow she had to climb up and over it, or force her way through. She made lists. She tried to see Ari's side of it. Wouldn't she do the same thing in his position? But somewhere under that was her own rebellious voice saying, I would not be so terrified that I would let my cousin die. They can save some of the cord blood. I don't need it all. I won't take it all. He's just being—Ari.

Ari had dropped out of college midsemester of his sophomore year. He had made his own way in the business world, working his way up from the bottom, fiercely, determinedly. He had learned to rely on his own resources. He trusted no one. "He's a force of nature," Mimi used to say, trying to explain Ari to strangers. When he shut you off, it was as if someone had turned off a faucet. Nicole worked up what seemed like the last remaining shred of her nerve and called Ari herself. She asked him to see her in person, to discuss it.

"I don't see the point," said Ari. His voice was the flat dismissive voice she remembered from when he was in his early twenties. It seemed to her that one minute he was a child, the next he had become an icy businessman.

"I know," she said, "but it might help us, anyway. Just to sit face-to-face and talk."

"I don't agree," Ari said. He knew if he had to sit across a table and look into his cousin's large brown eyes, flecked with gold, if he saw her mouth, her hair—her *wig*, he reminded himself, with a kind of horror—if he saw Nicole, his flesh, in the flesh, he would never be able to say no to her. He could not remember a time when he had ever refused his baby cousin anything.

"Please," she said. "We'll just talk."

"All right," he said, the words dragging themselves out of his mouth of their own accord.

They agreed she would come to his real estate office in Oyster Bay. Ari hoped the dull familiarity of the office, the formality of the posh surroundings, his own surroundings—his secretary, his waiting room, his face on the ads and business cards, the framed photos of him standing beside of his most famous clients, a gold-medal tennis player, a few TV stars—all of that would help strengthen him to keep to his word. He was not a villain. He was protecting his children, doing a father's job.

Except as it turned out, Nicole came down with bronchitis on the autumn day they were to have met. A freak snowstorm, a letter that gets stuck in a grate, a case of food poisoning, a cough, and history begins marching off in a different direction, regardless of who or what was in the lead.

The chemotherapy had made Nicole more vulnerable to every bug, and whenever she got sick, the sickness seemed to hold on a little longer, a little tighter, like a burr. She called to reschedule the meeting with Ari, but when her cousin heard Nicole's scratchy voice on the phone, it was with a kind of deep-down relief that he seized the opportunity to refuse. She did not sound like herself, but like a stranger. You could say no to a stranger.

"Look," he said. "There's no point dragging ourselves through this again." He pictured Julian, pale in the doctor's office. It could happen again, to either of his children. His voice sounded harder, edgier than she'd ever heard it in person. In fact, one of his big clients had just backed out of a deal that morning. He was sick to death of the economy. He was sick of business, sick of autumn.

"I just want—"

"I know what you want," Ari said. "Every sentence for you begins with 'I want.' But the answer is no. You had the same opportunity we did; the same technology is open to everyone. It's not my fault that you didn't take advantage of it."

"That's not fair," Nicole said. "It was so new. You were the first person we knew who stored cord blood. And it was expensive—we were living on one salary."

"Five thousand bucks," Ari said. His voice sounded exactly like his father's just then, even in his own ears, barking around the corner of his auto parts and repair store on the Lower East Side. "What's a few thousand bucks? You're saying that you and Jay never went on a vacation all those years? I told you it was a good idea, back when you were pregnant with Daisy. You never listen to me. You never *have* listened."

"If I had to do it over," Nicole said, "of course that's what we would choose. But we don't have that second chance. Ari, stop for a second and listen. This is me, Nikki. My leukemia is resisting all the treatments. It's some kind of genetic fluke. And I've tried every public source, every alternative."

"It's *genetic*?" She could hear the ring of fear in his voice. "So Julian and Arianna might have the same gene. What right have you got to steal from my children?" Ari was yelling now. He had gotten up from his chair and he was pacing, with the office phone in his sweaty hand. Normally he talked on the cell, through a Bluetooth headset. It felt weird to hold the phone in his hand, this appendage. "You've *had* your life. Why would you try to take away their safety net? What makes you so precious?"

"I'm—I'm not," Nicole said. "Jesus, Ari, aren't we all precious? I won't let them use all of the cord blood."

"You can't guarantee that. What if it gets contaminated? What if some moron drops the tube or tosses it? I can't risk my children's future for you."

"Ari, for God's sake. No one is going to drop or toss anything." Not just her voice, her whole body was shaking. She was looking out the west window in her living room. It seemed like the last bit of color or beauty left in the world lay in the branches of the Japanese maple whose brilliant quadrangles touched the glass, glittering with light, blood red and on fire. The branches scooped the air and flourished brilliant scarlet against gray-white arcs of sky in between like an ikebana flower arrangement. Fall was coming. Every tree would soon be bare, the piles of leaves swept up, carted away, burned, discarded.

"As for that goddamn letter," Ari went on, his voice menacing. "You'd better tear it up and send me the pieces, or I swear I'll come after you. I'll take every measly dime you've got left. Do you hear me? Do you under-stand me now?"

"I have to go," Nicole said. "I can't listen anymore." She hung up and tears burst from her eyes in a flood. Crying came as a relief, loosening the agony of holding on and listening. Surely he would change his mind. He was her cousin, she had known him forever. She felt closer to Ari in many ways than she did to her own sister. He was moody. He had a temper, granted. She was not going to give up hope. Her tears, like the leaves in the Japanese maple branches, seemed at least some form of life.

As for Ari, he felt a sick headache coming on as soon as he hung up the phone. His desk looked hazy, as if seen through fog. He punched a button and barked at his secretary, "No more calls today! No one. Nothing."

His temple throbbed, as if someone was trying to pound a nail into the right side of his head, and his stomach burned. The usual red aura began to collect around objects in the room—the chair, cars parked out in the office parking lot. He shut off the lamp by his desk to make the room dimmer. He thought he was going to throw up. He drew the blinds. He felt older than he'd ever felt in his life. There was barely enough energy left in his hands to pull the cords on the window blinds.

"What in God's name have I done," he said to himself, in a voice low enough not to stir the angry hornets buzzing in his head, not to raise the demons. "What have I started?"

That night, Nicole dreamed she was back at her senior prom. The wooden floors of the gym gleamed golden brown; the basketball hoops were so festooned and heaped with paper flowers that they seemed like blossoming trees. Ari was there, too, looking as he had in high school—his hair longer, his shoulders wider. He was dressed in some sort of elaborate purplish-red velvet jacket, edged with gold trim. But he didn't look ridiculous. He appeared regal, a king. On his head he wore a spiky gold crown. It was glowing with rubies, emeralds, topaz. He came toward her smiling in the dream and, removing the crown from his own head, held it out to her. She didn't want to accept it. She could imagine its weight, its spikiness, settling down on her. She hung back. But he smiled even more broadly—a beaming, mischievous grin that she hadn't seen in years—and held it out again, insisting. "It's yours," he said. "You have to take what belongs to you."

She woke up, and lay in the half-gloom of early morning, mulling it over. She felt calmer and saner. It had often been this way for her—whenever things were at their worst, at their darkest, she would have a supremely happy dream. Nicole wasn't sure why this was the case, but she supposed it was a gift. It was as if her nighttime life carried on joyfully with or without her, and the momentum of that dream happiness swept into her waking hours. After her mother died, she'd had a series of happy dreams where they were out biking, mountain climbing, picnicking in deep woods together—things they had never done in real life. She woke up laughing from one of the dreams and asked herself, Am I losing my mind?

In fact, she remembered, she and Ari had gone to his senior prom together. Not as a couple, of course, but with their own dates, together. Ari had been going around with a girl named Denise since his junior year. She was a short, tough-looking young woman with high blonde hair who chewed gum, smoked cigarettes, and cut class more often than not. Nicole was in awe of her. She'd just assumed that Ari and Denise would get married, but then something happened—a pregnancy scare, she thought—and it all fell apart abruptly after high school.

Nikki, a few years younger, had just started dating one of Ari's closest friends that spring of his senior year, a boy named—she fumbled for the name an instant. Darrell. A tall, skinny runner from upstate, shy and quiet. He wanted to be a veterinarian. He was crazy about animals. He'd worn a red tux to the prom, she remembered now, an orangey-red color that looked like a band uniform. He had been almost handsome enough to carry it off.

Nikki was just beginning to realize that things weren't going to work out between her and Darrell after all. Darrell was a nice guy, a truly sweet guy, but after a few mumbled sentences they had nothing to say to each other. The silence between them was paralyzing. And she didn't know any of the other kids at the prom—they went to different schools, and besides, they were all older than she was. In those days, three years felt like a century. Ari was her safety zone that night. As often as she could, Nikki crept over to him and stood in the comfort of his familiarity, nursing her punch in its plastic fake champagne glass. He seemed to realize that she felt out of place; he made a point of including her while he stood around talking to his friends. He'd asked her to dance a few times, and as long as she was at her cousin's side she didn't feel so hopelessly lost and awkward. Once, though, while they were dancing, Ari leaned his chin against the top of her head.

Nicole stiffened. "Are you smelling my hair?" she demanded.

"Sure," Ari said easily. "Why shouldn't I?" He moved her in a circle. "It smells nice," he added. "Like your mother's meatloaf."

She laughed. Her mother had indeed made meatloaf for dinner that night. Relieved, she punched him lightly on the arm.

"Denise's perfume is giving me a headache," he confided. "That and the smell of cigarette smoke."

"So hold your head farther away," she advised him.

"Naw. Are you kidding? Did you see her in that dress? I want to get *closer.* —But I might end up with a migraine."

"Other than that, Mrs. Lincoln," she teased him, "how did you enjoy the play?"

How did we come so far, she wondered now, from so much closeness? All the hours they had spent together, she and Ari, all the days and nights—it must add up to months of their lives spent in each other's company, playing cards, trying not to be sick in the back during long car rides, watching old movies, building intricate sand castles, just hanging around. Time that had seemed without end. She used to love wearing his outgrown sweaters because they smelled like him, and made her feel stronger, older, braver than she really was. And now this. They had come to this. Had some thread of their connection caught and held? she wondered. Wasn't there something unbreakable behind it all? Perhaps only in her dreaming life. But even that was enough to keep her buoyant for an hour or two.

———

Every family has one living patriarch or matriarch, the final arbiter and repository of ancient family history, and Nicole's aunt Patti was the last woman standing. It was to the formidable Patti that Nicole turned for help now. Her stage name was Patti Leeds, and she was best known to the world as Aunt Patti, a loudmouthed character she'd played seven years running on a TV sitcom.

Aunt Patti had never had a major breakthrough as an actress, no starring roles, never top billing, but she'd managed to capture the kind of small parts people remembered. She was the angry soup lady. She was the one on the cat food commercial who tangoed with the cat. She was the woman in the bakery who had bought the last cream puff and ate it while the main character watched and cried. She had been on Broadway and off-off-Broadway; she had appeared in movies, television shows, and scores of commercials.

"I'm the queen of the bit part," she used to brag. "If the Academy Awards ever handed out an award for Best Bit instead of those awards nobody gives a crap about, I'd have a gold statue over my fireplace."

Nicole's mother, Leslie, had been the brains of the family; Patti, Ari's mother, had been the wild one. Aunt Patti was brash, even vulgar. She was a short, round, dramatic-looking character with a snub nose and high cheekbones. Almost Mongolian looking. Her hair, even now, in her eighties, was jet black, and she swore it wasn't dyed. That meant nothing, of course. She swore to a lot of things that weren't remotely true. Born Esther Morgenstein, she had changed her stage name to Patricia Morgan. She still lived well off the residuals of Aunt Patti reruns and the occasional commercial.

She had stayed on in the house in Little Neck where she raised Ari and his brother, Al. After her husband passed away, she moved into one of the two big rooms downstairs, and treated the Cape Cod as a ranch. There was a large backyard, filled with a tangle of thorny raspberry bushes, and a church next door, which is why they'd been able to buy it cheaply back in the 1960s. Patti didn't start her acting career till she hit her forties; Nicole still remembered watching her aunt's early roles in tiny basements of makeshift theaters all over Manhattan, and how her mother had scoffed at them. Nicole and Ari both had painful memories of being dragged onstage to dance with the actors, or of being showered with colored confetti and, one memorable time, pelted with black feathers. Nicole still had one pasted into a photo album somewhere. She thought her aunt Esther brave, weird, and exotic, then and now.

So before she called Aunt Patti and told her what was going on, Nikki braced herself. Ari was the baby of her aunt's family and her favorite son.

Nicole could only imagine what her aunt would say to all this, but she steeled herself with her new stubborn will.

Or maybe it wasn't so new. Maybe she had just unearthed it, here in the last lap when she needed it most.

Nicole had been a rock-headed teenager, she knew that. She wondered uneasily if it had driven her father away, if it had led to her mother's early death. Despite the softness of her face, the roundness of her curves, Nicole was someone who stood her ground. Once she had warded off a would-be rapist by planting her feet and refusing to get inside his car. Her resistance seemed to confuse him. He finally gave up and drove away. Her shapely calves were round but large, as if from having rooted herself firmly to the earth all these years.

As soon as the doorbell rang, Aunt Patti threw open her front door. The old lady still drove, though time had shrunken her so she could barely see over the top of the steering wheel. She was wearing a long black cape, dripping wet at the fringes, and she drew Nicole inside out of the wind and rain.

"You look awful," Aunt Patti said, enfolding her niece in a hug. Her cape smelled heavily of musk perfume. "I just got in myself," she added, stamping her feet to shake off water. "My neighbors cornered me. Right outside my own house, here in the downpour. I was just getting out of the car when they hobbled up to me. 'Oh, Mrs. Leeds!

Mrs. Leeds!' they cried—and that's not even my real name, my name is Wiesenthal, same as my husband—'We've got colored people moving into the neighborhood!'

"'Colored people!' I said. 'Heavens, what colors *are* they?'

"'Oh, you know what we mean,' they said. 'African-Americans.' —As if I didn't know exactly what they meant. I know what they say behind my own back, too, the old cranks. 'But what are you going to *do* about it?' they wailed."

Aunt Patti struck a pose on the carpet. Her mouth dropped open in mock amazement. "'*Do*?' I said. 'What am I going to *do* about it?' And I looked those old women right in the eye. 'I shall treat them exactly the way I treat *all* of my neighbors,' I told them.—'I shall *ignore* them!'"

Nicole laughed, and Aunt Patti dragged her over to the sofa and made her sit down.

"Little Neck," Aunt Patti said. "Little brains, little souls. I would have moved out long ago, but I love my yard and the church bells next door. They practically conduct their funerals in my driveway. It's very baroque. Sometimes I sneak inside and take communion. They don't know what to think."

She bustled around, hanging Nicole's coat on a brass coatrack in the shape of an elephant with many trunks. She shook out her own long black cape and hung it on another brass trunk. "How about I make some tea," she said. It was not a question. She disappeared into the kitchen, a narrow galley-style room that was hardly used. Aunt Patti had never been a cook. Aunt Patti was the only woman Nicole knew who served her guests TV dinners and lasagnas still in their frozen-food foil trays.

She reappeared ten minutes later with a tea tray trembling in her arms. All of the dishes clattered together gently, and she set them down with a look of relief. A deep red teapot, two dark red cups, and a pack of Fig Newton cookies. "I adore Fig Newtons," she said. "These are my idea of health food."

She poured the tea, and Nicole pretended to nibble at one of the cookies. She forced herself to eat something every morning—usually fruit with yogurt—then didn't eat again till dinnertime, when Jay and Daisy watched her like hawks. She and her aunt sat in silence for a few minutes, drinking tea and eating the cookies. At least, Aunt Patti ate while Nicole hung on to hers. After a while Aunt Patti got up and turned on the NPR station on the radio. They were playing something with strings.

"So," she said at last, when she had finished her tea. "Tell me what's going on."

"How much do you know?" Nicole asked, stalling. She had always been terrified of Aunt Patti, who seemed so much larger than life, plump and tiny as she was.

"I know Ari promised you something you need, something medical, and changed his mind."

"That's right," Nicole said.

"What's it called, again?"

"Cord blood," Nicole said. "It's Julian's."

"Cord blood." Aunt Patti mused on it. "When I was born there was no such thing as a TV set. No computer. If you were a preemie, chances were you'd die. So Ari said yes, and then he backed out. Son of a bitch."

She put up one short, pudgy hand. She always wore several large rings, including one enormous square aquamarine. "And do you know why? —Because he's a frightened little man. Takes after his father. He clings to things. He was like that even as a little boy—a packrat. He collected everything. All kinds of useless crap." She turned the dark red teacup around and around on its little plate. "Baseball cards, shells, nails, paper clips, polished rocks. One time he decided to collect walnuts, hid them under his bed, and we ended up with white maggots all over his room. Maggots, in Little Neck." She barked out a laugh.

"He could never let go of anything. When he outgrew his clothes, I'd try to donate them to Goodwill, but he wouldn't let me give anything away. I might need them, he'd tell me. *When?* I asked. Probably it's my fault. I'm not what you call the maternal type. So now he hangs on to everything." She shook her head. "Like a dragon. Sits on a pile of crap and guards it. And that poor homely wife of his has to keep him company while he does. No wonder she tells jokes. I introduced those two, you know."

This was not true. Nicole had introduced them in college, but it was one of Aunt Patti's many myths. "Mimi is not homely," is all Nicole said.

"Suit yourself," Aunt Patti said. "A *meeskite*. Even on her wedding day. They say every bride is beautiful, but Mimi proved them wrong. She looked—what is it you say about an ugly baby? She looked *alert*." She patted Nicole's hand. "Now, now," she said. "Don't get upset. Everything you felt always showed in your face and it still does. Beauty isn't everything. —But it doesn't hurt, either. Right? I was a beauty. You were a beauty. Still are. But this." She looked down again. Nicole had the funny feeling her aunt could read her future in the bottom of that red teacup. There had always been something witchy about Aunt Patti. "This is a mess."

"What should I do?" Nicole asked.

Aunt Patti lifted her head. She'd had enough facelifts so that her features looked windblown; she always looked faintly surprised. One brown eye was wider than the other.

"Do? —You fight back. That's what you do. And you have to act as if nothing's wrong, as if you know everything is going to come out all right. You *have* to do it, for Daisy's sake. You can't just lie down on the carpet and die."

Nicole felt relief and dread. There were days when lying down and dying seemed easier than this endless struggle. And what if in the end she lost the battle anyway? She had read the statistics. They were not good, not for cases like hers. She sat up straighter against the lemon-yellow sofa. A Van Gogh painting of a woman's sharp face, also yellow, sat across the room from her, above the piano. The woman looked sickly. Nicole remembered the print from her childhood.

"Once upon a time," Aunt Patti said, "your mother and I were together, driving through the Catskills. We were only teenagers. I had just gotten my license. I took her out for a ride, and on one of those mountains around Ellenville the brakes just went kaput. I felt them go. The car kept rolling downhill faster and faster, picking up speed, zooming around curves. Your mother was terrified. She started screaming.

"What could I do? She was my little sister. It was my job to take care of her. So I just pretended it was on purpose, like an amusement park ride. 'Wheeeee!' I yelled. 'Isn't this *fun*?' —And I hung on like death till the road finally started to go uphill and I could pull over to the side.

"Sometimes you go through the motions. You bluff your way through. Act like you know it's all going to come out hunky-dory." She laughed and crammed another Fig Newton in her mouth, then dabbed daintily at her mouth with a paper napkin, orange, decorated for Halloween. "I understand there was something in writing. May I see it?"

Nicole unzipped her big pocketbook now and handed the letter over, still in its envelope. Her aunt examined the envelope first, front and back, then opened it. She wore her reading glasses around her neck on a beaded chain. She read slowly, moving her head from side to side. Despite all the plastic surgery, she had jowls, and age spots on the back of her hands. She looked young and old at the same time, angry and sugary. Nicole wanted to grab hold of her and hug her, the way you would an old tree that has survived a hundred storms. But you didn't do that sort of thing with Aunt Patti. Finally she frowned over the tops of her glasses at Nicole.

"Well, it looks legal to me. Signed by a lawyer. You have to shame him into this, my darling. That's the only way."

"How?" asked Nicole.

"He refuses to listen to reason, right? Drag him into the public eye. He'll hate that. Ari has always had an excessive sense of pride. When he was six years old he wet his bed. Not for the first time, mind you. And I drew myself up to my full height"—here Aunt Patti did a demonstration, and without rising from the chair, she appeared to grow several inches—"and I said, 'Oh, Ari! *Shame* on you. Such a big boy!' —That's all I had to say. It offended his dignity. He never had another accident again."

She folded the paper back into thirds, slid it into the envelope, and handed it back. "There's your weapon. Shame him. Take out an ad in the *New York Times*. Haul him into court if you have to. The public will lap it up, and Ari will hate that. He'll back down in a red-hot minute."

Nicole looked at her aunt. "Why are you taking my side?" she said.

"I'm not taking sides," Aunt Patti said. "This is a matter of life and death. If they invented this cord thing now, they'll invent something else next year, or two years from now. I'm not worried about the distant future. I'm talking about what's happening right now. Without this, the doctors say you are going to die. Leukemia and lymphoma. Correct?"

Nicole nodded. Without intending to, she touched the side of her neck.

"The purpose of family is to preserve life," Aunt Patti said. "We treat family members the way we're supposed to treat everyone else on the planet. Listen, Nikki—if you died, Ari would never forgive himself. I know my son—he has a good heart. I'm protecting both of you, I'm not taking sides."

"Jay says I can't give up," Nicole said.

Aunt Patti dismissed this with the wave of one hand. "Well, but Jay adores you. He's gaga over you. He would say or do anything. I'm telling you what you *have* to do."

Nicole shook her head. "It doesn't feel—natural."

"There's nothing natural about this," Aunt Patti said. "Maybe chewing each other to bloody stumps would be natural, I don't know. Your brakes have gone out," she said. "May as well pretend to enjoy the ride. All I can say is, it worked for me. —And now," she added, "I have to take a nap. I hate to admit that."

"I won't tell a soul," Nicole said. She got to her feet.

"Good," said Aunt Patti. "And you can tell Ari I'm on your side. He won't like that, either, but it may motivate him. That's all my boy needs—a little motivation."

Then, as if to demonstrate, she propelled her sick niece into her coat and out the door, into the fall sunlight.

SEPTEMBER 2011
The Age of Mandatory Retirement

"Oyez! Oyez!" Flannery sang out in his piercing tenor. Solomon's court chamber echoed like a swimming pool, though the smell in the room was one of something melting or burning.

Listen, listen. The way Flannery called it, the words sounded like *Oh yes, oh yes!* Ecstatic. Like a lover. It reminded the judge of the opening words to the most seminal prayer in Judaism, the shema, "Hear, O Israel!"

Of course Flannery need not have cried "Oyez" at all. The principal clerk was a standing joke at the Supreme Court offices of Mineola, clown of the third floor, of Part 301. There was no need for this bit of fancifying, this calling out of the "Oyez, oyez!" in New York, and it was normally the task of the part clerk anyway, a lowlier position, to bang in the judge and call out the "All rise," but try telling Flannery.

"The Honorable Justice Solomon Richter, Supreme Court of the State of New York! All ye draw near! Give your appearance and ye shall be heard."

A few heads turned. Sergeant Carter Johnson, tipstaff in charge of security, grinned at the judge and winked, his big arms folded across his dark blue uniform. The silver badge twinkled on his broad chest like a fallen star. It was not like him to be jovial. Two younger security officers shifted from foot to foot in front of the two exit signs. They reminded Sol of colts in a field—better to let them run. Sol gathered up the folds of his robe and moved behind the oak stand.

Solomon's courtroom seemed fuller than usual for a simple civil case. A married couple was suing a local caterer over an incident with a sprinkler system. Claimed it had ruined their wedding. The bride had slipped and fractured her ankle. The real question, Sol thought, was whether they'd allow it to ruin their whole marriage.

His elderly court recorder nodded and beamed at Sol over her stenotype machine, as if he were accomplishing something momentous simply by walking into the courtroom and mounting the three steps to his bench. He had always felt uncomfortable ascending those last few steps, unworthy.

There was a note at the bench, in his chief clerk's flourishing handwriting: "Important. Please recess for five minutes." The judge looked over at Flannery and frowned. Flannery beamed back. The smell of burning had grown stronger. Maybe there was a fire somewhere in the building.

"Good morning," the judge said, keeping his face unreadable. "Court will recess for five minutes." There was concern—near panic—among the people gathered, defendant and plaintiffs. The bride limped out exaggeratedly on the arm of her groom. It took just a few minutes to clear the room. Sergeant Johnson, in his dark blue uniform, kept everyone calm as if organizing a class trip for elementary school students. When he shut the heavy doors leading into the courtroom, however, he stayed inside. So did the judge's entire staff.

"Would you kindly step into your chambers a moment, Your Honor?" said Flannery.

"What the hell is going on here?" the judge asked.

He entered his chambers, saw the cake, and finally understood all the smiles and secret nods. He'd nearly forgotten what day it was.

Flannery turned and waved his bony arms like an orchestra conductor. "*Hummmm...Happy birthday to you, happy birthday to you...*" his voice sharp as a whistling teakettle. All the others joined in, even the judge's misanthropic secretary Myra.

Solomon grumbled, "You're lucky the smoke alarm didn't go off. That thing is a hazard."

"You're lucky we used long-burning candles!" Myra called back.

The court recorder said, "Make a wish!"

A few of the candles had already burned out. The birthday cake looked like a forest fire with small blackened trees; more the scene of a disaster than a celebration. Here he was, Justice Solomon Richter, seventy years old, the age of mandatory retirement. Three months left, and the clock ticking. It was the end of an era, his era.

He thought an instant, made his hopeless wish, bent at the knee, and blew out the candles.

———·———

That night, Sol had to run the gauntlet of a family party. His wife, Sarah, had organized it, and their daughter Abigail was there, along with her good-for-nothing live-in boyfriend, Tomas.

Sol's only living brother, Arthur, and his wife, Ruth, sat at the table; his clerk Flannery showed up wearing a bright blue vest and matching tie. Sarah had made roast leg of lamb, Sol's favorite.

"Lovely, lovely," his brother Arthur said, rubbing his hands—the chubby gourmand, though his blood pressure and cholesterol were lousy, and he'd already suffered one heart attack the winter before. The next blow might kill him, but he'd be happy if he died with his mouth full, Sol thought grimly.

"Is there any mint sauce, dear?" Arthur asked Sarah.

"Of course," Sarah said. She pushed a cut-glass bowl closer to Arthur's doughy hand. Arthur wore a diamond pinkie ring, and a ring with a red stone in it on his pointer finger. There was something damned effeminate about Arthur, in Sol's opinion—the way he gushed over food; the silly bright-colored clothes he wore. But his loudmouth wife seemed not to notice or to care.

Sol had stopped for wine on the way home. He went by way of Roslyn, a ghost town these days—more small businesses closed than open. Even the duck pond was deserted in the center of the park, though here it was the end of winter. Sol parked by the water and stood looking down at the bedraggled cattails. Wind cut at his face.

What next, he thought.

Bridge. Gin rummy. Four months a year sweating in exile down in Florida. Golf, chess—he had always hated games.

In Ray's liquor store Sol felt overwhelmed by choices. What kind of wine did he want? asked the man behind the counter. This was Ray, the owner, renowned for his foul temper and good heart. It was known he let drunks sleep it off in the back of the store. He glowered at Sol. "What'll it be—French, Italian, Californian?"

Sol rubbed his head. "Lamb," he said.

"Lamb," Ray snorted. "That tells me nothing. I know people who drink rosé with lamb."

"What do you recommend?" Sol asked.

"What do you like?" Ray countered.

"I would like," Sol said, "to be five years younger. What kind of wine do you have for that?"

Ray made a face, twisting his lips. "Let me suggest a syrah or a Côtes du Rhône," he said. "Not for you, for the lamb."

"Just give me two bottles of the best." Then Sol remembered that Flannery was coming to dinner. "Make that three," he said.

"Where were you when I was in real estate?" Ray asked. He limped to the back of the store and reappeared a few minutes later, thumping the bottles down on the counter. "So what is it, an anniversary?"

Sol dug out his wallet. "Birthday," he said.

"Oooh." Ray raised his eyebrows. "One of the big ones?"

"None of your goddamn business," Sol said. He wasn't smiling.

Ray wedged the wine bottles into a cardboard container. Then he took a tiny bottle of schnapps and tossed it into the paper bag. "Happy birthday," he said.

———

Sarah met Sol at the front door, took his coat and hat, kissed his cheek, and murmured, "Tomas got laid off again. Be nice."

"I'm always nice," Sol grumbled.

Sarah rolled her eyes.

"There's something wrong with a grown man who can't hold down a job," Sol said.

"Stop."

"I'm just saying," he said.

"Sol," she said, in a warning voice. "Make an effort. Please." Sarah was wearing the diamond necklace he'd bought for their twenty-fifth, and the matching earrings he'd purchased when she turned sixty. It reminded him of the old story of a millionaire, who, when he was first married, couldn't afford anything but some candy peanuts, which he gave to his wife with a note, saying, "I wish they were emeralds."

Years later, he gave her emeralds with the note, "I wish they were peanuts."

He kissed Sarah's soft cheek. "I promise I will make an effort."

She shook the cold air out of his coat. It fluttered across him like a ghost. Then she hung the coat in the closet and patted his hand. "Happy birthday," she told him.

He groaned.

———•———

Flannery was three sheets to the wind before the lamb was served. He sat so close to Sol's daughter Abigail that he was practically in her lap. He was in the process of demonstrating how limber he was. He performed this same trick at every dinner party; pulling his leg back behind his head and over his shoulder, like some contortionist elf. He looked like a trussed old turkey.

"Yoga," he said. "That's what keeps me young. Hatha yoga. Your Honor, you should give it a try."

Abigail regarded him with amazement. Her eyes were hazel, with orange circles around the iris, which gave her the bright-eyed look of a cat.

"I remember you did that once when I was a teenager," she said. "I think at my sweet sixteen. I can't believe you can still do it." Her long, ginger-colored hair was tied back in a bow, resting on the back of her slim neck.

"Oh, yes," Flannery said. "I'm extremely limber for my age. Extremely active." He managed to make it sound obscene.

"That's enough of that," Sarah said.

"I am willing to bet that no one else at this table can do this," Flannery said, still a human pretzel.

"I wouldn't want to!" called his sister-in-law Ruth in a loud, carrying voice. Her voice wobbled, her throat wobbled. She was wearing a baseball cap covered with gold sequins perched at a rakish angle on top of her bright orange-red hair. Ruth dressed in jeans two sizes too small, embroidered denim jackets, short skirts, and high heels. She still wore low-cut blouses to show off her ample bosom. Tonight she was wearing a gold miniskirt and a white T-shirt with gold lettering that read "Fort Lauderdale Yacht Club." You'd think she lived on a yacht, but in fact she and Arthur spent one month each winter in a one-bedroom condo rented by their son Morris, the lawyer.

Ruth patted Flannery on the shoulder. "But it's very impressive!" She sounded like she was hollering even when she spoke in her normal volume, her voice like that of Judy Holliday, the gangster's girlfriend in *Born Yesterday*. Ruth had grown up dirt poor in the worst area of Flatbush. For this reason she never left the house without matching jewelry—matching earrings, bracelets, rings, pins, shoes, bags, matching everything. No wonder she shrieked.

Flannery untied himself. He brought the foot back down to the floor and wriggled his shoulders to loosen them. His right arm rose in the air, holding a glass of wine.

"To the Right Honorable Justice Solomon Richter," he said. His voice trembled. "The best judge in the state of New York; the fairest, the smartest, the most committed judge it has ever been my pleasure and privilege to serve." He drained the glass and set it down.

"Hear, hear!" said Abigail with a delighted smile. "To Dad!" She clapped her hands together as she had when a child. The slender fingers were ringless, of course, a fact that bothered Sol more than he cared to say. Why wouldn't Tomas want to marry her? Why wouldn't any sane man?

Flannery leaned forward to look directly at Sol. "I promise," he said, "to find you the case of a lifetime this year. Something worthy of your valedictory term."

"I thought computers randomly assigned the cases," Sarah said.

Flannery laid one hand over his heart. His eyes fluttered closed. "The power of prayer, dear. My word of honor."

"This is it?" Arthur asked his brother. "They're forcing you to retire?"

"Age seventy. *Finito*," said Sol.

"It didn't used to be that way," Sarah said, distressed. "You were automatically granted the extra years, up to age seventy-five. But the Office of Court Administration changed the rules under the new director, Pescatori."

"Pescatori," Arthur mused. "Why is that name familiar?"

"I ran against him almost thirty years ago. It was an ugly race. No love lost there," Sol said shortly.

"It's a disgrace," Flannery said. His face was flushed. "A man at seventy has just reached his prime." He himself was seventy-one. "Damn the OCA. Injustice to justice!" He looked like he was about to cry. Poor drunken Flannery.

"Well," said Sarah uneasily. She was looking in Sol's direction, trying to gauge his mood. "Let's talk about something else."

"What's the big deal?" Ruth hollered. "I worked! I was happy to retire!"

Solomon turned his head to look at his sister-in-law. Beside him, he felt his daughter Abigail suck in her breath. "You sold lingerie at Lord & Taylor," he said.

"So?" Ruth's voice got even louder and sharper. "Work is work! You think I didn't work hard? We weren't even allowed to sit down!"

"Dear God," Sol said. He dropped his fork with a clatter onto his plate.

Abigail reached over and put her small hand on his wrist. Her skin was cool and calming to the touch. Even as a little child, she'd had that soothing effect on him.

"I made a savory pâté for an after-dinner treat," Sarah said. She rushed to the sideboard and lifted it in the air.

Arthur put one fat freckled hand on his heart. "My dear," he said. "After dinner. How European of us." He leaned forward to investigate. "I'd almost call it a timbale," he said. "What's in it?"

"Beef, veal, butter, spices," Sarah intoned. She raised a knife to cut it. "Wait," she said, putting the hand back down again. "I'll show you the recipe."

"I would love to see it," Arthur said. "It's glorious. Glossy. Beautiful."

"I found it online," she said.

"See how golden brown the pastry is on top," Arthur said. "Look, dear." He turned to his wife, Ruth. She still sulked.

"I'm not a chef," Ruth said. "It looks okay."

"Let me go get my camera," Arthur begged. "I want to take a picture before you slice into it."

"All right," Sarah said. "It is rather pretty."

Sarah frowned down at the recipe. "I can't read anything without my glasses. Tomas, would you be a dear and go get my glasses from the kitchen?"

"Does it have potato in it?" Flannery asked. "If it has potato it's more of a shepherd's pie."

"If my grandmother had wheels she'd be a wagon," Ruth said.

Tomas called back to Sarah from the kitchen, "Where do you keep your glasses?"

"I'll help—" Abigail began to rise, but Sol snapped, "Sit! For God's sake, why are we making such a stink about this!"

Arthur came back just then, aiming his camera. "Smile," he said. "Everyone crowd together and say, 'Pâté!'" He quickly changed his mind. "No. Let's all say—let me think. It's a sort of cross between a pâté and a terrine. Did you chill the butter?"

"For two hours," Sarah said. "Was that long enough?" She lowered the knife again.

"Lean in a little closer," Arthur said. "But don't cover the crust."

"Just cut it! Cut the goddamn meat loaf!" Sol exploded.

Sarah burst into tears.

"You are so nasty!" Ruth announced. "There's no fool like an old fool."

"What would you know?" Sol said. "You're an old sales clerk who dresses like a dead teenager."

"Dad!" Abigail said, outraged. Flannery laughed then tried to straighten his face again.

"Do I? —Do I look—like that?" Ruth demanded of her husband.

Arthur rubbed small circles on her back and said, "You look like a movie star. A glamorous movie star." He lumbered out of the dining room and brought back a box of tissues. He pulled one tissue out for his wife, and then slid the whole box over toward Sarah. "Sarah, my darling," he said. "I don't know how you put up with him all these years."

Sarah blew her nose, shaking her head. "Neither do I."

"There is no way to win in this world," Tomas said. "When you are too young they don't want you. When you become seasoned they throw you out. 'It so happens I am tired of being a man. It so happens I enter the shops and movie theaters, marchito, impenetrable, como un cisne de fieltro.'"

"What are you jabbering about?" Sol demanded.

"He's quoting Neruda," Abigail explained. "A Chilean poet. Don't you dare pick on Tomas!"

"You're tired of being a man?" Ruth shrilled. "What do you want to be, a little girl?"

Sarah announced, "I am going to go wash my face. When I come back I want every*one* to be normal and I want every*thing* to be normal, and then I will serve this stupid meat loaf. And then we can have cake. All right?"

"I apologize," Sol said meekly.

"As well you might," Arthur said.

"I didn't mean it," Sol said to Ruth. "Everyone knows you're a knockout."

"Screw you," Ruth said, but she looked pleased. "What kinda cake?" she asked.

Arthur stopped by Sol's house the next day holding a Bloomingdale's bag.

"Happy birthday, big brother," Arthur said. He stood in the front hall in his tan jacket with a plaid collar. He looked like he should be wearing knickers, a fat newsboy from the 1930s. He thrust the bag toward Sol.

"You shouldn't have," Sol said.

"It's nothing big," Arthur said. "But I've been looking for this for a while." He set down the bag at his feet and picked out one smaller flat object, wrapped in blue foil paper. Obviously a book.

When Sol tore off the wrapping and saw the cover, his heart gave an unexpected leap. It was an old hardcover of his favorite childhood novel, Ransome's *Swallows and Amazons*. He had not seen the book in forty years at least. Here again was the familiar beige cloth cover, covered with a map that suggested a river. He opened it and found it signed by the author in a strong and loopy hand.

"Thank you," Sol said. Without thinking about it, he pressed the book to his chest.

Arthur took a seat. He rested his checked cap on one round knee. He pointed at the book in Sol's hand. "If you remember that book at all, you remember it is full of small adventures. The very ordinary things of life. Ginger beer. Outings by the river. You were always trying to set things floating in the Brooklyn Bay, wearing that sailor's cap. You named your toy boat the *Kinship*, remember?" He laughed.

"What is your point," Sol said. "That I am about to enter my second childhood?"

Arthur pursed his lips. "Children know what's essential: friendships, our families. Those are the things that matter. We love what we love. Our hobbies—building toy boats, trying to figure out how to fit ships inside of bottles. Playing stickball. Listening to radios late into the night." He was citing all the things he had watched Solomon do, of course. "I used to spend hours on my back gazing up at clouds. Full of wonder. I was so sure I would see God come striding around the corner of a glorious sunset one day."

"And did you?" Sol asked.

"Not yet," said Arthur. He leaned forward in the chair, shifting his weight, trying to get comfortable. "Sol, all I am trying to say is that no one is taking your life away. Maybe they are giving it back. You've been driven so hard for so long. Ease up a little. Now you can pay attention again to the things that matter most."

"Is that it?" Sol said. "Is the lecture over?"

Arthur got to his feet. "It's over." He groaned a little, straightening up. "Enjoy the book, big brother." He held his arms out and tottered forward. Sol accepted the embrace. He felt himself fall into it, falling back into memory, like the cream-colored book he was still clutching in one hand.

"You were always the nice one of the family," Sol said.

"You were always the smart one," Arthur said. "We each have our cross to bear," he added and patted him on the cheek. Three soft pats, like being touched by bread dough. "Ah, Solly," he said. "It is never too late to be grateful for your life."

OCTOBER 2011
They Tried to Kill Us, We Won, Let's Eat

Nicole knew that their family lawyer, Peter Allister, had an innocent crush on her. He was easy on the eyes himself—he looked like the aging Robert Redford, a splash of the Sundance Kid about him. His eyes were a piercing blue. A shock of whitish-blond hair fell over his forehead. When he walked through a room, female heads turned.

Nicole watched it happen now as he stepped into the reception area to bring her back to his private office. It was decorated, if that was the word, with glass-cased chunks of rocks that he'd collected from rock-climbing expeditions, each crystal box lit from below by fancy track lighting. On one of those rock-climbing adventures years ago he'd slipped and fallen several feet, and as a result he walked with a slight limp—adding to the general romance and ruggedness of his appearance.

When he sat and faced her now, though, there was not much romantic bravado, and no smile. He searched her face, the brilliant blue eyes scanning her like a lighthouse beam.

"How you feeling?" he asked. He had a ream of papers in his hand and glanced down at them.

"All right," she said.

He looked up.

"Not so great," she admitted.

"I bet not," he said. "Well—let me tell you, I think our chances are very slim. It's a tough case. In fact I'm wondering if we have a chance to legally survive a motion to dismiss. They may toss it. It's all luck of the draw, really."

"But you're willing to give it a try?" she asked.

He nodded brusquely. "I am."

She hesitated. "Can I ask how much it will cost?" Her hand crept to her throat. This was where she had first felt the lump; somehow her fingers went back again and again to the spot of their own accord. Last thing at night, first thing when she woke.

"It could cost a fortune," he said, then seeing the frightened look on her face he added, "but it won't. It's my firm, I call the shots. We'll work something out with court costs if it comes to that, but basically, I'd say money's the least of your worries. I just don't want to lead you on with false hope as to the probable outcome."

"I appreciate your honesty," she said. Then she added, because he looked as if he didn't believe her, "I get tired of lying, and tired of being lied to."

"Well, I'll try to be straightforward," he said. "I'll get this filed in the Suffolk Supreme Court in Riverhead right away. I'll give you a call as soon as I know anything. All right?" he said. "Anything else?"

"No," she said. "Peter—I'm very grateful."

He waved that away. "Don't be grateful till I accomplish something," he said. "Meanwhile, try to take it easy. Don't worry about anything unless you have to. —Now I'd better run. Got a meeting to get to."

He was already halfway out of his chair, but he took her hand when she put it out to shake his, and he held on to it for a half instant longer than he absolutely had to. She was surprised by the warmth of his grasp—and then it was gone, and he was striding out of the room, favoring his good right leg over his left.

She took a little more time to get her pocketbook back over her shoulder, button up the lightweight jacket she was wearing. It was a warm fall day, she could see sunlight through his window, and the usual crush of traffic outside on the Turnpike. She'd have to hurry to get Daisy picked up from school on time.

Daisy hated to wait—she got a look of panic on her sharp little face when Nicole was one of the last mothers to arrive. "I like you to be early," Daisy had said the night before. "Please, tomorrow, can you be a little early?" So Nicole worked her day around that promise—it was a good way to organize a day, better than most. She would get there ten minutes early, fifteen, maybe, and read in the car while she waited. Or stand out on the blacktop by the door, so Daisy could see her face right away. Who was she fighting for, if not for Daisy? Then again, wasn't Ari fighting to protect his own two children? Funny how it boiled down to that. Trying to get to the bottom of a family schism was like peeling an onion—by the time you got to the end of it, there might be nothing left. And yet, here she was.

She looked around Peter's well-appointed office. "It's a start," she said aloud. She talked to herself more and more these days, as if cancer had given her permission to be eccentric. Her brakes had gone out, no question about it. "Now we'll see what happens when the car starts rolling downhill."

It rolled faster than she expected. Less than two weeks later, Peter was on the phone, giving her what he obviously considered to be the bad news. He spoke quietly, as if softening his voice could soften the blow.

"Your cousin has requested a change of venue," he said. "Says he can't get a fair trial in Suffolk, apparently there was a similar case a year ago. Prejudicial publicity. So he's requested that we move the case to Nassau—I suspect his lawyer knows someone or something about the Mineola Courts that we don't. The Supreme Court judges in Suffolk are a little more open to scientific cases. I was hoping we might keep it out east."

"What if we refuse the move?" Nicole asked.

Peter sounded impatient. "If we oppose the motion to change venue, that could drag out the decision for several more months. I don't think your situation can wait. They're bluffing, in a way, counting on that."

"Then the hell with it," Nicole said. "Let's agree to Mineola. You said it was a gamble either way."

"It is," Peter said.

"All right. So let's go for it."

"I agree with you," Peter said. "In addition, they've made one mistake they hadn't calculated on."

"What's that?"

"They've pissed me off now," he said. "And I am a far more effective lawyer when I'm angry."

That same afternoon Mimi called "just to talk, and because I miss you"—this was the message she left on Nikki's answering machine. Nicole was home, she recognized the caller ID even before Mimi began talking— Mimi had her own distinctive ring tone on their phone that played "You Are My Sunshine," an old joke between them. But Nicole let the machine pick up. She did not think she had ever, in the fifteen years she had known Mimi, let a call from her best friend go unanswered. But right now she was too wiped out to talk. This trial was taking everything out of her, and it hadn't even begun yet, not the ugly part.

She felt angry and bitter, though she knew none of this was her friend's fault. Somehow that didn't help. She didn't know what she would have said if she *had* picked up. That Daisy was trick-or-treating with someone else this year? Someone she didn't love one-tenth as much as Julian. That she, Nicole herself, felt like an orphan for the first time in her life, though her parents had been dead for years? She let the song play through four rings, then sat listening to Mimi's voice, its familiar hesitations, the slight nasal quality and tentative laugh in between the hesitations. The voice she would recognize ten thousand years from now. Mimi ended by saying, "I'm babbling here in the hope you might just pick up. So, here's a short summary of every Jewish holiday: 'They tried to kill us. We survived. Now, let's eat.' —Okay, so call me back soon, sweetie."

But Nicole did not call her back, not then, not soon. The silence stretched between them, a yawning abyss. And that seemed a kind of early death.

OCTOBER 2011
Good News, Bad News

The Supreme Court chambers in Mineola divided into two basic camps, if you didn't count the justices who simply hid in their chambers, uninvolved, and there were many of those. But among those inclined toward socializing, about half of the justices went down into the basement coffee shop, mostly the younger ones. You could hear the buzz of conversation and the clink of cups and cutlery before you'd stepped off the elevator; the smell of toast and coffee drifted out to meet you.

The fare in the coffee shop was basic: grilled cheese sandwiches, wraps, bagels, coffee, fruit, and dessert. The same ancient Chinese woman had been managing the place for ages. Judge Lieu, the most popular of the senior judges, held informal court here, sitting at one of the longer wood-veneer tables. It normally sat eight, but if one pushed in another smaller table right against it, it could fit as many as twelve. There were smaller tables, of course, for friends, coworkers, court-bound families, knots of secretaries, and loners. But Judge Thomas Lieu, even when he sat entirely alone, drinking the green tea he favored, sat at one corner of the long table that ran down the center of the room.

Judge Lieu was Vietnamese. He was a small man, his features so sharply chiseled they seemed carved with a knife, and his hair was still jet-black though he was in his midsixties. He was athletic, a sixth-degree black belt in tae kwon do, known for his long-distance running. Now and again you'd see him out running in a pair of gray sweat shorts and a sweat-soaked gray T-shirt, five or six miles from the center of Mineola, sprinting down Old Country Road with the traffic, or downhill on one of the smaller streets. Then he'd shower in the court officers' locker room, and dress in his dark suit again before driving home to his house in Oyster Bay.

Lieu was a quiet, thoughtful man. He'd made his name in family court, where he listened and sighed and said, "Terrible, terrible sadness," or "More civilities, please!" when tempers flared. He addressed everyone as sir or ma'am, including the janitorial staff. He was immensely popular with the younger judges, especially the women. Even those who appeared before him remarked that no matter how crowded the courtroom, they felt as if they were alone with Judge Lieu, and that his remarks were meant especially for them.

He had a melancholy streak that he hid behind a small, sad smile. He was a great kidder, always telling jokes and teasing the younger judges and lawyers. Women were drawn to him. He had been married for twenty years, and then one day his wife—a doctor with a family practice in Syosset—walked out, taking the two smaller children, leaving Lieu to the company of his eldest son, who had just entered high school. It was around this time that he left family court and became an elected member of the New York Supreme Court, the first Vietnamese to succeed in a power cartel run almost entirely by Italians.

One by one, the two younger children fled their mother's house and came to join him in Oyster Bay. He never spoke of his own private life. Sol learned all of this second- and thirdhand. Tom Lieu had a way not merely of removing but of erasing himself from all conversations. That may have been one reason why he became a father confessor to so many colleagues and coworkers. He was modest to a fault. The basement coffee shop suited him.

A very different group of judges socialized up in the posh space of the new law library. Here the scent was of new leather and lemon furniture polish. There were comfortable sofas, easy chairs, gold-embossed law books, and plush wall-to-wall carpeting. This was where Judge Michael DeNunzio held court unofficially. Unlike the basement, people didn't casually drop by for chitchat. Most sat at the computer desks, doing research, taking notes, scurrying back and forth on soft-soled shoes, the women secretaries and paralegals teetering in the thick carpeting on too-high heels.

DeNunzio could be found there many afternoons, at the center of a knot of men, deep in disputation. DeNunzio had been a law professor at St. Joseph's and some scent of academia clung to him, though he dressed better than any academic Sol had known. His suits were bespoke; he was given to electric blue shirts and expensive ties. He was a tall handsome man with sleek black hair, in his early fifties, but he seemed to hail from a much older generation. Perhaps even another century. He was soft-spoken; listeners had to bend their heads to hear each word.

Sol did not especially like DeNunzio, but he respected him. DeNunzio had worked his way through Princeton University, coming from an immigrant Italian family in Elizabeth, New Jersey. First in his family to attend college, DeNunzio had a sharp, clear legal mind. He knew the law, and more than that, he could penetrate to the subtleties beneath and around the law. You watched him run his finger across a page of a legal brief, and it was like a man running his finger across water; you sensed the depths of something moving underneath the surface.

So when Flannery came to Sol triumphantly waving *Greene vs. Wiesenthal*—the case Sol had quickly come to think of as simply "the blood case"—he was undecided about where to turn for a second opinion. It was a messy situation, the one dying cousin suing the other. There was the possibility of a breach of contract, and the larger question of whether one could force rescue. The case might or might not even be actionable. Sol studied the gathered materials and said, "I don't know. I have a bad feeling about it."

"What do you mean?" Flannery cried. "It's the case of a lifetime! Here is a question of individual rights—our own particular bailiwick." Over the years they had taken on a number of tough cases—a family fighting enforced seat belt use, another case about chlorinating the water in Bayville.

Still, Sol said, "Hard cases make for bad law. The defendant has already requested a change of venue to Nassau. Now he's making a motion to dismiss. His attorney insists that the letter he signed for his cousin is unenforceable. I'm inclined to agree." He shrugged. "I'll be honest, I don't like it. That's all."

"That's *all?*" Flannery said. "Have you seen what's on your calendar, Your Honor? One petty case after another. Most will never even make it to the courtroom. And the valedictory year is racing by."

"General jurisdiction ranges from the mundane to the complex," the judge said. "It always has, always will. And half the cases settle before going to court. You know that."

"I do know it," Flannery said stubbornly. "That's why I say we take this on. This case is worth trying. It's got meat on its bones."

"All I can promise is that I'll consider it," Sol said.

Flannery began to protest. "Your Honor, this is our big chance."

Sol narrowed his eyes at his chief clerk. "I'm not looking for a big chance," he said. He showed the clerk to the door.

After he sat down again, alone, he pressed the button on his phone. Myra answered, sounding bored. "Yes?"

"Myra, please keep Flannery out of my way for the rest of the day," he said.

"Gladly," Myra said.

The judge looked at the pile of papers on the blood case and sighed. He did not trust himself with this case—something made him hesitate. There was something ugly about it, something thorny. His closest friends among the judges had retired in the past few years—to Florida and the mountains of North Carolina. Should he go to Lieu or to DeNunzio for a second opinion? He had a feeling Lieu would advise against the case. DeNunzio was harder to read.

Feeling vaguely guilty, as if he were betraying Tom Lieu, Sol made his way an hour later to the law library on the second floor. It was nearly empty. One new young clerk, his eyes as red as a rabbit's from too much research, sat as if stapled into his seat in front of a computer in the corner. A pair of interns flirted over a pair of books at the center table. And there, in his corner of the room, sat DeNunzio, alone for a change. Sol nearly bolted. But DeNunzio spotted him immediately, as if he'd sensed him coming along the second-floor hallway.

"Ah," he said. "The Honorable Justice Solomon Richter"—gently mocking Flannery's calling-out in court—"What can I do for you?"

Sol had no choice but to take the leather chair catty-corner to DeNunzio, Sol's chair a shade smaller, a shade shorter—were these things deliberate? Sol wondered. With a sinking feeling he offered up a few pages of the numerous *Greene vs. Wiesenthal* motion papers that Flannery had given him.

"You'd like me to take a look?" DeNunzio said in his soft voice.

Sol almost said no. He hung on to the papers a few seconds longer than made any sense. But there was something in the sharpness of DeNunzio's eye that moved him. Did he serve justice or didn't he? Did he, Solomon Richter, desire to do the right thing, even the difficult thing, or would he slouch his way through these final months of public trust? He had earned his reputation on thorny cases like these. He'd upheld the rights of a deeply religious woman to refuse a needed blood transfusion. He had visited her in the hospital on her deathbed. But she died at peace with herself; he could not regret what he'd done.

"Give me a little time to study these," DeNunzio said. "I take it it's a difficult case."

"I'm not sure it's a case at all," Sol answered.

"All right, then." DeNunzio was already bundling the papers into his sleek tan Italian briefcase. There was no fishing them out now. Sol sensed that both Myra and Flannery would have been disappointed in him. God knew he was old enough to make up his own mind. He turned, like a schoolboy ordered out of the principal's office.

"We'll talk again," DeNunzio said, as a principal might have done.

Sol spent the day in an uneasy truce with himself. If DeNunzio said there was no case, then it was off his shoulders. He could move on to simpler matters, clearer and easier decisions. Not risk making a fool of himself here at the tail end of his career. The closer he drew to retirement, the less real his life's work seemed to him, as if none of it had ever happened. That's how easy it was, he thought, to lose one's footing in the world.

Sol knew how it was with blood relations. He himself had labored for seven years in family court, and he'd considered them the worst part of his working life. If people could only hear what went on behind the closed doors, the pulled curtains of suburbia. No wonder Judge Lieu was always crying out, "More civility! More civility!" The family was the last remaining savage tribe.

Finally, around four thirty in the afternoon, as the sun was sinking toward its wintry grave, the phone rang. It was DeNunzio. "Come up to my office," DeNunzio said in his soft, even voice. He never had a secretary make a phone call for him. When he ran for election for judge, he bragged, "I answer my own phones"—and it was true. He was not a delegator. He saved the best and worst work for himself.

DeNunzio's office was on the fourth floor, his courtroom the largest in the building, his chambers window with the widest view. A legal clerk had once been shot and killed there after hours by a jealous lover. Other judges would have avoided it. Not DeNunzio. He simply had it redecorated. His beige carpet was so thick, Sol felt his feet sinking at every step. He took the chair that DeNunzio gestured toward. It swung left, and he put his feet down to steady himself. DeNunzio was smiling, a tolerant smile, as if he were used to such shenanigans.

"Looks justiciable to me," he said, handing the papers back to Sol, neatly held together with a paper clip and slipped inside a file folder. The file folder made Sol homesick for Sarah and her common sense. You did not find much of it out in the so-called real world. Sol thought it was why many men his age had so few friends. He could count on the fingers of one hand the number of men who would ever say anything sensible to him: his brother Arthur, his neighbor Joe Iccarino, one or two inmates. But for the most part he turned to the women in his life for conversation, comfort, advice—Sarah or Abigail, or even Myra, for that matter. There was something almost feminine about DeNunzio—which may have led Sol to this judge's chambers in the first place.

DeNunzio placed the briefs where they both could see them. "There's an ipso facto contract, and wherever there is a legal contract, you have a shot at an interesting legal argument. The motion to dismiss can be denied. I'm not sure there's much doubt which way this will go, but you've always been interested in these cases. One might even say you've made your name on them. I'd say you've got a nice big fat one right up your alley." He tapped the pages with one tapered forefinger.

"Legally, then, you think the case has merit?"

DeNunzio shrugged. "That's for higher minds than ours to say. But I don't think there's much chance of it being overturned." He leaned forward. "Why not?" he urged. "Why not go for it?"

"Well, for one thing," Sol said. "I'm due to retire in December. This case could drag on into next year."

DeNunzio waved away the objection. He wore a gold ring with a seal on it, as if he were a pope. "An extension is easily granted in these situations," he said. "You can't swap judges in the middle of a case. Let me make a phone call to my friend Pescatori in New York. We went to Princeton together. There shouldn't be a problem."

"I ran against Pescatori back in eighty-two," Sol said. "It's unlikely he'll grant me any favors."

DeNunzio shrugged and smiled. "Who says this is a favor?" he said. "Pescatori might not see it that way. Besides, if I tell you this thing will go through—it will go." He held out his hand, and for one brief instant Sol wondered if he was supposed to kiss the ring, the way you would with the pope. Instead they shook on it.

"Thank you," Sol said.

"Good luck," DeNunzio answered.

————

"I have something to tell you about Abigail," Sarah said that evening without preamble. Sol had not even had time to take off his coat. In the morning, frost had coated the lawn. By evening, he drove through a summer storm. Climate changes, volcanoes, everything upside down. He'd thought to outwit the weather by avoiding the parkway. Instead he'd been crawling down Jericho Turnpike for what seemed like hours, skidding in puddles, gripping the steering wheel so hard that even now his fingers could not unclench themselves. Sarah had begun a conversation the exact same way about a month earlier, only that time she had said, "Tomas is gone."

"Gone, as in—"

"He's not dead, if that's what you mean."

"He walked out on her?"

"Let's just say that they agree to disagree."

In Solomon's opinion, Tomas's departure was good news. He had never approved of the relationship; too haphazard, too unsettled.

"She's going to have a baby," Sarah said now.

"She's *pregnant*?" he asked. "The son of a bitch knocked her up and then left?"

"No! —She's not exactly pregnant," Sarah said. "That's the thing."

"Not exactly pregnant," the judge said. "Tell me how that works."

"She's *adopting*," Sarah said. "She just got the phone call last week—she was going to tell us."

"She was going to tell us—when?" said the judge. "When the kid arrived with a suitcase in its hand? Where is it from?"

"It's not an it, it's a she. She's nearly a year old. And she's from Thailand. Her name is going to be Iris."

Sol sat with both hands on his knees. He felt like a statue. He felt he looked like a statue. He could not identify all the emotions he was feeling. Chief among them was confusion. "Thailand," he said.

He knew little about the country, except that it bordered on Cambodia, somewhere near Laos and Vietnam. He had lived through the era of the Vietnam War as a lawyer—too old to be drafted, too young to be indifferent. His image of Southeast Asian children was limited to a vision of one small child running down the street, burning, her mouth twisted open in fear and pain. A famous news photo at the time. He rubbed the palms of his hands over his kneecaps and stood up. He shuffled in his slippers past Sarah and into the kitchen. "I need a drink," he said.

"I already poured you one," she called after him.

A half tumbler of whiskey sat waiting on the kitchen table. Unless she had been drinking, too—but that was unlikely. For one thing, Sarah seldom drank. For another, there would have been lipstick around the rim of the glass. She thought he didn't notice that kind of thing, but he did.

"I'm not sure I approve," Sol said, after he had taken a slug of the whiskey. "I'm not sure it's a good idea."

"Well, *I* think it's a great idea. And so does Abigail. And that's what matters." She sat across from him defiantly, and drew a cup of tea closer to her.

He looked up and nodded sardonically. "I see," he said. "How long have *you* known?"

Sarah flushed a little but held her ground. "Nothing for sure," she said. "I had my suspicions. Abigail and I had a few talks—they were very general. She's not getting any younger, Sol, and she desperately wants a family."

"We're her family," Sol said. Sarah didn't bother to answer. She looked at him over the rim of her teacup, just her sharp brown eyes showing. "And a single woman with an adopted daughter is not a traditional family."

"Traditional is a matter of perspective," Sarah said. "And let me remind you, buster, this will not be her *adopted* daughter. This will be her daughter, period. And your granddaughter."

The judge let this sink in. He tilted his head right, and then left, as he often did in court, unconsciously, weighing out a situation. He curled his fingers over his mouth, another habitual gesture, to hide his expression.

"When does this baby arrive?" he asked.

"In about three weeks," Sarah said. "We're scheduled to leave in late November. They don't give you much advance warning." She held up one hand. "Not you. I know you're busy with the court. I'll go. She needs me. A mother is not the same as a husband, but it's something. We'll only be gone about ten days. I'll leave you plenty of food in the freezer. We still have that lasagna from a few weeks ago, I'll make a few of your favorites. Maybe a pot roast."

"I am not worried about food," Sol said. "For Christ's sake."

"And I'm sure Arthur and Ruth will have you over for dinner. Maybe the Iccarinos, too."

"Yes, I'm sure." The judge frowned.

"Well, when Abigail calls, it would be nice if you could act delighted," she said. "She's scared to death to tell you."

"Delighted might be stretching it," Sol said.

"I would settle for happy."

"Happy...and surprised, I take it."

"Yes, she wanted to tell you herself."

"Thank you for the advance warning," Sol said.

"A baby! Isn't that wonderful," Sol said on the phone to his daughter a few days later. Abigail had called after supper.

"You mean it?" Abigail said.

"Oh, yes," the judge said.

"Really?"

"Absolutely."

out adoption lately."

why you're so enthusiastic."

t a word. I'm just—so surprised."

, finally."

apparently. There was the briefest

"I mean, she'll *be* our own. Of course we'll love her." He could not resist. "Are you sure you've thought this all through carefully?"

Abigail laughed drily. "Now, that sounds more like the father I know," she said.

———·———

"Don't get excited," Peter Allister said. "But I have a bit of good news."

Nicole was back in his office, looking into the piercing blue eyes of her lawyer.

"They've agreed to take on the case in the Mineola Supreme Court. Judge Richter denied the motion to dismiss. We're going to trial."

"Wow," she said. "Okay. Wow." She tried to smile but felt, actually, as if she'd been knocked sideways.

Peter held up one hand. "It's a situation with a judge, not a jury, you understand. You can't hope for sympathy from fellow mothers, or men who—well, men who might want to take your side. This judge is a tough old bird, ready to retire soon. His name is Solomon Richter. And"—he took a deep breath—"he's famous for upholding the rights of the individual. Which is not good for us, in this case. We're trying to force one individual—your cousin—to give up something that belongs to him, and bring the weight of the legal system to make him do so against his will. I've read several of the cases that Judge Richter has been involved in—and his written opinions." Peter managed a wry smile.

"You're saying he's likely to judge against us."

"I'm not saying anything. In thirty years of practicing law," Peter said, "I've learned never to predict human behavior. People will surprise you. But yes, Nicole. I'm trying to warn you not to get your hopes up too high."

He sat back in his chair and swiveled it back and forth a little to each side, twisting like a boy on a swing. "You also need to prepare yourself for all the possible publicity. The media gets a hold of a story like this, they're likely to run with it. No one but the judge can keep them out—and I'm not convinced even Judge Richter can control it. It could turn into a circus. I'm having serious second thoughts about the wisdom of pressing on. Do you really want to be the center of a media blitz for an unlikely outcome?"

"No," said Nicole. "No, of course not."

Peter stopped twisting his chair back and forth. His face showed visible relief. "All right, then," he said. "That's that."

"But I also don't want to die and abandon my eight-year-old daughter," she said. "Or Jay. So I can't back down now, no matter what. This is the only chance I've got."

He gave a flicker of a smile. "And I just broke my own rule," he said. "Asking a question to which I did not already know the answer."

NOVEMBER 2011
Like a Dog

Sarah had charge of the paperwork and government forms, while Abigail took care of everything else. She had found a nice apartment in Manhasset, thanks to Sarah's synagogue connections. She had hired a nanny. At Sol's house there were oceans of adoption paperwork to fill out, a list of rules and regulations as long as your arm, checks to write in advance, little gifts to wrap in pink and green—because Thailand had a different lucky color for each day of the week. Sarah wrapped key chains and American makeup, Hello Kitty T-shirts, and coin purses filled with pendants or little beaded bracelets.

"Bribes," the judge said grimly.

"Not bribes—gifts," Sarah said. "You don't understand the culture."

"There's a lot I don't understand."

The agency had provided a list of cultural dos and don'ts that Sarah studied with great care. No touching any statues in a Buddhist temple. No blowing your nose loudly. Sitting in a temple with your feet pointing toward Buddha was considered an insult, but so was sitting with your feet pointing toward a person. If you picked your teeth, you were supposed to cover your mouth with your other hand.

"I hope you'll remember that one," Sol said.

"Very funny," she snapped.

Sarah kept the precious file folders inside an old backpack that must have been left over from Abigail's early college days. It had paisley designs all over it, painted on fire-engine-red leather. It looked unlike anything else Sarah owned. "I can't possibly confuse it with anyone else's," was all Sarah said. After a while, the red paisley bag seemed like an appendage to her body. She was afraid to carry it outside with her, but more afraid to leave it at home. She woke during the night asking Sol, "Where is the N16 form? What did I do with the FR886432 papers?"

"You're getting yourself too worked up over this," Sol told her. "You'll have a heart attack."

"I'm just being careful," Sarah said. "If I ruin this for Abigail, I'll never forgive myself."

Then, the Friday right before they were to leave, disaster seemed to strike all at once. The judge had come home from court early. He wished he were accompanying his wife and child. He was anxious about long-distance travel. Even Myra, his cranky secretary, told him, "For God's sake get out of the office." She was a childless woman in her early forties, with waist-length black hair and a smoker's husky voice. "There's nothing that can't wait till Monday," she said. "Go. It'll give me a chance to catch up. Kisses to the family. Tell them bon voyage." She blew an air kiss into the atmosphere, like a smoke ring.

Sol found Sarah practically in a puddle on the sewing room floor. The familiar red paisley leather backpack was wide open like a yelling mouth. Adoption papers spilled in a circle around it, tumbling out of their folders. The little canary-colored room, normally so tidy, looked as if it had been burglarized.

"What's going on?" Sol asked.

Sarah was wild-eyed. He could not remember the last time he'd seen her like this. She was gasping like a fish. "I can't find the N6 paper! I've looked all over."

"Calm down," Sol said, sinking down beside her. That floor got harder every day, the carpet thinner under his flanks. "We'll find it."

Sarah's hands pawed through the papers. "I'm telling you, I've searched everywhere—I can't find it! My body is going numb. I can't feel my arms. We can't go without the N6 form!"

"Take it easy," Sol said. "It's just one more piece of paper."

"It's the form giving permission to adopt from the INS," she said hoarsely.

"Jesus," Sol said. He, too, began searching through the folders, but there no longer seemed to be any order to anything. "Call the adoption agency," he said.

"It's Friday afternoon, after four o'clock. No one is going to be there. Oh, Sol. Sol. What have I *done*?"

Sol went to the little phone on the corner table—it, too, was canary yellow—and lifted the receiver. "Give me the number," he ordered.

"No one is going to be there," Sarah repeated. "Let me call. I'll call." She had the agency's number on speed dial. She listened to it ring once, twice. She held the phone out toward him, as if to dry it, tilting it. "See?" she said. "No one."

Just then someone answered. Sol heard the voice with a flood of relief in his own chest. He did not approve of this adoption, but he did not want it to fall apart at the eleventh hour. Feeling like a hypocrite, he said a small prayer. He promised to do tefillin, faithfully, if this thing would go all right. Every day, if necessary.

"You do?" Sarah was saying. "You have a copy?" Sol was shocked by his own sense of relief. He wanted to run over and kiss her, kiss the ground, do something foolish.

"Yes," she said. "We have a fax. —I'm sorry you lost your keys, but thank God you were there." She laughed. "Oh? I'm glad you found them! Then it's a very good day, isn't it? I'll turn on the fax right now. Would you? Just till I'm sure it's come in? Thank you so much—Jane, is it? Thanks so much."

She practically collapsed into Sol's arms. "I could feel my body losing sensation. I've never been so frightened in my life, never." He hurried downstairs and turned on the fax machine in the den. They sat in the kitchen to wait, and within two minutes heard the high, shrill familiar ringing sound of a fax coming through.

"Don't ever tell Abigail about this," she said, flopping down opposite him.

"I won't," he said.

"Ever," she said. "I'm supposed to be the capable one. That's my only strength."

Sol was touched and taken aback. "You have many strengths," he said.

"No." She shook her head. "Hypercompetently flying by the seat of my pants," she said. "I've been doing it all my life."

That night Sarah made a traditional Shabbos supper—roast chicken, noodle kugel, kosher wine. She used the tablecloth her mother had cross-stitched in moss-green thread, the linen starched within an inch of its life.

Abigail took all this in with a single sweeping glance. She had her mother's way of absorbing the mood of a scene, her father's way of keeping her own counsel.

"What's going on here?" she asked. "Is someone converting? Are we praying to the God of international long-distance flights?"

"We just felt like celebrating," Sarah said, going over to embrace her daughter, draw her into the dining room, take off her jacket, and smooth her hair, all in one fluid gesture. "We have a lot to be grateful for." She had put all of the papers back into the files, the files back into the red backpack, which hung from her own dining room chair. She was not about to let it out of her sight again. And of course, five minutes after the fax arrived, they'd found the missing form in the back of a different file folder.

They all lined up by the kitchen window for the lighting of the candles. It was a ritual they had not performed as a family in a long time. Sarah lit the candles, one after the other, five in all. She acted as if each candle was a separate person, someone she knew intimately. Sol knew she would use this moment to remember anyone in their extended circle who might be sick, or suffering, or in pain. He would not hurry her. He thought of his brother Arthur and wished he would lose some weight. He thought of Prissy Gardino, his court recorder, battling with her second bout of lung cancer. Of his wife and daughter about to leave for a foreign country, to bring home a little stranger. Worry for him was a form of prayer. Keep them safe, he thought, reminding himself to think of the baby as well. Keep them all safe and bring them home safe.

Sarah murmured the Hebrew blessing into her hands. The words were muffled by her fingers but grew clearer at the end: "Ner shel Shabbos Kodesh!"

"Let's eat!" Abigail said. "I'm starving." She slowed down just when she reached her chair, and pulled it out slowly, looking around the room, neat as a pin. "This is the last time I'll be eating here without

Iris." She shook her head. "I don't know how you do it all," she said to her mother.

A look passed between husband and wife. "Oh, it just happens," Sarah said airily.

"Well, I'll never be able to," Abigail said. "I hope you're prepared to feed us."

"You'll be surprised what you can do for a child," her mother said. "Trust me."

———

Nicole came downstairs and planted a kiss on her husband Jay's blond head. His hair was so curly it had always reminded her of Jason and the golden fleece. She handed him a small piece of paper. Jay was watching a college football game, but he clicked off the sound and looked up at her immediately, his light blue eyes attentive. "What is this, a shopping list? Is there something you need me to get?"

"Sort of," she said.

"I'll go right away."

She put one hand on his shoulder and laughed. "There's no great rush."

He picked up the paper and looked at it. First he looked puzzled. Then his expression darkened. His shoulders drew in. "Please tell me," he said, "this is not what it looks like."

"Shhh," she said. Daisy was upstairs playing with her best school friend, Claudia. They were playing some noisy make-believe game. Still, their girl had supersonic hearing, like a bat.

He read off the list of women's names. "Jesus," he said.

"I just want you to know that there are some nice women out there in the world," she said. "You know, in case worse comes to worst."

"For God's sake, Nikki." His eyes were pleading. He stuck his hand out sideways, holding the list between thumb and forefinger, like something contaminated. The football game flickered on the muted TV. Someone had just done something. They were showing it again, the ball flying out of bounds.

She took the list from Jay and sat in his lap. She wrapped her arms around him, but read the list over his shoulder. "Shelley Needham," she said. "The girl's basketball coach is a very nice woman. Daisy adores her."

He laughed bitterly, but did not push her away. "Shelley Needham is gay," he said.

She leaned her head back. "Are you sure?"

"Well, Shelley's life partner Gloria seems pretty sure. They just bought a house together in Northport."

"Okay," she said, "what about Maura Carter?"

"What about her," he said tonelessly. He was watching the silent TV. The strain of the past several months was starting to show. He was going gray at the top of his hair, the gold color losing some of its luster.

"She's attractive, she's lonely, she's a nice person. You always say that yourself."

"She looks like a rodent," Jay said. "Her pigtails stick up on either side, exactly like a rat's ears. Why are we even discussing this? You are the only one I want. You are the only woman I have ever wanted." He kissed her neck. He put one hand on the small of her back.

She wriggled out of his arms. "Jay, listen to me," she said. "I can't stand the idea of you being lonely the rest of your life. It's not right. And Daisy is going to need a mother."

"Daisy *has* a mother," he said stubbornly.

"Okay, Jay, but at some point you're going to need to move on."

"Move on?" He lifted the remote and clicked off the TV. The screen went grayish black. "Listen to me, Nicole. If anything happens to you—and I do not believe that it will, we're going to win this case and get you the cord blood you need and then you're going to be back on track—but if anything should happen, don't expect heroics. If you go anywhere without me, I'm going to cry like a dog. That's it. Like a goddamn dog."

———·—·———

Sarah phoned the judge from Los Angeles to say that their connecting flight had been delayed, and they were still having trouble locating the baggage. Sol should plan on coming to the airport at least four hours later than he'd intended. "And by this," she said, "I do not mean that I want you to get there six hours *early.*"

"Don't be ridiculous," he said—but Sarah was right, as usual. He always worried that some road would be closed, the expressway would be backed up, he'd be sent to the Van Wyck or some other crazy route, and find himself driving around in circles. He hated rushing to get to airports and train stations. He had planned to leave several hours early, just in case.

"I promise not to leave till after noon," he said.

"Two o'clock would be better, but okay," she said. "If there are any further delays, I can still reach you there at the house. I wish to heaven you'd get a cell phone. You must be the last man on earth without one."

"Call if there are any problems," he said. "I'll wait here by the phone."

"It'll take an extra hour to get through customs," she said. "So don't panic. They're being very careful these days coming into the United States."

"Well, that's one dangerous-looking baby you've got there." He'd seen the photos on the computer, e-mailed by Sarah with subject labels like "First bath!" "Beautiful in red dress!" "Clapping hands!" Being a grandparent apparently brought on the exclamation points. Sol wished he could feel as excited. What he saw in the photos was a hopelessly scrawny little being with a solemn expression, often worried, with one eyebrow curved in a fishhook. She looked undernourished and possibly ill—though that might have been the effect of the bilious green shade of the umbrella stroller they had purchased in Thailand. A top-of-the-line Maclaren awaited her in America—the judge had already loaded it into the back of his Volvo.

"I can't wait to see you," Sarah said. "And Abigail sends her love."

"Good," he said.

"You're going to adore Iris," Sarah said. "You'll surprise yourself."

"Mm," said Sol, unwilling to perjure himself. "Travel safe."

He could hear Abigail in the background, calling "Love you, Dad!"

"Okay," he said. He was famous within the family for never responding to an "I love you" with one of his own. But there they were, still three thousand miles away, an entire continent between them, about to climb into a piece of steel machinery that was supposed to fly them home. "I love you, too," he said.

What if Sarah was wrong about him as a grandfather? he thought. What if he didn't adore his granddaughter? What if he didn't even like her? It was like adopting a young dog from the pound instead of a puppy. They'd missed the first year of her life—first smile, first step. Some things were hardwired. But they would never know with this baby what that hardwiring might be. Possible genetic defects. Personality disorders, disease, psychological history. Who knew what led a mother to abandon her child?

And then there was the matter of foreignness. Iris looked nothing like any of them. Her skin was a dark yellowish color, her eyes unreadable slits in all the photos Sarah sent. In the orphanage she wore a plain off-white nightdress that hung straight to the floor; her hair had been close-cropped, the front cut into a severe V. She looked like a little Buddhist monk. It took Sol a long time to warm up to people. What if he never warmed up to this girl at all? What if he felt like a stranger holding her, taking her out in public, giving her a bath?

He instructed himself to get a grip. He had a cup of tea and a bowl of oatmeal, steel-cut, cooked from scratch. Yet once the oatmeal was cooked and in the bowl, covered with a dollop of yogurt, he barely touched it. He drank his tea plain, without cream, without sugar. He remembered his grandmother holding a sugar cube between her teeth, sipping hot bitter tea from a glass. He had fond memories of her, though she had been a tough *balabust*, a force to contend with. He remembered her running her rough hands through his hair. She would let him roll out his own batch of noodles and bake them, though somehow they never ate those noodles—grimy from the dirt of his hands. They were too special to eat, she told him. Once, a wasp had been flying around his head in the Bucks County boardinghouse, and she killed it with her own forefinger, jabbing it down on the windowsill. That was courage, he thought. That was a true grandparent.

He read the *New York Times* and *Newsday* cover to cover. It was a Thursday. He did the crosswords in pen. Then, still at a loss for a way to kill some time, he took out the book Arthur had given him for his birthday, *Swallows and Amazons*. It was as enchanting as he remembered. Only the illustrations seemed different—they had once loomed so large, and now he found tiny figures, some of them barely more than sketches. He fell asleep in the middle of chapter four, the book hanging from his hand, and was awakened by the sound of the doorbell. He marked his place in the book with a scrap of the *New York Times* and went to open the door.

No one was there. At least, that was his first impression. He looked out into a blue morning, milder than one had any right to expect in late November, the sun climbing. Then he looked down. Sitting in a vivid green stroller, all by herself, was an Asian baby girl with the most exquisite face he had ever seen, the color of gold, with a pair of sparkling eyes so dark they looked almost black.

"Oh, God," Sol said. "Oh, my God."

Abigail and Sarah, laughing, popped out of their hiding places, but his eyes were riveted on Iris. He never would have believed this. It was love at first sight.

DECEMBER 2011
Let the Games Begin

DeNunzio had been correct. Sol's extension glided through the Office of Court Administration without a hitch, more quickly than things usually moved in judicial administrative affairs. The letter came stamped with a dark blue OCA seal on the letterhead, and Albert Pescatori's signature at the bottom. Solomon Richter's tenure as Supreme Court judge was extended till the end of *Greene vs. Wiesenthal,* with a deadline generously set at two years in the future. Sol could have seen it as a new lease on his working life, but he was surprisingly depressed by the whole thing—the case itself, the ease with which this exception had gone through by the hand of his former adversary, a man he did not admire.

The initial meeting took place in chambers with the judge and lawyers only. Sol was old-fashioned that way. He'd found that even lawyers tended to be on their best behavior in his chambers.

The lawyer for Nicole Greene, the plaintiff, was Peter Allister, a man he did not know. Sol was surprised that that the plaintiff hadn't hired a larger law firm for the case, with a specialist in medical malpractice or contract law. As far as he could tell, this lawyer worked alone. He was soft-spoken, his sandy hair touched with gray. He presented the case simply—almost too simply, Sol thought, not trying to tug on the judge's heartstrings as most lawyers would have done, but simply pressing the urgency of moving forward quickly, and emphasizing the contractual nature of the letter that the cousin, Ari Wiesenthal, had signed.

The defendant's lawyer, Sol did unfortunately know quite well. She was famous, or infamous, depending on your point of view. A few jurists admired her; many did not. Katrina Turock was a junior partner at Singular and Prescott, a large prestigious law firm located in Great Neck, with branches in two of the Five Towns. Turock was in her early thirties but had already made her name with a few well-publicized cases. Her client was always the big guy, the five-hundred-pound canary. Her beauty tended toward the showy side, with long, wavy blonde hair. It was said she was a bodybuilder, but she was too muscular, almost bulky-looking, and, he noticed, her hair was starting to thin. She was also high-strung, smart, ruthless, sarcastic to her opponents, and had had numerous affairs with older men in high places. None of these ended well for the men.

As he'd expected, the first thing she did was reargue the motion to dismiss. She called the case "ludicrous, based on old-fashioned notions of gallantry that have nothing to do with law." She did not shake Flannery's hand when introduced, and spoke insultingly in front of Peter Allister about "little firms that had nothing better to do with their time than to waste it." Peter bared his teeth in a smile.

"The court has already decided to keep the case," Sol said. "So let's move on to scheduling."

Katrina rolled her eyes and took out her BlackBerry. "I'm not free till March or April, at the earliest," she said.

"That's unfortunate," said the judge, "as the case will commence in two weeks, time being a key factor. Perhaps another lawyer in your firm can take your place." He hoped that this was true.

Her pale eyes flashed. "It's *my* case," she said. "I'll rearrange my schedule." She was wearing a low-slung belt with many brass studs over a short skirt, over a pair of leggings. Over this she wore a jacket that he supposed was stylish, but the whole effect was vaguely military. If Arnold Schwarzenegger became a woman and a lawyer, this was what he'd be wearing.

"Thank you," said Peter Allister, gathering up his papers. "I'd better mosey on back to my little office."

"Let the games begin," said Katrina Turock.

———·•·———

"I've been thinking," Sarah said one morning at breakfast. Sol knew from experience that this was never a good sign. "I did some thinking while I was in Thailand, and I realized…" She bit into her bagel and chewed it in thoughtful silence.

As usual, she made him ask her. "Realized what?" When he was younger and newly married, he would begin to panic inwardly. *I just realized that I want a divorce. I realized that I hate this house. I realized that we should move to Alaska.* In reality it was likely to be, *I realized no one in my family was ever a Republican.* Sol had learned not to guess. So he laid down his morning paper and waited.

"I have a choice," she said. "I can settle down and become a grandmother and devote myself entirely to that—and it's very tempting, with Iris so close. Or I can try to develop myself in some way. It doesn't mean I won't be available for my family. But I realized something is missing."

Another long silence. Another question. "What's missing?" he said, tempted to make a joke.

"Spirituality," she said. "I go through the motions on Friday night, but I barely feel it anymore. You know, we took Iris to a Buddhist temple for a blessing—they do that with all the orphans—and I felt very uncomfortable. But I didn't know why I should be uncomfortable. What does it mean for me to be a Jew?"

It was not a question he could answer.

She plowed on. "You know that nice young rabbi who's renting the apartment to Abigail?" she said. He nodded, though he'd never met the man. "He's running a study group for older women—women my age who never really had a Jewish education. At the end of it we're all going to get bat-mitzvahed."

Now he did laugh.

She frowned. "What's so funny about that? You think we're too old?"

"Are you going to have a disc jockey?" he asked. "A theme? Maybe the Golden Girls?"

She swatted him with the newspaper. "It's not *about* the bat mitzvah. It's about learning. As long as you're learning, you still feel alive. Learning is the greatest defense against despair."

"Are you in danger of despair?" Sol asked. He was taken aback, looking at his wife more closely, like a man searching for symptoms of an illness.

"I want to feel alive—and not just through other people. I have the time now, I'd like to"—she glanced at him shyly—"to connect myself to something higher."

"You should," he said.

"Really? You're not just saying that?"

"You deserve this."

"The class meets Tuesday and Thursday nights."

He frowned, unable to control his face.

"I'll make dinner ahead of time."

"It's not that," he said. "I don't care about food, you know that."

"Then what?"

"I'll miss you," he said.

She patted his hand. "I'll be back," she said. "As long as you're sticking around, I'm sticking around."

———————

In the weeks after first meeting the lawyers involved in *Greene vs. Wiesenthal,* Sol had time to remind himself that it didn't matter how he felt about law firms, or the behavior of particular lawyers, so long as they did not overstep the law; what mattered was the case itself, and the facts and history pertaining to it.

Flannery had been particularly conscientious and diligent in collating his research. This had always been his strong point as clerk. He was sure of the results. "The case is cut-and-dried," the chief clerk said with a slash of one thin hand. "Cut, dried, and hung up to wash." He had pages of notes, "in his back pocket," he claimed, but Sol waved him off. All of his staff seemed to sense something unusual in this case, some excitement. The thrill of a blood sport, Sol thought morosely. Even Myra made no complaints about putting in overtime typing up notes and running searches online in the various libraries. Frank Zimmer, the young part-clerk, helped Sol upgrade his computer for the task.

Sol could not get used to the speed at which even the most arcane knowledge could be accessed. At times he felt he must be dreaming it. When did Google become a verb? He remembered sitting around the family dining room table with the *Encyclopaedia Britannica* to settle questions. It must have felt like this when man, who could only walk or run, suddenly got behind the wheels of a car and watched the landscape speeding by.

Sol had been born before TV existed, before a man stepped on the moon, even before private telephones were common. He remembered life without those things. He was a mere blip on an enormous screen of time and circumstance. Some people felt larger looking at the ocean, while others felt smaller. The vastness of things had always disturbed Sol, while they always exalted Sarah. It came as no great surprise that she wanted to draw closer to the Infinite, even as he shrank away from it.

The lawyers for the blood case had met twice more, alone in conference with Flannery. Katrina Turock kept dragging her heels, trying to slow things down. Diligent, quiet, Ned, Sol's part lawyer, kept stubbornly moving things along. He was young and, despite his baldness, handsome, with delicate, clear-cut features. No doubt, Sol thought cynically, that also helped keep even Katrina Turock in line. Sol's immediate problem, one he had never faced to this degree before, was how to keep this case from turning into a circus.

Turock was a notorious publicity hound. She was well connected, a media darling, photogenic. Clever, caustic sound bites were her specialty. When the judge pulled into his usual reserved parking spot on the day he was to first meet with the defendant and plaintiff, he saw all the cameramen and their trucks assembled and his heart sank.

He got out of his car, registering the heavy clunk of the Volvo's door as he shut it behind him. He walked the gauntlet of a dozen reporters jabbing their mikes at him. He shook them off, saying, "No comment, no comment," as he shouldered his way into the courthouse. He had wanted this first meeting between the cousins as informal as possible, which is why he'd deliberately scheduled it in Flannery's smaller office. Sometimes all it took was for the people involved to get a good look at one another, and things could be resolved outside the courtroom. But this—this was a nightmare.

"It's a private meeting," he instructed the court public relations officer. He tried not to show his exasperation. She knew all this. "No media access." It was her job to tell the crowd that had assembled outside the outer office doors of Part 18. They piled their camera equipment on the white marble benches and they obstructed the hallway. They jostled and shoved and ignored the public relations officer, a sweet grandmotherly-looking woman named Stephanie Korziack. Her gray hair was flattened on one side. Myra was signaling to Sol through the glass, though he had no idea what she was trying to indicate, and Flannery was right beside her, nodding and smiling like the welcoming committee.

"Do you have any comments on this case?" a reporter asked Sol. "We know that this is a fraught situation, charged with family—"

"Get out," the judge said. "Anyone who is not immediately involved in the case. In future I'll thank you to listen to Mrs. Korziack." His harassed elderly court officer smiled at him weakly.

"But after the trial actually begins—"

"Out!" he barked.

"You can't keep us out once the legal process begins," a young reporter from *Newsday* began. He was tall and thin, with a hawkish, aggressive look.

"We'll cross that bridge when we come to it," Sol said. He knew he was on thin ice, but he didn't give a damn. "Now get going. I mean it. I'll start taking names in another thirty seconds." He spotted Sergeant Carter Johnson making his way down the hall, looking larger and grimmer than ever.

The reporters turned and scurried away, even the young Turk from *Newsday*. Through the glass doorway Sol saw Flannery's face fall. Myra, on the other hand, nodded approvingly.

"I'm sorry," Stephanie apologized. "I told them three or four times. They just wouldn't listen."

"I don't understand why you would deny yourself a little publicity," Flannery said softly, as the judge walked past him. "A moment in the spotlight, so to speak."

"Apparently there's a lot you don't understand," Sol answered. "Is everyone here?" he asked Myra.

"Everyone but Nicole Greene, the plaintiff. Her lawyer's inside. So is everyone else. Including that muscle-bound broad on her broomstick."

Sol nodded without smiling. "All right," he said. "Call security. Get someone to escort Mrs. Greene up here when she comes."

Inside Flannery's office sat the plaintiff's handsome lawyer, wearing a camel-hair coat and looking like an irate movie star. Katrina Turock sported a patterned dress. A big belt. She wore high red heels. Beside her sat a man looking extremely grim and down in the mouth. If the judge hadn't known better, he would have thought that this was the one who was ill. His hair, his suit, and even his face, were all ashen.

"I won't have a circus in my courtroom," Sol said. "I want to make that clear."

"Thank God," Peter said. "And thank you, Your Honor."

Katrina Turock said, "Well, *we* have nothing to hide. Justice Richter, this is my client, Ari Wiesenthal."

The man, Ari, half rose from his seat and shook the judge's hand. Then he slumped back into his chair, eyes on the floor.

"Is there any good reason to deny the media access to this case?" Katrina said.

Sol ignored her tone. "That's one of things we're here to find out. Will there be any children involved as witnesses?"

"Absolutely not," said Peter. "My client is emphatic that her daughter not be exposed to this."

Ari looked up with a hopeful expression. "Yes," he said. "My son, Julian. He's only eleven. I think you need to meet with him. You need to see what's at stake for *me* and *my* family." The pronouns were slightly pronounced.

"But that doesn't necessarily mean we block the media—" Katrina began. She put one hand on her client's arm.

"It does," Ari said. "I don't want Julian in the middle of a crowd like that. My goal is to protect my children."

Katrina's high-heeled foot began to bounce up and down. "We can keep the media away when your son appears."

"No," said Ari. He turned to face her. "We went through all this. No. I want a closed case."

Katrina rolled her eyes and let out a sigh.

"As does my client," said Peter.

"Fine. I'll take that under advisement," said the judge. "And to the best of our ability we will keep the media away."

"Thank you," the man named Ari said. A little color returned to his face. But the relaxation lasted barely a moment. There was a flurry at the door, and a woman in a puffy blue winter coat appeared through the window in the door, flanked by Carter Johnson and one of the younger court officers. Johnson's chest was puffed out; he looked like one of those birds who becomes twice as large in the face of danger.

The judge suspected they had pushed through a crowd downstairs. The way the tipstaff shook his head at Sol confirmed this. The other court officer was sweating, though it was the dead of winter. Johnson knocked on the door. "We have the plaintiff," he announced. His voice was loud enough to be heard through the oak doors.

The woman in the blue down coat practically fell into the judge's office. She took off a winter hat and shook out a mane of reddish hair. When she unzipped her coat, Sol saw that she was wearing a sweater exactly like one that his daughter Abigail owned—dark blue, with a thin stripe of black across the chest. He was staggered by the resemblance. No matter what happened in this life, he thought, he should know better than to be surprised. This woman Nicole looked like the ghost of his own daughter. Slim, red haired, brown eyed. Her hair singed his eyes, as if she were on fire there in front of him. He felt sick at heart. Flannery made the formal introductions, but the judge's attention was riveted by the young woman. She looked at the defendant, her cousin, but his eyes were fixed on the carpet. He held his head, using his hands as a shield.

"Hello, Ari," the woman said softly. He nodded without answering.

This whole case, the judge saw in a flash, was going to be harder than he had dreamed.

Mid-December 2011

In the Middle of the Longest Night

The judge's daughter had made arrangements for her new apartment online and without meeting a single human being. Her landlord was a Rabbi Theodore Lewin, but most of the e-mail correspondence came by way of his assistant, J. D. Pakul, an efficient but officious fellow. He had some kind of obsession about animals. Abigail was not to have any pets, the man wrote. No, nothing, not even a bird or a goldfish. Even after he'd run a background check on Abigail, he'd demanded written assurance that she had no pets and no plans to acquire any pets.

"Not unless you count my baby as a pet," she finally e-mailed back, a touch crabbily.

"Only if it's a baby cat or alligator," J. D. fired back.

When she went to pick up her keys, neither the rabbi nor J. D. were in the office, and a smiling young woman spent twenty minutes apologizing and searching through the drawers till she finally, triumphantly produced the set of keys. "J. D. would have had these right away. I'm so sorry."

"It's fine," Abigail said. Iris had been unusually fussy all day, and the last thing she wanted was for someone to walk in and find her with a howling baby in her arms. If no goldfish were allowed, probably no crying babies were allowed either.

When she finally met Rabbi Lewin, she could not tell if he was thirty-five years old or sixty-five. He was balding, and had a potbelly. The bags under his eyes were a bluish purple, with grayish lines around the deep circles, as if he had not slept since seminary school. But there was something youthful about him, too. When they met she had the impression that he was actually running forward to shake her hand. He was wearing tennis shoes under his black suit.

"Ah! My new tenant!" He beamed. "You must be Abigail."

She was carrying Iris in one of those front-slung baby carriers. Iris was almost hidden from view, even to the top of her infant head, her black hair under a knitted cap as fine as the tip of a paintbrush. The rabbi bounded forward a step, took in the bundle at a glance, and smilingly corrected himself.

"I mean tenant*s*," he said, emphasizing the plural. "Iris, isn't it?"

"Yes," she said. "The apartment is lovely. I wanted to thank you for the flowers, and the food in the fridge, Rabbi Lewin—"

"Please, call me Teddy. The only person who calls me Rabbi Lewin is my mother." He might really be in his early thirties, but with a terrible case of insomnia. "As for the flowers and the food"—he waved one large paw-like hand—"you can thank the temple sisterhood. They're very good about that kind of thing."

"Okay," she said. "I'll definitely thank them."

"Sisterhood is always looking for active new members." He must have seen the alarmed look on her face because he immediately added. "It's not required. Just a thought... —Well," he said, rocking back on his heels, "I shouldn't hold you up. You must be very busy, settling in with Iris, getting used to a new place, all of that."

"Yes," she said, though she had another month of maternity leave, and with Iris asleep and breathing against her chest, she could not think of a single thing she had to do today. Take a longer walk, maybe? How many times had they already gone out into the neighborhood today? As long as she moved along slowly and steadily, Iris slept in the front-slung carrier. But as soon as Abigail stopped and sat down, her daughter would startle awake, crying as if she'd just realized she had landed in a foreign country.

"If you have any problems or concerns, I'm right there"—he pointed at the Jewish Center down the block, past all the evergreen shrubs—"I'm available. To talk. Or just to listen, for that matter."

"Thank you," she said. The rabbi's offer sounded genuine—so unlike anything she had ever heard as a child at her parents' old synagogue, where the rabbi harangued them to attend services more often, show more dedication to their Torah studies, contribute more money to Israel. "That's— lovely—of you." Lovely seemed like the wrong word, but there didn't seem to be a right one.

The rabbi—Teddy—shrugged, embarrassed. He shoved both big hands into his pockets and looked off toward the Center again, as if someone were there and waiting for him. Probably, she realized, someone really was. *He* was not on maternity leave, after all.

"*Lovely* is not a word I often hear in regard to myself," he said. "So you've given me something very nice to think about." Above the enormous sleepless rings, his eyes were large, brown, and intelligent. "See you." He turned with that same light swing in his step and headed back down the walk.

Abigail walked around the block once, twice more, then circled back to her apartment. Half their things were still in cardboard boxes. It was the apartment of a woman who looked as if she might still change her mind about everything. Who did she think she was kidding? She and Iris were in this thing together; there was no backing out now.

Iris looked at her now as if she expected something to happen. Going to services once in a while might not be such a bad idea. If only Abigail had asked when they were. That would have been a friendly thing to do. She'd meant to ask about the nearest health food store, too, and if there were any good restaurants within walking distance.

Iris stared at her with eyes as black as two shining mirrors. In their hotel in Thailand, her daughter had sat happily through long meals playing with the different kinds of sugar packets—blue, yellow, pink. Stacking them like playing cards or spreading them over the table. She'd never tried to tear one open.

"This is one very easy baby," her mother had said, "you're being spoiled," and Abigail didn't argue. She had a feeling she was blessed; almost as if she were cheating. Other babies from the orphanage cried all night. Some threw tantrums in the hotel. Iris watched Abigail with those intelligent thirteen-month-old eyes that seemed to drink in everything at once. Abigail had the feeling she was storing up language, soaking that in as well, and that when she began speaking, it would be in phrases or sentences instead of in single words. Once Abigail dreamed that Iris explained a complicated math formula to her father, the judge, and she woke up relieved that it was only a dream. That was all she needed, a baby prodigy.

Abigail checked her hair in the mirror, brushed and redid it, parting it on the side, which made her look—what? Older? Younger? Less matronly, anyway.

"Out we go again," Abigail said, trying to make it sound normal. They walked across the frozen lawns and tiny paths toward the Jewish Center.

"Yes?" said a young woman. "May I help you?" She was clearly Asian, and Abigail thought she might have been imagining it, but it seemed as if the woman were Thai.

"I'm here to see the rabbi," Abigail said.

"New to the congregation?" the woman asked.

"Yes. —No," Abigail said. "I'm the new tenant, in the apartment building the Center owns. Three B."

"Ah! Well, I'm J. D. Pakul," the woman said. She leaned through the open sliding glass window to shake hands, then thought better of it and stepped out of her office into the hall. "It's spelled J-a-i-d-e-e."

"I'm Abigail."

"And who might this be?" the young woman asked, peeking at Iris. She was wearing high heels of an unusual plum color, which matched the plum-colored belt she wore around her black dress. Chic but modest. Her long black hair was pulled back in a long braid down her back. She could not have been more than five feet tall without the heels. Abigail felt like a giant. "Your little girl looks Thai," she said.

"She is," said Abigail.

"You know," Jaidee said slowly, tentatively, "there's a small but tight-knit Thai community right here in Manhasset. There are two good Asian groceries. Sometimes we bring in musicians or folk dancers from Thailand. You and your daughter would be welcome to come to those events—if you're interested."

"I would love it," Abigail said.

Jaidee grabbed a pad of paper off her desk and began writing in neat, spiky handwriting. "I'm going to put down my name and phone number, and also the names and addresses of the two stores."

She tore off the sheet of paper and handed it to Abigail. "The rabbi is in a meeting," she added. "His schedule is fairly full. Was it anything urgent?"

"No," Abigail said. She could feel herself beginning to blush, the curse of the red haired. "I just wanted to—ask him a few things."

"What you're doing for this little girl is an enormous blessing," Jaidee said. "Giving her so many opportunities."

"Actually," Abigail said, "I'm the one who feels blessed."

Jaidee nodded, studying Abigail a long moment, pursing her lips. Her daughter had a similar small smile, the ends of her lips tucked up. "If you had one small pet in that apartment," she said slyly, "I think that would be acceptable."

Nicole awoke in the middle of the night as if someone or something were crouching on her chest. Her teeth were chattering, but she had been sweating in her sleep. Sometimes she could not distinguish between night terrors and the side effects of the chemo.

Jay held her hand in a tight grip. His long fingers wrapped around hers. She gently extricated her hand. He looked so much younger asleep. The dimness of their bedroom at night disguised the white strands in his hair, making it all a shining blond again.

"Jay," she said. "Are you asleep?"

"No," he said immediately. "I was just thinking."

She shifted onto her side to see him better. "What were you thinking about?"

"If I move the boxes onto the court, the kids won't have to run through the mirror."

He was dreaming again about coaching. She was used to that. She smiled. "Good idea," she said.

"I love you madly," he said.

"I love you, too," she answered. But she could not stop shivering. She sat now with her arms around her knees, looking out over the winter view of the harbor, past the streetlamp on the corner of Potter's Lane. Snow fell softly around it, blowing like a white scarf. How many nights, she thought. How many nights had she sat there in bed like this, taking everything for granted, reading a book instead of talking to Jay, going to sleep without making love? Why had she wasted a single hour? Now lovemaking exhausted her; she felt her body struggle to rise, only to fall back again, worn out and weak. More often than not these days she lacked the energy even to try.

"I'm so sorry," she'd told Jay, but he'd assured her, "I'd rather hold you than make love with anyone else."

In some strange way even that made her sad. Jay had few friends—men didn't seem to need close friends the same way women did. There was a math teacher in his block that Jay hung out with once in a while. He talked now and then to his best friend from elementary school, but that friend lived in Seattle; they had not seen each other in five years at least. Jay's mom was a worrier, his dad had left the scene decades earlier; he wasn't close to either of his brothers. She wasn't sure Jay confided in anyone. She worried about him being lonely when she was gone. He would not listen to her. "You're not going anywhere," he said. "Not without me."

He thought he was making things easier on her. He did not realize how much harder it was this way. It meant she could not tell him the truth. Not really. Not the bad parts. She couldn't tell him that she was terrified much of the time; she couldn't tell him when she felt like crying. She could not picture a future. Sometimes the thought of the world going on without her—simple daily chores and errands, school days and summer months, spreading out with her a zero, erased, like a child marked absent—just froze her in her tracks. She changed now out of her sweat-soaked T-shirt and pulled on one of Jay's old sweatshirts. She padded down the hall to Daisy's room.

Daisy's one white-socked foot was sticking out of bed. As usual, she was sleeping cockeyed, at some crazy angle, her head far down from the pillow. The little girl was getting so long. A skinny beanpole. Nicole could remember when the whole length of Daisy's newborn spine was shorter than the span of Jay's outspread hand. She remembered Jay flying Daisy around the room, still asleep, wearing one of those footed infant onesies. Now Daisy slept wearing one white sock and one colored one—in honor of the superstition that one white sock would bring a snow day. Nicole gazed over her daughter's sleeping head out through the sheer curtains. Yes, the snow was still falling, but not heavily enough to cancel school. She brought her hand down lightly on top of Daisy's mass of wavy hair. In the darkness it might have been any color, but of course it was that almost pinkish strawberry blonde, a color Nicole thought far more beautiful than her own had ever been.

Daisy slept soundly, breathing in and out. Just the hint of a rasp, the remnant of a winter cold that lingered. Nicole slowed her own breathing to match her little girl's. This is eternity, she thought. Right here this minute.

This girl, this room, this love. She felt calmer almost at once and edged a little closer to the bed, as if to bring the safety closer as well. It doesn't matter so much, she thought, whether I live or die. Daisy will be all right, Jay will be all right. Life will go on. Someone else might have thought it with resentment, but she said it over and over to herself, like a mantra. A new thought that gave her room to move. Breathing again. Life will go on. Life will go on.

Late December 2011
Doing the Job to the Best of Your Ability

All of Sol's efforts to bring the cousins to some agreement had fallen on deaf ears. In fact Ari Wiesenthal, the defendant, kept his hands literally over his ears or cupped over his eyes all during the first meetings. Flannery raised his bushy eyebrows at the judge as if to say, "This is what we've got," but the judge persisted. Whatever the law might dictate, there was no logical reason to deny this woman some amount of the cord blood. It was highly unlikely to be contaminated in the process, unlikely even that she would need all that had been stored. But there was something impenetrable about Ari Wiesenthal, as if he had retreated into some private walled-off space, a private logic of his own.

"I'm protecting my family," he kept saying. "Family first." Wasn't his cousin also family? the judge wondered. He saw no obvious enmity between the two. They sat mirroring each other, arms identically folded, their legs crossed and facing. But families are like icebergs—only a fraction shows above the surface. "I have rights under the law, too," Ari insisted.

Katrina Turock glowered. That high-heeled foot bounced impatiently, like the smart kid in the class having to listen to someone else's boring homework assignment read aloud.

"Why don't you ask the *plaintiff* to reconsider her selfish position?" she said, jerking her head toward Nicole. "This case is going to judgment. Despite our best efforts. Over our protests. If you were hoping for some happy family reconciliation scene here, you're going to be disappointed."

The judge was disappointed but not really surprised. For every rare instance where a family situation resolved peaceably outside the law, there were three where each side stubbornly held its ground. He was used to this, if saddened by what it said about humanity—and about family. Sol was by now resigned to human nature as he found it. Only in someone as young as Iris could you hope for purity.

What did surprise him was DeNunzio's reaction to his calling off the press. DeNunzio phoned his chambers that same afternoon. Disappointment appeared to be the word of the day.

"Disturbed and disappointed," DeNunzio said in his quiet, sibilant voice. He sounded, looked, and behaved a good deal like the most powerful man then on the US Supreme Court. Sol had a flash of intuition that one day DeNunzio himself might become part of that august body. DeNunzio was only in his fifties, he was well connected, and he was a politico. Somehow the idea made Sol shudder.

"To lose an opportunity to bring attention to the work we do here..." DeNunzio said. "It is unusual to shut out the media so absolutely—on what basis?" he added.

"There's a child involved," Sol said shortly.

"There are ways to protect the interests of children without it seeming as if the Supreme Court of Nassau County has something to hide. The OCA is surprised. Pescatori is surprised. I must say, it puts me in an awkward position."

"That's unfortunate," Sol said.

DeNunzio sighed, a sound that traveled clearly through the receiver. "You may be making more trouble for yourself than it's worth," he said. It was almost but not exactly a threat.

Sol said nothing.

"Well, good luck with it," DeNunzio said in his soft voice, and then hung up.

———

Flannery was less subtle. "Why? Why? You deserve this attention and approbation," Flannery said. "We all do. We labor in silence. Anonymously. All the briefs, the *ratio decidendi*, judicial opinions carefully worked out and written—no one reads them. Not a word. Stones down a well. Unless the media brings the world's attention to bear upon the case. Of course a trial with a jury would create more attention, but even so—"

"I am not," the judge said icily, "looking for attention."

"That's right," Myra said. "You know what it would be like around here, the press swarming up our asses day in and day out? Pardon my French," she added.

"It would be invigorating!" Flannery said. "Lively." He appealed to Myra. "Tell me, wouldn't you like to see your face on TV?"

"Flannery," Myra said, "I don't even like to see my face in the mirror."

Being barred from the courtroom did not keep the media's attention entirely away from the case. The local papers kept up a running commentary on Judge Richter's advanced age: he was, they said, scheduled to have retired that December and had barred the press from this important case to hide his disabilities as an adjudicator. They played up the human interest aspect, milking it for all it was worth. Nicole's photos showed her as a young beauty, or as someone so thin and haggard it was amazing she hadn't yet expired. They ran the same photo of Ari Wiesenthal each time, a picture in which he seemed to be snarling. There were plenty of glamour shots of Katrina Turock and one or two thumbnail photos of Sol himself, looking ancient and palsied. Sarah assured her husband, "You don't look like that. Not even first thing in the morning."

"The dogs bark, but the caravan moves on," Sol said. Vanity, vanity, all is vanity, he reminded himself. His one commitment had been to uphold the law, to be the most informed and unbiased judge possible. This case was his last, and his worst. He dreamed about it, brooded about it, felt helpless in the face of it. Logic, philosophical inclination, precedent, led him in one direction, and one direction alone. He knew that; his clerk Flannery knew it; he sometimes suspected that everyone involved knew. But still, he felt himself pulled elsewhere. The impulse to rescue. It was unfathomable at his age. A mystery. It did not help, this uncanny resemblance between the plaintiff and his own red-haired daughter. Even her last name, Greene, reminded him of his own long-lost grandfather, the one-armed tailor, Nathan Greenplotz.

"Is there anything that might allow us to consider the merits of her case?" he asked his attorney, Ned, in private. Ned was young, but bright and diligent. Flannery appeared at just that moment, of course, carrying a large pile of briefs that he dropped onto the table with a thunk.

Before Ned could answer, Flannery piped up. "You know there isn't. That's the beauty of the case! It's airtight."

"How about the duty to rescue? Ned—what about the letter?"

Again Flannery jumped in. "A letter is not a contract. What if someone signed a contract to chop off his own leg and then changed his mind? This is not a *contractual* issue. Justice can punish a man for behaving illegally. It cannot force a man to do the right thing."

"Then what is the point of it?" Ned asked, unexpectedly. He seldom entered into theoretical disputes; he never got between the judge and his chief clerk in one of their arguments. "Justice should be more than a matter of punishment."

"Justice *is* more than a matter of punishment!" Flannery cried. "The law prevents antisocial behaviors. It creates a structure of acceptable and unacceptable rules. And, in case you never got past fifth-grade civics class, the judiciary balances out the powers of the executive and legislative branches."

"I got past the fifth grade," Ned said mildly. He never bragged about the Stanford degree. Sol doubted if anyone else in his court even knew about it.

Flannery turned his attention back to the judge. "You'll get your feet back under you. I haven't worked for you all these years without learning how you operate. But you can't become a humanist at the expense of being a great legal mind."

"I have never been a great legal mind," Sol said. "I'm someone who's done his job to the best of his ability."

"But Your Honor—" Flannery sputtered.

Sol held up his hand to stop him. "And the best of my ability was never anything to write home about. Go find yourself another hero, Flannery. It's hard enough just being a human being. I wish I'd had more practice at it."

———·———

That afternoon Sol drove the crowded expressway inch by inch, and then hazarded the fantastically crowded and gnarled twisting back streets of Brooklyn to visit his last remaining inmate at the Brooklyn Federal Detention Center. He himself, twenty years earlier, had sentenced her. She was in for capital crimes, or she'd have been away from Brooklyn Federal long ago. As it was, she was an anomaly in an aging federal prison that was most often used as a holding tank.

By the time he arrived at the prison it was already pitch-dark in the early winter night. The only hint of brightness came from the colored lights strung on houses and apartments, reindeer with flashing red noses, traffic lights going from green to yellow to red in an endless circle. He could barely remember when Long Island was a place one could actually drive from one end to the other—the potato farms of his early marriage were long gone; even back then, cars and trucks were beginning to swell each of the veins that ran the length and breadth of this fish-shaped island. Parkways filled, new ones sprang up like weeds. These, too, came to a standstill, and still more farmland, more greenery, was torn away. More cars spilled into it and stalled in traffic. Eventually Long Island would turn into one enormous, overtaxed parking lot.

Once inside Brooklyn Federal he relaxed. The ritual of unburdening began at once, the shedding of keys, penknives, loose change, the handing over of one's identity, emptying of pockets. It reminded Sol of going to the synagogue mikvah, where he'd gone to take the ritual bath before his marriage to Sarah. One entered the mikvah as stripped of adornment, as naked and unburdened, as a newborn. So too would he leave it, when the Burial Society came to wrap his body in white linen.

He gave over his belt, and removed his winter shoes for inspection before he was permitted entry. He sat without a wallet, without even a pencil. Sometimes he brought paperback books in a see-through bag, which were duly inspected and stamped. Today he had brought a candy bar and a self-help book for the woman—a volume Sarah had chosen. He could not bear to come empty-handed. It was a Jewish rule of visiting: Never go anywhere without some dessert wrapped up in a box with string. Neither the boxed treat nor the string was permitted here.

———

His inmate in Brooklyn was Naveen Abou. She'd been barely out of her teens when he judged her case. A devout Muslim, she had strapped bombs across her body and headed into Times Square the day she turned eighteen, ready to greet Allah in glory. She had stopped at a fabric store, paused to finger the silks as a last gesture of affection for the things of this world—"I was saying good-bye with my fingertips," she told the judge later—when her coat opened and the manager called the cops. Even then, she was obedient. She sat down on a hard chair and waited for them to arrest her. She could have blown up the manager and the store, but "it was a little shop," she explained, "with only one man and his daughter working in it. That would have been murder, not jihad."

Her transformation inside Brooklyn Federal had been gradual and steady. First she gave up the name she had taken in her fiercer days, Mujahid, "freedom fighter." She called herself Naveen, Pakistani for "new." There had always been something childlike about her; she stood barely over five feet tall, and spoke with a lisp. It seemed as if she tried to use the letter *s* more than any other. "So you thee, Tholomon," was how she began many sentences. She used his name repeatedly, affectionately. And she loved "thweets," so he brought candy each time he visited. Naveen remained a devout Muslim, but now she focused on other aspects of Islam—on generosity toward others, for instance, and charity, festivals where people brought food for the poor. She talked about obedience, diligence; her greatest treasure was the leather-bound copy of the Koran she kept on a high shelf in her room. Her second-most-treasured book was Dale Carnegie's *How to Win Friends and Influence People.*

Over time Sol had watched Naveen morph from a fiery, solitary teenager to a middle-aged spinster reaching out to others in small kindnesses— the only ones available now. She was often rebuffed. She spoke softly, and had a characteristic way of covering her mouth with her hand, as if to hide her lisp. She remained solitary by force and habit, not by choice. And she was wildly enthusiastic over the smallest things. For instance, she had stumbled on a way to order ordinary household products cheaply over the Internet—cellophane wrap and cleaners—and she had the judge fill out an order each visit. "Think of all the money you are thaving!" she would say, her eyes shining. "And you know, Tholomon, they are of very good quality." Naveen greeted the candy bar and self-help book today with a cry of delight, covering her mouth.

He was not sure how it came about, but after the usual chitchat, and after placing a large order for plastic wrap (Three for the price of one! she enthused), he began talking around this last case. He presented it simply as a matter of a family where one member needed something from another, and a life was at stake. He could share none of the specific details, of course. He changed some of the facts and kept the rest sketchy. He was afraid, even so, that the story would distress her. Naveen listened and her large dark eyes filled till they were overbrimming. She wiped her eyes on her sleeve— she wore long sleeves and a head covering all year round. Yet she preferred sandals even in winter. She wore prison shoes only to walk out in the yard, and only because it was required. She stared down at her feet now, the long brown toes red with cold, and shook her head. "It is very thad, Tholomon," she said. "It mutht be very hard for all of you."

"It's not an easy case," Sol admitted. "She reminds me too much of my own daughter."

"Is there no way to thpeak to the family privately?" she asked. "Perhaps they can be reconthiled. —And you know, Tholomon," she added, "I will pray for you. And I will pray for every one of them."

"We'll need it," the judge growled, to cover the fact that he was touched by her concern.

"Ah. Well, Tholomon, you at least can thstill be reconthiled. Keep praying, and never give up hope." Her face brightened. "And once thith is over," she said, "you can retire in peath and quiet. You can thpend more time with your new grandchild." Her eyes shone at him. "Now show me the pictures of the little girl. I will thee if I can get permission to make something for her, maybe a little head scarf."

"Don't go to any trouble," Sol said.

She looked around the bare cell, smiling. "Here, there ith no trouble," she said. "I have you to thank for that." She nudged him with one sandaled foot and laughed.

HANUKKAH 2011
Traditions

There was a long-held family tradition of gathering at Aunt Patti's house for the eighth night of Hanukkah, the final night of the holiday. Nicole had celebrated at her Aunt Patti's as long as she could remember, even as a little girl. Never a cook—normally she'd order in soggy pizzas or greasy Chinese food and pronounce them delicious—Aunt Patti on this one night of the year grated potatoes from scratch, fried onions in chicken fat, turned the latkes herself, served separate bowls of sour cream and apple sauce. Half the potato pancakes came out scorched, the others raw in the middle, but it was the tradition that mattered, the gathering of family—along with a few of her old actor friends, most of them gay, Jewish, and without a place to go. Just watching their great-aunt Patti lurch around the kitchen, cursing like a sailor, was always entertainment enough for Julian and Daisy.

Because Patti hated sentimentality, and also because she was cheap, she insisted on joke presents—some awful piece of kitsch that no one could possibly want: cheap plastic Christmas platters, tacky posters from old Broadway shows, the ugliest hats imaginable. They took turns passing from household to household an exceptionally large and hideous salt-and-pepper shaker in the shape of a chicken. Whoever won this gift had to care for it till the following Hanukkah, when it could be dumped into someone else's hands.

Nicole had gotten the ceramic chicken the year before, and while she had always hated the thing, for some reason this year she was loath to part with it. And the idea of giving—and getting—tacky, useless, ugly things was beginning to bother eight-year-old Daisy. "Why can't we give nice presents like everybody else?" she asked plaintively.

"We do with each other, sweetie," Nicole said. If anything, she over-compensated by buying too much too lavishly. She'd stored up so many gifts in the months leading up to Hanukkah, it was hard not to make every night look like Christmas morning—exactly what she and Jay wanted to avoid. She had bought and hidden enough gifts, she thought grimly, that some of them would end up being given out posthumously. She was always unearthing old gifts from the dark corners of the backs of closets.

This Hanukkah would be different from all the others. There would be no loud, raucous family gathering at Aunt Patti's. Patti understood that the two families could not be in one house at the same time. To Nicole's surprise, however, it was her own family who received the invitation for the eighth night. Ari wasn't in the mood for a big party, he'd told his mother, and had already made plans to go skiing in Vermont.

"It'll be terrific," Aunt Patti assured Nicole over the phone. "It seems like no one I know has any place to go this year. We're all getting old. Maybe I'll include that new black family that just moved into the neighborhood. They won't be getting other invites. I think they're being boycotted from the neighborhood. From the Christmas caroling, too."

"Are you sure?" Nicole said.

"Well, no, I can't be *sure*," Patti said. "Those singers are so desperate for attention they might be willing to perform for *schvartzes*. Half the carolers are Jewish anyway. Toss a stick in this neighborhood and you hit another Jew."

"I mean about Ari and his family. Are you sure they don't want to come for the eighth night?"

"Ari made it very clear," Aunt Patti said. She sounded edgy, which meant her feelings had been hurt. "Loud and clear. He's skiing at some overpriced resort."

"Okay," Nicole said. "Well—I have one favor to ask this year."

"Ask away," Patti said.

"Can I...can I keep the ceramic chicken?"

To her surprise, Aunt Patti didn't mock her. She didn't hesitate—as if she had expected the request. "You hang on to it," she said. "You can always give it back next year."

"All right," Nicole said. "Next year. —What I can bring instead?"

"Find something really tacky," she said. "And bring along some Manischewitz wine. The cheap stuff. Maybe a bottle of Cherry Heering. This year I won't have Ari sneaking in any fancy wines, looking down his nose at me."

"Nothing but the worst for you," Nicole promised.

"Thanks, doll," Patti said. "I knew you'd understand."

———•———

Patti's house was controlled chaos at the calmest of times. On this eighth night of Hanukkah she'd hung multiple plastic mini-Santas around her living room, and was wearing a silver tiara that lit up at the ends, flashing purple, yellow, and green. Her theater friends milled around, arranging plastic flowers in cheap glass vases. Eight-year-old Daisy wore a wine-colored velvet dress with a lace collar. This was, strictly speaking, against the rules, but the friends oohed and ahhed over her. "Oh, she is *gorgeous*," one man said. "Look at that glorious red hair. I've never seen anything so stunning." And a small man, a former children's show host wearing a red velvet jumpsuit, said, "Look, we practically match."

Daisy smiled politely, and asked Nicole in a low voice, "Are you *sure* Julian isn't coming?"

"I'm sure," Nicole said. How many weeks had it been since she'd even laid eyes on her best friend—eight weeks, ten? Ever since she'd let that first phone call go unanswered, she had ignored all subsequent calls, increasingly pleading on Mimi's part, increasingly desperate—but Nikki could not bring herself to breach the silence. The court case required all the energy she had to spare. And eventually, the phone calls stopped coming. They had never before gone eight or ten *days* without seeing each other. Mimi's absence had become a chronic, nagging ache lodged behind Nikki's breastbone. A few times every single day she saw or heard something and thought, I have to tell Mimi that! And then thought, Oh. No. The way amputees feel phantom pain long after the limb is gone. She never got used to it.

"Maybe they'll show up later?" Daisy insisted.

"Afraid not this year, sugar plum," Nicole said. She could not bear the disappointment in her daughter's face. She was tempted to lie and say, Yes, maybe they'll come. Let me call Mimi. Let's make it happen.

"Lucky thing, too," Jay said. He'd already started into the Cherry Heering, mixing it with vodka. "I could do some serious damage to that bastard's BMW."

"Julian is not a bastard," Daisy said with some spirit. "And he doesn't drive yet."

"Daddy didn't mean Julian. And he's just kidding," Nicole said.

"Well, it's not funny," Daisy said. "Plus he used a bad word, too." She went off into a corner to sulk and play with Aunt Patti's china figurines.

"Take it easy on the booze, okay?" Nicole said to Jay. She of course could not drink. Everything mixed badly with her medications, which mixed badly with each other. Her veins always felt like they were filled with ice water these days.

The new black neighbors showed up a little after seven, looking confused. The house had so many tacky decorations, it was hard to tell which holiday was being celebrated. They had brought along an elegant stained-glass menorah in a Saks Fifth Avenue box.

"I'm so sorry," the man said to Aunt Patti. "We had heard you—we had thought—maybe you'd like to exchange this for something else." He turned to his wife, a tall, regal-looking woman in a red coat, holding the hands of her two solemn-looking daughters, toddler twins. "You still have the gift receipt?"

"Yes, of course," she said. "I can run back home and get it."

"I'm a Jew!" Aunt Patti said. She roared it so loudly that the whole house went temporarily silent. "This is a Hanukkah party, isn't it? Come on in. Wait till you taste my latkes. Delicious! No one makes anything like them."

"That's for sure," Jay muttered under his breath.

"But you might want to run home and get that gift receipt anyway. This thing looks expensive."

The wife hesitated, still holding both her girls' hands, already turning back to the door.

"*Kidding!*" Aunt Patti bellowed. "It's beautiful. You shouldn't have. Everyone, these are our new neighbors, the Rogerses. The Rogerses, everyone." She handed the menorah, still inside its box, to Nicole, and whispered sotto voce, "Put this in the back bedroom. Maybe I can exchange it without a receipt."

———·—

Late, long after the menorah candles had burned out and the tacky gifts had been opened and distributed, long after Aunt Patti had sung "Happy Birthday to Jesus"—luckily, the Rogerses were gone by then—the doorbell rang. It was after ten o'clock. No one made a move for the door. Aunt Patti made a quick scan of the room with her uneven round brown eyes, and then, when the knocking began, said, "Oh shit," and hobbled to the entrance.

Mimi was first through the door. She held a bundled-up Arianna in her arms, looking something like a pink marshmallow Peep. Rianna had lost her baby look, Nicole thought; she had moved straight through toddlerhood and somehow already looked like a little girl, with her father's strong features and dark complexion. Mimi and Rianna were covered with snow—the sky had begun to drop large, wet flakes about an hour earlier; guests were making jokes about curling up in various corners and spending the night.

"Are we too late?" Mimi asked. "I'm sorry, I couldn't get Ari moving—" And then she stopped, having spotted Nicole and her family. Her mouth opened but nothing came out. Her arms tightened on her baby daughter, either to protect the little girl or to gain protection from her.

Nicole's heart leaped into her mouth. She stepped forward automatically, her arms rising, forming an embrace in the air. There was her best friend Mimi, her darling, standing at the door, snowy, bedraggled, and wet, her daughter in her arms, looking like a modern-day Madonna. Nicole hoped that her auburn wig hadn't come crooked. She wished she had dressed a little better; she could not for the life of her have said what she had on without looking down at herself, and she could not bring herself to take her eyes even for an instant off Mimi's face. Mimi. She looked thinner, she'd cut her hair shorter. The beloved face she had not seen in months—longer than they'd ever been apart since the day they met. All these thoughts went through Nicole's head in less than ten seconds. Her arms rose to make a half circle with which to embrace Mimi, and hung there, futile, when Ari crashed drunkenly through the door, reeling sideways.

"I am so sorry," Mimi said. She spoke to Aunt Patti, but didn't take her eyes off Nicole. "I didn't know about any of this. Ari didn't tell me—"

Julian loped past his father. "Hey!" he said joyfully. "Daisy, you're here!" He lifted her off her feet and swung her around in a circle. She shrieked and protested, laughing, her narrow feet pointed like a ballerina's as they swung.

"See, Mom?" Daisy said. "See?"

"Ari," said Aunt Patti, her eyes blazing, "what are you doing here?"

He brushed past her, his arms loaded with packages. "I *belong* here, remember?" He sat down heavily on the sofa, next to the man in the red velvet suit. "And you," he said. "One of Santa's faggot elves, I take it."

"You do not belong here," Aunt Patti said. "Not tonight, and you know it."

Julian stopped twirling Daisy around. Both children stared at the grown-ups.

"Get the hell out," Jay said. His mouth barely moved when he spoke.

"You can't talk to me like that," Ari said. "This is my mother's house."

"I don't give a crap whose house it is," Jay said. "Just turn around. For your own sake. For the kids'."

"Oh, you're thinking about my *kids*, aren't you? Both of you. You've certainly proven that."

"You went skiing," Aunt Patti said. "What happened?"

"Snow happened. Ice. Wasn't about to risk my family's life. Because I actually do care what happens to my family. I've proven that, allowing my good name to be dragged through the mud."

"Ari," Mimi said. "We are leaving right now."

"No, we aren't," he said.

The man in the red velvet suit got up from the couch and stood there.

"What are you going to do, Tinker Bell?" Ari challenged him. "Throw me out?"

"No," said the man. "I just don't want to be near anything so ugly."

"Then don't look in a mirror," Ari sneered.

Aunt Patti put an arm around the man in red and spoke with her voice shaking. "You may be my son, but you are not welcome in my house. Not like this. Not tonight."

"I *may* be your son?"

"Ari," said Nicole, as gently as she could. "You need to go."

He looked at her with bleary eyes. "Why aren't you dead yet?"

Jay hit him so hard, so fast that no one saw it coming. One minute Ari was on the sofa, the next minute he was on the floor, staring up. Jay stood over him, looking like he might kick him.

"Jay," Nicole yelled. "Stop it! Stop!"

Daisy was sobbing. Julian and Aunt Patti were crying. The man in the red velvet suit was dabbing at his eyes, saying, "Oh, this is so awful. So awful!" Baby Rianna was wailing.

Mimi said in a calm voice, "Ari, get up and go to the car." To Aunt Patti she said, "Mom, I'm so sorry. I had no idea. Absolutely no idea."

Patti said, "I know you didn't, and I'm not your mother."

Mimi and Nicole helped Ari to his feet. He looked dazed. He was holding the side of his head but he wasn't bleeding. He looked as white as he had the long-ago day the strange mongrel had attacked Nicole. "Are you all right?" Nicole asked.

"Like you care," he said.

He pushed both women away and staggered to the door. He had never removed his coat or his boots.

"I don't even know you anymore," Mimi said to Ari in a husky voice. She was still hanging on to the wailing Rianna with one arm.

"I'm your husband," Ari said. "I am the father of your children and the guy who busts his ass for all of you." Then he walked out, slamming the door.

That seemed to waken something in Mimi. "Julian," she said. "Julian, honey, put your coat back on and get in the car."

"No," he said. "I'm not coming."

"You have to," she said.

"No, I don't."

"Let him spend the night with me," Aunt Patti said. "You can pick him up tomorrow morning."

Mimi looked to Nicole, who nodded just barely. Mimi looked at her son, Julian, still body-blocking Daisy, weeping behind him. She glanced around the room, hoisted Rianna a little higher in both arms, and shrugged. "All right," she said.

"I'll call tomorrow," Aunt Patti said. "Just don't let Ari drive. Keep waking him every few hours, make him tell you his name and address. Make sure he doesn't have a concussion."

Jay was rubbing his hand as if he had hurt it. He kept his head down.

"I will," Mimi said. Her boots were still dripping on the rug. "Well—good night."

Nearly everyone in the room out called a weak good-night. Julian's voice came last. "Night, Mom," he said. "I love you."

"I love you, too," she said. She looked at Nicole, but neither of them said another word.

"Well," said Aunt Patti, after the door had closed behind her. "I certainly do know how to throw a party."

———

Out in the car Ari was weeping. He sat on the passenger side of the front seat, his seat belt already fastened. He was shivering, with cold or from shock. When Mimi had opened the back door and settled Rianna into her infant seat and got her buckled and ready, he said thickly, "Have to go back inside and apologize." He opened the car door but then closed it again.

"No, you don't," Mimi said.

"Yes."

"I think you've done enough damage for one night."

"She thinks I hate her," Ari said. "She thinks I'm a monster. I'm killing my own baby cousin. Did you see her? I can't go on like this."

"Oh, Ari," Mimi said. She sounded exhausted.

"Where's Julian?" he asked.

"He's spending the night here with your mother."

Tears crept down the sides of Ari's face. "I want my son," he wailed drunkenly.

"Well, you'll have him tomorrow." Her voice was kinder than she intended.

"I have to do the right thing," Ari said. "Mimi, you have to help me. This is too hard. It's killing everything."

"We'll do it together," Mimi told him. She put her hand on his coat sleeve. "It's not too late."

He turned in the seat to face her. "Do you believe that? Really?" His face was streaked with tears.

"I'm sure of it, Ari."

"I will, I swear to God," he said. "What difference does it make? Did you see her? Did you see Nikki? Jesus. —I can't stand myself. I'm so sick and tired of it."

She stroked the hair back from his forehead. "I know," she said. "It's exhausting, behaving badly. It really takes it out of you."

"My head hurts," he said. "That Jay bastard really packs a wallop."

"We'll call your lawyer tomorrow," Mimi said. "We'll put an end to all this." She could not even bear to say Katrina Turock's name aloud. She kept stroking his head. "We'll give her the cord blood, we'll act like a family again."

"Please don't leave me," Ari said. "I'm going to do the right thing. I will. I promise."

But the next morning Ari woke sober, with the right side of his head throbbing and burning as if someone had shot fire through it, and his heart dead set against the whole family. Mimi had betrayed him. And his mother. All of them were against him. He remembered the night before only in patches, like scenes from a violent movie. He felt a dull fury. His mouth was dry as sand. Last night he had been humiliated in front of a room full of strangers, and his own mother—his own flesh and blood had turned against him. She had kidnapped his son. He talked about a lawsuit against Jay. He was going to get X-rays taken, he said. He thought his jaw was broken. Then he decided he had punctured an eardrum, because he wasn't hearing clearly. He was going to take care of that son of a bitch once and for all. Katrina Turock would be thrilled, he said. Furthermore, he was going straight to the press with the whole story.

"You do any of that," Mimi told him, "and I'm leaving you. Today. With both kids." There was no softness in her face, no room for negotiation.

Ari felt himself alone at the edge of some abyss. He did not know how to step forward or back. Instead he just looked at his wife, his mouth opening and closing without words, his arms dangling at his sides like a hanged man's.

Mimi turned and left him standing there. The door closed with a quiet click, but it charged the room like the striking of a match.

WINTER 2012
The Price of Love

Daisy and Julian continued to see each other, secretly. It was not so secret, since both mothers knew about it. The children were too young to manage on their own. Every Thursday afternoon Julian came to Daisy's house in Huntington after school. He dutifully spent a half hour playing chess with a neighboring kid his own age named Max, and then he would knock at Nicole's door.

Daisy would always be there, anxiously waiting. She hustled Nicole home on Thursdays, insisting that they drive the quarter mile instead of walking as they did nearly every other day. Wednesday nights were her happiest night of the week. Thursday nights were the hardest, because it meant another full week before Daisy saw Julian again. "How many days before I see him?" she'd ask. "How many hours?"

Julian was unfailingly polite to Nicole. He called her "Aunt Nicole," and acted as if nothing was wrong between the families. Nikki, in turn, kept Julian's favorite treats in the house—mini Oreos, pretzel chips, and black currant juice she bought at a local Russian grocery.

It was the next best thing to coddling her best friend; Julian and Mimi shared a lot of the same taste in snack foods. And it seemed the least she could do to repay Julian for his loyalty to Daisy, the endless games of playing house and Barbie and hide-and-seek that he endured for her daughter's sake.

In between visits, he would call, between three and five o'clock, when Ari was still at work. Nicole imagined Mimi kept up a charade even more elaborately at her end, focusing on the fact that Julian played chess once a week, never revealing where he went to do it. Ari was eagle-eyed. Nicole could not imagine how they managed to fool him, but he must have believed his son was on his way to becoming a chess prodigy. Thursdays Jay coached the junior varsity basketball at his school, and Nikki, feeling guilty, kept the secret from him as well. So it was all elaborately orchestrated without words or explanations, and only the women and children knew what was going on.

Mimi no longer called the house or Nikki's cell phone to leave messages. She didn't send out e-cards or e-mail Jewish jokes. What was there to say? The chasm between them took on a life of its own and kept on growing. Nicole saw Mimi's familiar silver Saab parked at the corner, blue smoke puffing from the back of the car while she waited for Julian to emerge from Nicole's house. Mimi sat in that car for at least an hour, most Thursdays, with the engine running. Listening to one of her comedy tapes, Nicole was sure, or to National Public Radio. Once or twice when Nicole had peeked out the window—she had even used her birding binoculars one time—she saw Mimi asleep in the car, wrapped in a coat, a knitted cap, two scarves, and a pair of gloves. That loved, plain face, so familiar and so distant, broke her heart. Time after time she thought of running out and tapping on the window, inviting her best friend inside. But something held her back each time. It wasn't anger. It wasn't to punish her. It was more like the widening of a canyon. She no longer knew how to call across the distance, which grew every day that passed in silence. She tried to make other friends, but she felt too separate from the healthy young mothers, and couldn't quite bear to bind herself to the others in the infusion room.

One afternoon when Julian wandered down for a second glass of black currant juice he stopped at the kitchen table and turned his round dark eyes—so much like his mother's—directly on Nicole's. "I want you to know," he said, "that I miss you—that we *all* miss you. And I am completely on your side."

"Oh, Julian," she said, reaching out to brush the hair out of his eyes. "You're too young to have to take sides."

"Sometimes I wish I could just stay and live here with you in this house. It's a whole lot more peaceful than mine." He said it softly and matter-of-factly.

"I'm sorry to hear that," Nicole said. "Though you know you're welcome here any time, all the time. You have an open invitation." She wanted to ask more about what was going on at his home, but felt it impossible. Those dark brown eyes were trying to tell her—something—but Julian's lips were clamped firmly shut, as if intent on making sure the mouth did not reveal what the eyes did. She ruffled his thick, wavy hair. "Love you, guy," she said, and left the room. She sat on her bed and looked through her old picture albums. There were more pictures of Mimi than there were of herself. Mimi skinny right after a bout of mono in college. Mimi pregnant with Julian. Mimi clowning around onstage in front of a bunch of people somewhere. Mimi and Nicole, arm in arm on the beach, in matching polka-dot swimsuits. Mimi and Nicole in large floppy sun hats down in Florida. Nicole reached out one finger and touched her friend's head. The photo was slick and flat, nothing more than a sliver of plastic. Then Daisy knocked on her bedroom door to ask whether she and Julian could have hot chocolate, and Nicole jumped as if she'd been caught doing something shameful. She wedged the photo albums back into the bottom of her bookshelf, spines out, and went downstairs.

Nicole could hear the steady murmuring of her daughter's voice, high-pitched and quick, and the answering, comforting rumble of Julian's. His voice at age eleven was already deepening, he was shooting up in height, his face had lost all remnants of its baby look. He'd gotten new steel-rimmed glasses, which only added to the adult owlishness of his handsome face.

"I wish Julian lived with us," Daisy said. "I wish he was my brother." She'd been saying things like that since she was three or four: I wish Julian was my twin, I wish he lived across the street. But Nicole now felt the full poignancy of her daughter's desire. If Julian had in fact been her brother, none of this would be happening. Families had their hierarchies of loyalty. Ari would never have considered turning down his brother Al for cord blood or anything else, as badly as they'd gotten along. It was strange, the way families worked. It was stranger still that they functioned at all.

She often thought that if the parents of her students had seen how easily she lost patience at home, they'd have thought twice before they'd entrusted their own children with her. Ms. Greene, as her students had called her, was considered calm, even-tempered. She had been a popular and much-requested teacher, she knew. She had a reputation for never raising her voice to a student. Thank heaven for doors that shut and walls that kept your private life from public view.

What she felt these days was just plain lonely. Empty. She'd never had an easy time making friends, and now it was worse. She had most in common with the other patients in the oncologist's waiting room; she'd shared detailed, touchingly intimate stories with the others who went through chemo. One of her favorite patients was a woman in her eighties whose goal was to see one last Super Bowl. Another was a trucker who had lost his right leg to cancer. They compared numbers and spoke in a language no one else could understand. T-cells and PETs; Kidrolase versus Leukeran; 6-MP or 6TG. When she met up with her fellow chemo patients on the second round, then the third, the fourth, it was like meeting up with old army buddies—and like old army buddies, they joked about old war wounds, the side effects that no one ever warned you about: aching teeth, loss of memory, arthritic pains, vertigo, and insomnia; a lingering metallic taste that spoiled your appetite for the things you'd loved best: coffee, chocolate. If you complained to the healthy people around you about these things, you'd never stop complaining, and they'd still have no idea what you were talking about.

But she was done with chemo now. That was one decision she could make without lawyers or a judge. That had been her New Year's resolution. She'd been through six cycles. She wasn't responding to any of it anyway, and they'd tried every new drug in the book. If she lost this case, if she was refused the cord blood and never could get well enough for a bone marrow transfusion, she would die in peace rather than keep subjecting herself to one procedure after another. She'd seen women in the infusion room lose parts of limbs, holding up bandaged stumps, death taking them one small bite at a time. She would not go through that. She could not put her family through that.

Jay said he understood, though she wasn't sure he did. She was ready to walk away from all of it, including the fight over the cord blood. She was only going through the motions now for Jay's sake. By the time the court case was over it would likely be too late. She might not even make it to learn the outcome—she knew that now. When she looked in the mirror, her eyes had a hollow-socketed haunted look, as if someone else had moved in with her, behind her eyeballs. Death had already staked its claim. It was too early to be apparent to the others, but Nicole saw it—or imagined she did, the therapist reminded her.

"You have no reason to be this pessimistic," he said. He was a nice man. He collected seashells; they were all over his office shelves, small ones, large conches, mostly delicate little spirals. Nicole supposed she should have requested a female therapist, but she feared that might make her miss Mimi even more. It would seem pathetic—paying some woman to be her friend.

"Why do you assume you are dying?" he asked her. "Is it possible that you secretly want to die?"

"No," she said. "I secretly want to live." This was why therapists kept boxes of tissues in their offices, discreetly scattered all over the room, like vases of flowers. She blew her nose into a tissue from the box on the little table to her right. "I assume I'm dying because I can see it in my own face. I'm just astonished that everyone else doesn't see it, too."

Maybe they did and just couldn't admit it. Daisy didn't want to snuggle as much anymore—though this might have been a function of her growing up. Nicole didn't think so. Daisy still climbed into her father's lap at night to watch TV; it was her father she requested to put her to bed, while it had always been Mommy this and Mommy that. So much so that it was almost a family joke. And Jay treated Nicole as something breakable. Even his touch on the rare nights they made love was lighter, less certain, as if he sensed she was merely renting her body now, not fully occupying it.

But there were still good days. Sunny days, even in the depths of winter. Snow days curiously airy and empty and free of school when she and Jay and Daisy all stayed home, huddled around the fireplace in their little purple house, light bouncing blindingly off the snow. She loved her house, she loved her people crowded around her. On such a day she could almost forget that she was dying. One of her favorite poets had written, "There are good days, and there are fair days." Any day she didn't have to drag herself to the courthouse in Mineola she counted as a pretty fair day. Even the infusion room was better than that. She could not bear the hours spent with her cousin Ari sitting like a statue. He never looked at her. She hated that Turock woman. Even Peter no longer provided good company; she suspected his interest in her and in the case was flagging. For a man who had never lost a major case, he was closing in on his first defeat, and it made him cranky and impatient. The judge himself regarded her, or so she imagined, with some strange combination of pity and horror. It seemed to her that he avoided eye contact as much as he could, and she had watched enough televised court cases to know this was a bad sign.

Even now, a few journalists hung around the cavernous lobby, buzzing in circles like the last bees of summer, hoping she'd change her mind and grant an interview, hoping the judge would break down and open his chambers, or at the very least, that they could scoop his decision, which, Nicole thought, must surely be coming any time now. She thought of these journalists as early-bird vultures. She was tired. She was ready to let them land. And when she thought of the inevitable it was no longer with fear, but only with a piercing sadness. If that was the price of love, it was worth paying.

Flannery waylaid the judge one day in late February. There had been a thaw and the world seemed to be melting at their feet. Snowdrops and crocuses appeared, where only yesterday there had been nothing but a crust of dirty traffic-blackened snow.

"I've never asked you for a favor," Flannery said, as soon as Sol walked in. "Never a personal favor, in all these years."

The judge hung up his cashmere winter coat, and then sat down, facing his court clerk. Flannery seemed to be aging and shrinking before his eyes.

"What do you need?" the judge said.

"I've met someone," Flannery said. When Sol continued to look at him uncomprehendingly, he added, "An extraordinarily beautiful and cultured woman, a widow who recently moved up here from Clearwater, Florida. She's a few years younger than I am, still working."

"How much younger?" the judge asked.

"In her forties," Flannery admitted. "But wise beyond her years. — What's more," he added, "she is extremely interested in politics and current affairs, which is highly unusual, especially for a woman with school-age children."

"I can imagine," the judge said drily.

Flannery began to walk around the chambers in small circles. The last time Sol had seen him act this way was when his cat had died, years earlier.

"Unfortunately, I am not the only suitor," Flannery said. The slight Irish lilt in his voice had become more pronounced as he worked himself up. "The lady is much sought-after," Flannery said. "Beautiful, intelligent, well-en—" Flannery began to make a rolling gesture with both hands in front of his chest.

The judge snorted.

"I was going to say, well-*informed*," the clerk said, offended.

"I'm sure you'll win her over," Sol said. "You have more charm than a barrel of monkeys."

Flannery stopped circling and looked dead-on at the judge. "I don't wish to be a laughingstock," he said. "Not to you, Your Honor, nor to anyone else."

"Of course not," Sol said. "Sorry."

"I want to make an impression," said Flannery. "I *need* to make an impression."

Sol sensed he was treading on thin ice, and wisely said nothing.

Flannery said, "You know I've been a confirmed bachelor all these years. Lonely as it's been, I've occasionally found female company"—Sol knew his chief clerk wasn't above calling an occasional escort service between lady friends—"but I never found my true match. I know you think I'm just a romantic Irishman, but I've fallen head over heels. Bridget is unlike any woman I've ever met in all my life. I consider her perfection itself."

Sol, who did not trust himself to speak, merely nodded.

"She is hesitant because she's had two bad marriages, and as I say, there are other men courting her, somewhat my junior. And she is—" He waved his hand over his head.

"Crazy?" Sol suggested.

"Statuesque. Bridget is a tall woman, over five foot nine in her stocking feet. She is sensitive to appearances. Doesn't want to look foolish, that sort of thing. She reads two newspapers a day, every day. The *New York Times*, of course, and then also…" He hesitated briefly. "*Newsday*."

Sol finally saw where all of this had been leading.

"I have never asked you a personal favor in all the years we've worked together. But I need to come out right in this woman's eyes."

"What is it exactly you're asking for?" Sol said.

"I'd like you to open this whole case to the press. Let it be televised, if they wish. I want you to have the advantage of presenting our side of things, not to let conjecture and rumor ruin years of work, years of the most sterling reputation in the Supreme Court of New York State."

"That's not going to happen," Sol said. "What's your second choice?" Sol suspected Flannery would have come up with a backup plan.

"Allow me to speak to the press," Flannery said. "Stephanie can't handle this. She's close to a nervous breakdown. I won't reveal anything you wish to keep concealed. Simply matters of public record—when the case is going to be on the calendar, procedural matters, a brief overview of legal philosophy. Your Honor, I could be—as, I hope I may say, I *have* been, on many occasions, in my labors over countless years—your voice."

"Granted," Sol said.

Flannery stared at him, his lips parted.

"I'm saying yes. Fine," Sol clarified.

Flannery's eyes squeezed shut, and to Sol's dismay, the chief clerk began to weep. He grasped the judge's hand and squeezed it. "Thank you!" he said. "I knew you wouldn't let me down."

"I just hope you won't be disappointed," the judge said. "The media can twist anything. Be aware of that. Say as little as possible."

"Indeed." Flannery nodded vigorously. He was still teary with relief. "I'll be the very soul of discretion. I promise you won't regret this. Thank you."

At this inopportune moment Myra walked by, carrying a heavy armload of files. "I'd love to know why I always carry the heaviest files," she said. Then she stopped in her tracks. "What's going on?" she asked. "What is he blubbering about?" Her face showed more concern than her words.

"I believe I am getting married," Flannery said.

"Holy crap," Myra said. "I mean—congratulations."

Flannery reached for a tissue and blew his nose loudly. "Thank you again, Your Honor," Flannery said. "From the bottom of my heart, I thank you." He bowed himself out of the room.

Myra rolled her eyes at the judge. "What did you do?" she asked. "Provide the dowry?"

"Something like that," Sol said. He turned his back on Myra. She wasn't going to worm another word out of him.

———·——

Strangely enough, the media took to Flannery. Sol had feared they would mock him, caricature his Irish accent, those pointed ears halfway between a Keebler elf's and Mr. Spock's. But they reported his every announcement with respect. He became a weekly sight on the Long Island news. He managed to make it seem as if he were giving away valuable information when all he provided was dates, procedures, and legal truisms.

"Justice is the law tempered by mercy," he announced.

"The law is not only a necessary counterbalance in government, it is the capstone and truest measure of any society."

Having written other men's briefs most of his adult working life, Flannery now had the chance to demonstrate his own eloquence, and canny instinct for sound bites. "We are bound to serve the law, and we are bound and *determined* to serve the law with diligence."

His popularity reflected back onto the Nassau Supreme Court in general, and even DeNunzio softened a little in the glow it cast over all of them. Only Tom Lieu said to Sol, in the basement coffee shop, "You will be relieved, I think, when this case is over."

Sol nodded, tight-lipped. "All over" to him meant the death of the young red-haired plaintiff. He never forgot that. He suspected most of the people around him did. "Human beings," he said, "are always crying out for justice. What they really want is something else. And they won't find it here in this building."

"Had you asked me," Lieu said, "I would have advised that sometimes it's best to let go. You might have been happier stepping down at the end of last year, as intended." There was no reproach hidden in that "had you asked me." It was merely a statement of fact. "But you have never been one to accept any of that. Has any good come of it? Could any good come of it? You would have had more time of your own."

"Soon," Sol said.

Tom Lieu patted him on the shoulder. "Yes, soon."

"I should have come to you instead of going to DeNunzio," said Sol.

"That's not what I meant," Lieu said, coloring a little.

"I know that," Sol said. "There were many mistakes—I just had to acknowledge that one."

———

Sol remembered that when he and Sarah first moved into the big, gracious house in Roslyn Heights, some stranger had driven by, honking, just as Sol was moving things from the van.

"Watch out for your new neighbors!" the man hollered. He was driving a Buick. "I hear they're crazy!"

Solomon had laughed as he watched the man pull into the driveway right next door.

Joe Iccarino had retired early—he was still in his sixties, his ulcer had gone out of control, he was done working, he claimed. Yet Joe was forever busy with one project or another. He volunteered at the Catholic church, the local hospital. He painted the inside of his garage silver-white and outlined the shapes of hand tools on the walls, then hung the tools inside those shapes. You could have eaten off the gleaming floors of that garage. He fussed and fretted over his lawn the way new mothers did about their babies. Joe kept the hedges perfectly manicured between their two houses. He came out dressed for the job like a man on combat duty. He wore the kind of helmet beekeepers wear. He sported an old but meticulously clean green coverall, goggles, enormous thick leather gloves, and leather work boots. The hedges were covered with red berries in summer, auburn leaves in fall, and sharp spiky thorns all year round. The day his Christmas decorations came down, Joe set straight to work again on the tangle of thorns. Sol would have hacked them down ages ago.

Joe's new power clippers were bright orange. The things made a tremendous amount of noise and dust. If Sol startled him, Joe was likely to jump in the air and chop off his own hand. So he waited till Joe had paused, and cut off the machine, then offered the mug of hot chocolate Sarah had sent him out to deliver. Two large cinnamon sticks clinked pleasantly in the ceramic mug. Compared to the roar of the machinery—it had been vaguely irritating the judge all morning—it sounded like chimes in an orchestra, or the first few notes of a harp. Joe smiled. He had a wide smile and even white teeth. "Thanks," he said.

"I wish you'd let me hire someone to do this," Sol said.

"I like the work," Joe said. "I like being outside in the fresh air." He raised the mug. "Salut."

"Well, there's plenty more where that came from," Sol said. "Sarah made it from scratch. Real cocoa, real sugar, real everything."

"Tell her I appreciate it. Especially I love the cinnamon." He bent his head over the mug and breathed in. When he breathed out again, his breath made a ghost in the morning air.

"Come by if you want more," Sol said. "I'm not doing anything much. Nothing that means anything. Reading the paper."

Joe cocked his head. Sol sometimes had the eerie sense that his neighbor could read his mind. "Might do that," he said. But Sol and Joe both relied on their wives for any sort of social life. That was their generation. This moment, standing together on the pavement, was the best the two men could manage on their own.

So Sol was surprised when Joe showed up an hour later, holding the empty mug in his hand, so clean and sparkling it looked new. He handed it back and said, "Why don't you come over?" The judge could count on the fingers of one hand the number of times Joe had invited him anywhere.

"Come on," Joe added. "Helen made cheesecake. Italian style. You've never tasted anything like it, not even in Italy."

Sol put down the crossword puzzle. He'd come to the door holding on to it; he was stuck anyway. Sunday puzzles had become another chore; once they had relaxed him. Now he preferred the *Newsday* Monday and Tuesday puzzles—what he used to call contemptuously "idiot's puzzles." First signs of old age.

He shrugged into his winter coat, and followed Joe down the pristine patch of sidewalk outside the Iccarinos' house—no snow or ice allowed to linger there—and up the equally spotless front path.

"Helen's out marketing," Joe said. "She acts like we're still living in the old country; shops every few days. I think she's just avoiding the big supermarkets. They look like warehouses. Who can blame her?"

He'd been watching TV, and instead of turning it off, he hit the mute button. He gestured at the set. "There's an accident in Hicksville on the Southern State, backed up all the way to Valley Stream. I don't know what's going on anymore—if they don't have enough lights, enough cops, or if it's just too many cars, like too many rats in the cage. We're all jammed in together—I remember when Long Island was one flat stretch of land," Joe said. "Farm country. That's how long we've been living here. The expressway was actually the fastest way into the city. The northern was the scenic route. No more."

He went into the kitchen and came back with two black lacquered plates, each with its serving of cake sprinkled with crushed almonds on top, and biscotti jutting out in half moons. The forks felt heavy, real sterling. The Iccarinos lived well; not ostentatiously, like Europeans. No junk food. No junk.

"Thank you," Sol said. "This is a treat."

"Five-car pileup outside Plainview," Joe said, sighing. "Stuck. Look at that." He clicked off the TV. "Did you know there's a station that shows you Long Island traffic, day and night?"

Sol shook his head, his mouth already filled with cheesecake, sweet and creamy, with a slight hint of liqueur.

"I watch it too much," Joe said. "It fascinates me, seeing how things have changed, how everything gets all snarled up. One person makes a mistake and everyone on the road pays for it. No one can move. You realize how interconnected we are. You see it so clearly on that screen. Late at night whenever I can't sleep, I find it soothing. Like a Christmas tree in a dark room. Blinking lights. Cars whooshing by. —My father-in-law in Ohio," he added, shifting in his chair, "used to watch the Weather Channel, day in and day out. I hate to think how I used to make fun of him. —Chin-chin!" he said, raising the plate.

"My daughter used to love TV infomercials," Sol admitted. "I'm embarrassed to tell you what we have in our closets, bought from those things. She used to beg us to buy the craziest items when she was a kid. A food dehydrator. Some kind of spinning fishing pole, for Christ's sake. Rock polishing kits. She was going to make her fortune with that one. If you watch anything for more than twenty minutes on TV, you begin to believe it."

Joe said, "I've been reading about that case between the cousins in the paper. Must be tough, a situation like that."

Sol's mouth tightened. "All cases involving family are tough," he said.

Joe waved his fork. "I know you can't discuss it with me," he said. "I respect that. Believe it or not, there were trade secrets in the furniture business as well." He scraped at the top of his cake as if he thought there might be something hiding underneath the surface. "I hope you won't take this the wrong way."

Sol said nothing. He laid the biscotti untouched next to the morsel of cake he hadn't polished off.

"Eat," Joe said. "Have seconds." He himself was doing more construction work than eating at the moment, rearranging the top of his cake and the crushed almonds. Sol remembered that Joe had started out as a bricklayer. "There's something you probably don't know about me," Joe said. "Most people don't."

This sounded ominous. Sol's mind went in ten directions at once, none of them happy. The crossword puzzle was beginning to look easy.

"Relax yourself," Joe said. "It's no big deal—I was a kidney donor. A couple of years ago you might remember I went into the hospital for a few weeks."

"I thought that was your ulcer," Sol said.

Joe waved the hand holding the fork. "I didn't want to advertise it. I went on one of those sites where you find a stranger in need of a kidney, and I donated mine. People found that sort of thing very strange, especially at the time. I'm not sure Helen ever really understood it. She worried." He took one tiny bite of the cake, then laid the fork down altogether. "I never knew the young man I donated to. We corresponded briefly by e-mail. Maybe there was one phone call, a few Christmas cards. I didn't do it to be thanked. Some people expect a relationship, they end up disappointed. But I didn't go into it with any ideas like that. I just relished a feeling of—purpose. Does that sound foolish to you?"

"Not at all," Sol said.

"Helen and I were never able to have children," Joe admitted. "I designed and sold furniture all my life. I wanted something else, something that would make me feel as if I had been given my life for a reason."

"I understand," Sol said. "You can't reach our age and not have some of those thoughts."

"Please don't think I'm trying to influence you one way or the other. This is none of my business, I know nothing about the law. I just wanted to tell you that giving up that kidney made me the happiest I've ever been in my life. I never regretted it for a second. It wasn't such a big deal. Everyone was against it. I had to follow my own conscience, and it ended up all right. People get so frightened for no reason, but I'll tell you, to live with no purpose is a far more frightening proposition." He looked out the large picture window of his house as if his thoughts were standing on the spotless front lawn. "You bring yourself to say yes when you always thought the only possible answer was no, and your whole world changes. That's all I can tell you."

A red bird landed on a feeder a few feet from the big window, and both men watched it for a moment.

"I'm sorry about all this, Sol, because I know you're a good man and you've worked hard all these years, even if you don't always keep up with the yard work. I hope you don't feel like I've been bragging. I'd just as soon you keep this whole kidney donation thing under your hat."

"Of course." Sol pushed back his chair and stood up. "Well, thanks for the delicious cake—and the chat," he said. "I'll try to do a little better with the leaves, come spring."

"That father—the cousin of the sick woman—he's the one I feel sorry for. Talk about being stuck." He mimed sitting helpless behind a steering wheel.

It occurred to the judge on his way out the door that he had been fighting traffic for the past forty years at least, and was more than a little weary of it himself.

FEBRUARY 2012
The Last and Only Chance

The case was drawing to a close. Nothing new was showing up, or likely to. The plaintiff had trotted in the usual medical experts, and Nicole's oncologist, wearing a bright purple tie, testified that the cord blood might do some good, might even be, in his words, "her last and only chance." Sol watched the woman Nicole wince when he said this. She rested her thin, still-beautiful face in her hands as if it had no place else to go. The relentless stampede of witnesses for the defense had ebbed, and Sol thought the worst was behind them when Turock announced she had one last witness who wished to address the court, but they would need the judge's permission to move on.

"And who might that be?" asked Sol.

"My son," said Ari, who seldom spoke at all these days.

Nicole's head came up.

"Since it is his cord blood, and he has an opinion on the subject, the least we can do is to let him speak," added Turock.

"Does the boy want to address the court? Is this his own idea?" Sol asked.

"He says he does," said Ari. "I have to believe him."

"And his age is—"

"Eleven," said Ari.

"Eleven. That's very young."

"He's old enough to know his own mind," Ari said stubbornly.

"And you," Sol said, turning to Nicole. "You have a daughter, don't you?"

She nodded.

"How old is the girl?"

"She's eight."

"Do you also want her to speak?"

"Absolutely not," said Nicole. "That is the last thing I'd want, dragging her in here. No. No way."

"Take it easy," her lawyer said, putting his hand on her arm in a steadying way. "I promised we wouldn't do anything of the kind."

The judge turned to Turock. "You're sure about the boy?"

She shrugged.

"We're sure," said Ari stubbornly. "Absolutely."

"All right, then," said the judge. "He can come in next week. He can speak to the court, *briefly*. But that will be a media blackout day. No press conferences, no leaks, no nothing." He spoke directly to Turock. "Am I understood?"

"Loud and clear," she said. She tugged at her short skirt, looking irritable. Perhaps she, too, was bored. Ready to win the case and move on to something more glamorous, more popular. Despite the efforts of the besotted Long Island reporter, the blood case had taken a toll on her reputation, tarnished a little of the pristine shine of her name. In future cases, Sol suspected, she would be making amends. Taking on the cause of some charity. Defending someone with no arms and no legs.

"All right, then," he said. "Court adjourned until next week." Out of habit, he lifted the gavel that was not even in his hand, and brought it down, which simply meant that he ended up slapping the side of his fist on the table, like Khrushchev.

———·———

"So," said the rabbi. He was toting two giant shopping bags, made out of some woven material, the name of a local health food store printed in green on the front. Each bag seemed to pull him slightly off balance; he wobbled as he stood in the watery sunshine outside Abigail's apartment. "How's it going?"

They were in the midst of a February thaw. She and Rabbi Teddy Lewin were wearing matching rubber boots from L.L.Bean, Abigail noticed. Iris still rode in the front-rigged baby sack, but she was getting bigger, she sagged a little, and her booted little feet merrily kicked Abigail in the ribs. Sunlight was bright around them. A few foolhardy crocuses poked up their purple-and-white-striped heads.

Abigail gestured around at the sunshine, the snow disappearing into puddles. "The ice caps are probably melting thanks to global warming, but we, personally, are grateful for the warm weather."

"I know what you mean," he said. "Winter lasts twice as long as summer."

"At least," she agreed.

"So I see you're not joining the bat-mitzvah group," he said, shifting his weight again from foot to foot.

"With my mother, you mean? I just don't have time." She realized she was just standing there, apparently with all the time in the world. And didn't her mother's study group meet on Fridays, her day off? "I mean"—she shifted Iris in her arms—"I honestly don't have the focus right now. With Iris and all."

"Bring her to Shabbat services," he said. "Lots of children come. Babies, too. Nobody minds. It's not that kind of congregation. It's a nice way to end the week. We have cake and coffee right after."

"It sounds nice," she said.

Her voice and face must have looked wistful, because he said, "So come tonight. It starts at seven." He put out his big hand and took Iris's tiny, mittened one. "Iris, you are very welcome. Everyone has been anxious to meet you. Your grandmother speaks about nothing else."

"All right," said Abigail, convinced by Iris's sudden wide toothless smile. "We'll come."

"Great!" he said heartily. "It's a date." Then he looked embarrassed. "I mean—it's a deal."

The judge and his wife were not at the Friday night services. But several of her mother's cohorts recognized little Iris and rushed over to greet her afterward, to ooh and ahh over the baby and reproach Abigail for not having shown up at synagogue earlier.

Then they lined up, either for coffee and cake or to chat with the rabbi. The line to greet him was as long as the line for food—which meant he was extremely popular. There were several braided loaves of egg challah, with raisins and without. There was coffee cake and Danish, and juice for the little ones who ran around the room. Teddy made sure Abigail and Iris had something they liked to eat or drink, and then stayed by their side for the rest of the *oneg.* The congregants' expressions went from amused to interested to something else entirely. Now they were scrutinizing Abigail, though they used Iris as a kind of prop, an excuse to draw nearer.

"How old did you say she was?" she was asked. "Which country? Have you had her converted yet? That's very important, the conversion."

"Happy to do it," Teddy said. "It's a simple ceremony—no trauma, no drowning, I promise."

The group interrogation went on. "Where do you work? Where do you live? How old did you say you are?"

"I didn't," said Abigail, her father's closemouthed child.

"Why don't you join your mother in our bat-mitzvah group? Unless you've already been bat-mitzvahed?"

"As a matter of fact, I have," Abigail said. "North Shore Synagogue."

The elderly woman talking to her made a face. "North Shore," she said contemptuously. "Ultrareform. But that must have been a long time ago. Now you can do it with intention, with full *ruach.*"

"Mm," Abigail said noncommittally.

"Good girl," the woman said, patting her hand and moving away. "And that Chinese baby daughter of yours looks like a doll. A real little China doll."

She's from Thailand! Abigail wanted to call after her, but just then the rabbi closed his hand around her arm. She felt both irritated and grateful. She was a big girl, she could look after herself—which is what she nearly said when he offered to walk them home after services. It was dark, and bitter cold. He insisted. She demurred—then caught the look of disappointment on his face. He was only being kind.

"Fine," she said. "If it's really no trouble."

"No trouble at all," he said, his young-old face lighting up. "Just let me say my good-nights and grab my coat."

"Take your time," she said. "We're in no hurry." She walked up and down the synagogue halls, bouncing Iris gently in her front pouch. She did not read Hebrew; the strange letters curled in red and gold. They strolled up and down, up and down, Iris blinking more sleepily.

The rabbi had pulled a navy wool watch cap on over his yarmulke, which made him look more like a college kid than a holy man. He wore a puffy blue down jacket that nearly matched hers.

"We dress a lot alike," she said. "Have you noticed?"

He looked at the hem of her long dress, flowered and ruffled at the edges. "I don't look as good in that dress as you do."

At her front door—which in some sense was *his* door, she realized; the temple owned the whole apartment building—she invited him in for tea or coffee.

"Thank you," he said. "I won't stay long." He took off his coat and wool cap—careful that his yarmulke was still in place—and hung them on the coatrack by the door. He hesitated, then untied and removed his boots as well, leaving them on the rubber mat.

She went down the hall to Iris's little room, three of its walls painted pale pink, one a deep, vibrant rose. She slipped her sleeping daughter out of the carrier, changed her diaper, and put her into a fresh onesie, all without waking her. She came back to the kitchen with the monitor in her hand, sizzling static.

"Is that a walkie-talkie?" the rabbi asked. "I haven't seen one of those in years."

"It's a monitor for the nursery. If Iris wakes up, I can hear her."

"Right. Because she doesn't have much to say on a walkie-talkie yet."

"No, but I have a feeling she's going to be a chatterbox. —Tea or coffee sound good?" she asked. "I can make hot chocolate, too."

"I'll have tea," he said. "Herbal tea, if you have it. I don't sleep well."

"I can tell."

He smiled ruefully. "I know. I look like a seventy-year-old man. Actually," he added, "I'm only thirty-eight."

"I'm thirty-two," she said. "Which doesn't feel very 'only' to me."

He said, "Please don't boil any water. Just hot water from the tap will be fine."

She had taken the teakettle to the spring-water jug to fill it.

"Shabbos," he said. "You're not allowed to light the stove."

She felt herself blushing. This was one of the hard parts of being a redhead—everything showed. "Right, sorry. —So. Why can't you sleep?"

"Oh—the usual things. The past. The present, too, but mostly the past." He waved, as if at invisible gnats. His broad shoulders slumped.

"How long ago did your wife pass away?" she asked.

He nodded. He looked away. "Actually," he said. "I'm going to tell you something most people don't know. My wife didn't pass away. She left me four years ago."

"Oh," said Abigail.

"The wife of a rabbi—it's almost a full-time job. And she already had a full-time job. Lawyer."

"My father's a judge," Abigail said.

"So you understand the intensity, the long hours. And as the rabbi's wife, you're always expected to be *on*. —When I got hired here, the congregants misunderstood the situation, and I never corrected them. I think they prefer the idea of a widower to a divorcé, anyway. So when people ask me, 'When did you lose your wife,' I just say, 'I lost her four years ago.' Which is the truth. Jaidee knows the real story. The board of trustees, of course. But they like to keep things quiet."

"I see," Abigail said.

He traced his finger on the wood grain of her kitchen table. "When she and I met, I was a law student. Things took another turn. It was hard for her. My life is not wholly my own."

"Whose is?" Abigail said. "At least you're doing something useful with yours."

"I don't know about that—but thanks." He looked straight into her eyes. "You manage to make me feel uplifted. I think it's supposed to be the other way around. Do you always know the right thing to say? Or do you just know the right thing to say to me?"

Abigail just smiled, embarrassed.

As he stood up to go a little later, he said, "I'm afraid I can't call you tomorrow."

Abigail felt the blood rush to her face. She was surprised at the way disappointment seemed to hit her so hard. "Of course not," she said. "That's fine. I didn't expect—"

"I mean because it's Shabbos," he said. "Can't use the phone. But if it's all right with you, I'll call you after."

"Oh," she said. "Yes, it's all right."

"We should talk about your daughter's conversion," he said. "Esther was right, it is important—if it's important to you."

"It could be important to my parents," she said. "Is that good enough?"

"Good enough for me," he said. "So—we'll talk." He bent over, and she nearly turned her face up for a kiss. Luckily she didn't close her eyes. He shook her hand and said, "Shabbat Shalom."

"Shabbat Shalom," she answered.

FEBRUARY 2012
Julian Takes the Stand

Sol would never know what made him go so early into court that morning. Normally he arrived at eight thirty like clockwork. No sooner, no later. Over the years he'd timed it nearly to a science. But that morning he woke just after dawn, and try as he might, he could not get back to sleep. The sky was a shimmering deep-blue screen outside the window; for once it had not snowed. There was no sense puttering around the house, he thought. He might as well go straight to the courthouse and get some work done.

When he pulled into the Supreme Court parking lot, he thought some terrible event had occurred. It looked like a full-fledged crime scene, with police lights flashing, four or five white Nassau County police cars parked in a line, and the parking lot jammed with newspaper reporters. A decade earlier, a jealous lover had murdered one of the clerks in the Supreme Court building after hours, and it had looked like this—pure chaos.

But when Judge Richter climbed out of his car, five or six flashbulbs went off in his face, and with a sinking heart he realized what had happened: Flannery had tipped off the press. He had told them a minor was going to testify. For an instant he couldn't tell if he was blinded by the flash or by his own fury.

"Judge Richter! Judge Richter!" A dozen reporters shouted his name, but he heard them only dimly, as if under water. A crowd had gathered on the courthouse front steps around one thin scarecrowish figure dressed in a dapper blue suit with red stripes. He knew that figure and that suit, and he headed toward it so forcefully that even the reporters and cameramen fell back.

He pushed his way up the courthouse stairs and dragged Flannery inside. He steered his chief clerk by the elbow, past the security guards, past the gaping reporters, the gawking passersby—crowd begets crowd, he thought, and it would take forever to get rid of them all. It was a miracle that neither the plaintiff nor defendant had yet arrived. Another ten minutes and the whole case would have blown up. The judge was four inches shorter than his clerk, but he had the energy of righteous anger driving them both.

"I'll be right back!" Flannery called to the reporters. Then to Sol, "What's wrong? Your Honor, what is it? I'm needed here," but Sol shook his head grimly till he'd steered them both straight into the men's room next to the lobby, closed the door, and locked it.

Then he stopped to face his clerk. "Pack your things," he said, his voice low. When Sol was truly angry his voice dropped. If you had to strain to hear him you were in trouble. But Flannery had heard him.

He goggled at the judge. "What do you mean?" he said. "Pack?"

"I mean you're fired. As of today. This moment. I want you out of here."

"Justice Richter," said Flannery. "There must be some mistake."

"You nearly caused a mistrial. Do you understand that? A woman's life is at stake! And now a young boy's future and reputation are on the line as well. Today's hearing was closed to the press, to protect a child and to preserve the law. But you had to be out there grandstanding. So I'm telling you to take your fat-assed fiancée and get out of this courthouse before I wring your skinny neck." Sol found his hands on the clerk's shoulders as if he were about to make good on his threat.

Flannery shook him off and moved gracefully backward, offended dignity personified. His face was brick red. He tugged down his suit coat and quickly checked himself out in the men's room mirror. "My fiancée does *not* have a fat ass."

"Get out!" Sol roared. Flannery bolted. Despite his rage, Sol could not watch him go without some feeling of pity and of loss. He had to steel himself, actually clench his fists, to keep himself from calling after the clerk. He watched the skinny figure cross the parking lot in five or six long strides and climb into his car, an older model Cadillac. Flannery had attached a set of Mickey Mouse ears to his car, he once explained, to make it recognizable in a crowd. Sol watched the Disney head bobble as it wove out of sight.

———·———

It took nearly an hour to clear away the crowd from outside the courtroom. Stephanie had intercepted both the defendant and plaintiff and told them to stay away. The police started handing out written citations and parking tickets, and that seemed to do the trick. The journalists scattered, taking their cameras and equipment with them. Sol was more shaken by his run-in with Flannery than he cared to admit. What a fool he was, to have put his trust in such a man! He had considered Flannery almost a friend. Sol asked Frank Zimmer to cover for him, and looking a bit puzzled, the young part clerk had done the "All rise" in his quiet, even voice. He had pulled together all the needed files for the day; Myra pitched in, too. When she started to ask about Flannery, though, he cut her off. No one had filed a formal complaint about the morning's disaster, but the judge knew he had a ticking time bomb on his hands. Katrina Turock looked like the cat who'd eaten the canary. For her, this was simply another opportunity. They managed to get the boy safely upstairs without further interference or publicity.

The young witness sat beside his father, his hands folded in his lap. He was doing something curious with the hands, the judge realized, lacing and unlacing them, as if rearranging some design with his fingers. He looked like a nice kid—the kind of grandson he himself would have liked to have. Might conceivably still have. This boy was built just like his father beside him—the same broad shoulders, the same broad nose and deep brown level eyes. His hair was a bit darker and curlier, and he was wearing a navy blue blazer instead of a blue suit like his father. The father's suit must have cost a thousand dollars, but the kid's jacket was no bargain either. The boy kept his eyes on his hands.

Nicole saw him come in, and she smiled at Julian, despite herself, but when he didn't smile back she felt exhausted, as if she'd suddenly run out of gas. She felt that way a lot these days. When she put a halt to all the chemo treatments, she'd stopped feeling so nauseated, and some of the side effects went away, but inside, it was as if her body had dropped another floor on an elevator. The lump on her neck had returned. She had recurring nightmares now, where she came to a stone wall and could not get across it, though she could see Jay and Daisy on the other side, walking in the snow. The court case seemed more and more irrelevant. She kept on with it because she had said that she would, and stubbornness, it seemed, was the very last thing to go. Besides, to walk away from it now would be a betrayal of her husband

and daughter. She'd fight this thing out to the end and try to leave them behind without bitterness. That was what she thought about now. How to exit gracefully, how to leave behind as little damage as possible.

Peter had always prepared her for how this trial was likely to turn out. Another judge might have gone with the first motion to dismiss it altogether. She sometimes wished this one had. She had no false expectations. Still, having Julian testify against her in court brought more bitterness than she'd have expected. It knocked the wind right out of her. Mimi was nowhere in sight. Ari sat stolidly beside his son, one arm curved around his shoulder. He looked more alert, more solidly *there*, than he had for months.

"This," said the father, gesturing toward the boy, "is what we are trying to protect. This boy and his baby sister, who is too young to be here today."

Katrina called Ari to the stand. "Please state the age of your children."

"Julian is eleven," the father said. "The baby—Arianna—is twenty-two months old."

"And can you describe the health of your children?"

"Objection," said Peter. "Compound question."

"Objection sustained," said the judge. "The court will hear about one child's health at a time."

Katrina rolled her eyes. "How would you describe the health of your daughter?" she asked with deliberate slowness.

"It's fine," Ari said.

"And the health of your son?"

"Good," the father said. "Their health is good. But some months ago, Julian got a lump"—his hand went instinctively to his own throat—"on his neck. A big hard lump on the side of his neck." One hand hovered toward his son, as if to reassure himself. "The doctor thought it might be

Hodgkin's. We have the records. We had a biopsy done. That's when I realized I could not go through with this thing. Life is too uncertain. Things go wrong when you least expect them. What if he really had been sick? What if we needed that cord blood for our own boy, and we had given it away?"

"Objection to everything after 'We had a biopsy done,' Your Honor," said Peter. "We request that it be stricken from the record. Witness may testify only to facts, not opinions."

"Objection sustained," said the judge.

"Is it a fact that you decided to withhold the cord blood after this biopsy?" asked Katrina Turock.

"Yes, it is," said Ari.

"Thank you," said Katrina. "Your witness," she added, as she walked back to reclaim her seat. She said it the way a cat flicks its tail.

"Mr. Wiesenthal," said Peter. "What was the result of that biopsy?"

"Benign," the father said. "Something called a teratoma. —Like a hairball, the doctor said. It happens sometimes. Still, it could have been much worse. Much, much worse."

"Objection," said Peter. "Witness cannot speculate."

"Objection sustained," said Sol.

Katrina Turock was glaring at Peter.

Ari looked rattled. His mouth opened and closed twice. "You understand," he said. His fingers were gripping the edge of the wood table so hard that the blood left his fingertips. "I'm a father. I only—"

"Objection again, Your Honor," said Peter.

"Sustained," said Sol. "Mr. Wiesenthal, you are not to say anything unless you are asked a question."

Ari nodded.

"I'm done here," said Peter.

Ari hurried back to his seat. His son kept his head down, the hair falling forward over his eyes.

Katrina rose. "Defendant calls Julian Wiesenthal to the stand," she said. She looked defiantly at Peter.

"Objection," said Peter. "Julian is too young to understand the oath."

"I'm not a baby," Julian said. He did not say it impolitely.

He looked like a nice boy, the judge thought. Unreadable, that half-babyish, half-teenage face. He felt the wrench inside his own gut when he looked at Nicole's expression, her lowered head. Had any good come of it? Lieu had asked. Could any good come of it? This rending of flesh from flesh.

"Julian," the judge said. "Do you know what the truth is?"

"Does anyone?" the boy asked.

"Do you know that it is wrong to tell a lie?"

"Of course," said Julian.

"So," Sol continued, in a gentler voice. "You want to testify?"

"I *do*," the boy said, though his voice shivered a little on the word *do*.

"And you've come of your own free will? No one has forced or coerced you to be here?"

Julian shook his moppy head. His mouth was drawn tight. "No one," he said. His father patted his arm with the hand that draped down over his shoulder.

"All right, then," the judge said. "Come on up to the stand, and we'll swear you in."

The boy looked extremely solemn all during the procedure. He did not glance around the room, nor did he show the slightest inclination to dramatize or show off. He kept his hands clasped together and his eyes fixed on the judge's face, which Sol found unusual in someone so young and inexperienced. His granddaughter Iris also had a preternaturally solemn face. Maybe this whole generation was born old. Aside from the small group, the court recorder tapping away, taking notes, and Carter Johnson himself standing guard at the back, the room was empty. Katrina Turock tapped her pencil rapidly on the wood desk in front of her, and then, hearing the sound rebound in the room, stopped.

"Julian," the judge said. "Is there any reason you feel you can't speak freely?" He inclined his head toward Nicole and her lawyer without mentioning them by name.

"It's fine," Julian said. "I don't care who hears me."

The judge nodded at Katrina, who strode toward Julian. "How old are you?" she asked

"I'm eleven," he said. He frowned at her as if to say, *We already established that.*

"Do you know Nicole Greene?" she asked.

"She's my father's cousin," he said.

"Her children are your cousins?"

"She only has one child, but yes. Daisy is my cousin."

"Do you know what cord blood is, Julian?"

"I looked it up on Wikipedia," he answered. "Cord blood is blood that stays in the placenta and the umbilical cord after birth."

"Very good," she said. Katrina laughed, and her laughter was rich and silvery, like bracelets jangling together. "Do you understand that you might need a cord blood transfusion someday?"

"I don't want it," said Julian. "I wouldn't touch it with a ten-foot pole."

Ari jolted upright as if someone had administered an electric shock. The elderly court recorder stopped typing on her machine and looked at the judge for an instant, her eyebrow raised. Katrina moved forward, quick as a snake. "Your Honor, I object," she said.

"Overruled," Sol said, just as quickly.

"I don't want the blood," said Julian. "It's mine, and I should have some say in the matter. I want it to go to Aunt Nicole. She needs it. I don't."

"She is not your aunt!" Ari called.

"My cousin," Julian corrected himself, his voice shaking now.

"You understand that this cord blood is being kept for your own benefit?" Katrina said. "Yours and your sister's."

"I understand that," Julian said. "But I really don't give a crap." For the first time now, he sounded like his father. "One of these days I'm going to turn twenty-one, and it's going to belong to me. And I swear to God I'll flush it down the toilet. I swear I will. —Arianna doesn't need it. I don't need it, I'm not sick. I wish I'd never been born!"

The judge thought of the famous Jewish dictum, "Best of all never to have been." He said nothing. The boy's hands had come unclasped and were now leaning on the edge of the table, gripping the wood.

"I don't want it!" he shouted. "Will someone please, please listen to me?"

"Calm down," Katrina said stiffly. "We are listening very carefully to your testimony—including, most importantly, Judge Richter."

"You're hearing my voice, but I don't believe any of you are listening. I don't want the goddamn cord blood!"

"Shhh," the father interrupted. "You are too young to know what you're saying. You're too young to know what you really want." He seemed more stricken than angry.

"Maybe you are too old to know what you want," Sol said, taking himself by surprise. It was not his way to speak like this. Perhaps it was himself he was really talking about. He felt everything slipping away, out of his control. "Mr. Wiesenthal, I am not going to tell you again not to comment on the witness's testimony. Order in the court!" he added curtly, again speaking mostly to himself.

Nicole's face was shining. She mouthed the words *Thank you* to Julian. He nodded, unsmiling. This was every bit as brave as the long-ago day she had dashed forward to protect her cousin and his dogs against the mongrel. Braver, she thought. Braver. We did all right with these kids. They're going to be fine in the end. We did our job well. She was proud of herself, proud even of poor Ari. She wanted to throw her arms around them and go home.

"I'm done with this witness," Katrina said with disgust.

"Counsel waives cross-examination," Peter said.

Julian began weeping like the child he really was as he stumbled out of the court, Ari hurrying after him.

"I'm sorry!" Julian called tearfully to Nicole over his shoulder. "I'm so sorry. Nothing I say makes any difference to anyone!" That wasn't entirely true. Carter Johnson stepped out of the way when Julian passed, and opened the door for the boy. He gave just the smallest hint of a salute, but it was a real salute nonetheless.

———

As soon as Nicole came home that afternoon, she dropped her bag on the floor and headed for the telephone. She didn't allow herself time to think. She pressed the numbers of Mimi's phone.

"We have to stop this," she said, as soon as Mimi picked up. "We can't let them do this to us anymore. I've never wanted to live without you, and I'm damned if I'm going to die without you."

That Thursday when Julian came by to visit Daisy, he held a big wrapped box in his hands. Daisy was dancing by the front window, watching him come up the front walk.

"What is it, what is it, what could it be?" she asked.

"It's a Wii!" Julian announced as soon as Daisy had yanked open the door. "With a sports game and a racing car game and a dancing game. I'm not doing the dancing game."

Daisy was too busy screaming to hear the rest.

"Julian, thank you," Nicole said. She couldn't bring herself to say any more. She hugged him instead, tears in her eyes—but she hadn't taken her eyes off Mimi, who was still inside the car, trying to get the parallel parking right. She never has learned how to line up the wheels of her car, Nicole thought. That's something I can still teach her.

"I don't know how to set it up," Daisy said.

"It's easy as lemon pie," Julian said, with eleven-year-old superiority. "Come on, I'll show you."

Mimi managed to get the car more or less parallel to the curb and was struggling out, holding her own bag of packages, in the kind of enormous bright foil gift bag Nicole's mother had always used. She was wearing a shearling jacket and a boy's-style gray watch cap—in fact, probably one of Julian's hats. Nicole had to keep herself from running out into the snow. She waited for Mimi to get to the front steps, then flung the door open. Her heart was beating joyfully.

"I brought presents," Mimi said, setting down the bag.

"So I see," said Nicole. "What for?" She watched Mimi sizing her up, trying to hide her shock, her dismay at the change in Nicole, trying simply to smile. I know I'm dying, she wanted to say. It's all right, it's not as bad as you think.

"Oh, I don't know," Mimi said, swiping the hat off her head and cramming it into her jacket pocket. "For the new year. Valentine's Day. Something."

Nicole put both hands on her friend's shoulders. She looked straight into those familiar brown eyes, the straight dark brows above them, her slightly crooked nose. "Lordy, lordy," Nicole said. "You're a sight for sore eyes."

Mimi half smiled, but her eyes filled with tears.

"I'm so sorry," Nicole said. "I've missed you."

"No. I'm the one who's sorry." Mimi pressed her wet face against Nicole's shoulder.

"Okay, it's a tie," Nicole said. The two friends hugged and swayed back and forth a long time as if dancing, without speaking. They didn't let go till the kids hollered at them to come downstairs. Daisy stood at the bottom of the stairway, studying them. She rolled her eyes at Julian, but looked triumphant.

"Look!" she yelled. "Our mothers are in love."

———·—·———

Sol had decided to write the blood case decision without help. He wanted this last case to be entirely in his own words. Flannery had composed a draft weeks before, and Sol tossed it in the garbage now without looking at it. Then, thinking of Sarah, he relented and put it into the paper recycling bin, still unread.

Sol struggled over the wording of this decision as if finding the right language might give him a clear conscience and direction. Justice, he knew, often depended on making the least damaging of two choices. Sol had given up his wide-eyed idealism long ago. Before he even got out of law school. Legal idealists were demagogues. They were more dangerous than the worst legal mind. The law was fallible because it was an invention of fallible creatures.

He had built his professional life on logic and precedent, and as long as he followed where they led, he felt he was in relatively safe territory. This had happened time and time again, over the years. Truth will spring forth from the earth, in the words of the Old Testament. But it evaded him now. He could not wrestle any meaning from the tangle of legalese. The harder he tried, the worse it sagged, snared in formal language like an animal caught in a trap.

His judgment was a death sentence, he knew that, written in what felt like a dead language. He tried to add something of Flannery's ornate style, but somehow that only made matters worse. Now the thing was not only dead but flowery. A eulogy. In despair one night, Sol showed Sarah what he had written.

Sarah was in the midst of what Sol thought of as her Jewish phase. Twice a week she attended the bat-mitzvah class, but the rest of the time she studied on her own, head down, reading glasses falling to the end of her nose. Between her studies and the time she spent with Iris, she seemed happier, more self-sufficient, than she'd been in years. Now she examined her husband's written notes closely, as if they, too, were Talmudic commentary, her chin propped in her hand. The lamplight glinted on her short gray hair. Finally she looked up.

"What are you trying to say?" she said.

Sol groaned and reached for the papers. "That bad," he sighed. "Jeez."

"No. Sol. Forget the writing a minute. Just tell me what it is you're trying to say."

He felt like an unprepared actor whose script had been snatched away. He tried to remember how the written decision began. "After due deliberation, it is the opinion of the Supreme Court of Nassau County, in accordance with—"

"In your own words," she interrupted. "Say it in English."

"Okay." He started again. "I'm trying to say—I *want* to say that it's impossible to force body parts or bodily fluids to be taken from one person and given to another without consent. Even if it saves a life. Legally speaking, it's a slippery slope with horror at the end of it. Nonetheless, I want the defendant to carefully consider what he is doing. It's up to him, we can't force him from his path no matter how much we may detest him for it."

"I don't think you can say 'detest,'" Sarah said. "But I get the idea."

"How about 'despise'?"

She pointed at the sheaf of papers in his hand. "Start fresh. You have nobody to impress; just be as clear as possible. Tear up the old draft. Write it down pretty much the way you just said it to me, add anything else you think you've left out, and let Ned take care of the legal language. It's a hard thing, Solly. I'm sorry your last case had to be so hard."

She hardly ever called him Solly. Only in their tenderest moments. "Thanks," he said gruffly. "This is why you were such a good teacher."

She looked at him over her glasses, her eyes wide. "Was I?"

"Oh, Sarah," he said. "Love of my life. If you knew even the half of it."

February 2012
The Decision

"All rise," Zimmer, the part clerk, said. "All manner of Men who stand bound by recognizance or who otherwise have proceedings before the Honorable, the Justice of the Supreme Court of New York, here holden this day for Nassau County, may now appear and they shall be heard."

Sol walked from his chambers into the short hall connecting it to his courtroom. He felt like a schoolboy his very last day of school. Done, finished. The absolute familiarity of the hallway made it seem unfamiliar. His robes swayed around his ankles as he turned the corner and entered the courtroom for the last time. Carter Johnson opened the door for him.

The faces inside were by now also familiar. Ari sat beside Katrina Turock and one of her young assistants, both of them wearing suits with short, slit skirts and high heels. Nicole sat between her lawyer and her husband, Jay.

Sol supposed that if he had not seen her week after week, he might have realized how much the plaintiff's condition had deteriorated over the past months. Perhaps it was the pale blue sweater she was wearing, belted, over a long skirt, that seemed nearly to match the pale bluish tint of her skin, but he saw it with his own eyes. The process had begun with or without his decision. The sweater was short-sleeved and her arms hung thin and without muscle tone. The lipstick she wore only seemed to emphasize the prominence of her teeth, as if the skull was beginning to show through the mask of her face. She looked more frightened than Sol had expected, and her fear infected him. Always, she reminded him of his own Abigail—even now, when she was so sick and so colorless, she appeared like the ghost of one he loved. What if it were his daughter, Abigail, dying? Or his little granddaughter, Iris? What did it take to save a life? He thought for one brief, heart-stopping moment, as he took the stand and looked down at his clerks, the court recorder and Carter Johnson, the defendant and plaintiff, all looking up at him, that he could still change his mind: rule in her favor and let all hell break loose. His career was over anyway, what did it matter? But to do this would only prolong the inevitable; Turock would take it to the next court up. Nicole would die, was already dying. If he wanted to save people, he should have become a doctor, a miracle worker. As in every other case, he must follow the law. He looked down at the papers in his hands and read:

"The Plaintiff, Nicole Greene, suffers from a rare form of leukemia and lymphoma and the prognosis for her survival is dim unless she receives a cord blood transplant from a compatible donor, paving the way for a bone marrow transplant and further treatment. Finding a compatible cord blood donor is especially difficult in her case. After a nationwide search and numerous tests, it has been determined that the Defendant possesses the suitable match from his son Julian's cord blood. Mr. Wiesenthal refuses the necessary transplant and before this Court is a request for a mandatory injunction that would compel the Defendant to relinquish cord blood against his will.

"The Plaintiff poses the question of whether, in order to save the life of one of its members by the only means available, society may infringe upon one's right to his 'bodily security,' and further urges, that since the cord blood exists independent of the body, there is no danger involved either to the Defendant or to the Defendant's son. In brief, the immediate risk to the Plaintiff is in no way matched by an immediate threat to the Defendant.

"Common law has consistently held to a rule that provides that no human being is under legal compulsion to give aid or to take action to save or rescue another. Precedent was set in England in 1594 when Thomas Aiken witnessed his neighbor fall through the ice and drown, and failed to rescue the man. He could not be prosecuted under a duty to rescue. Volumes have been written about this rule, and its seeming anomaly in a society that believes that justice travels hand in hand with mercy.

"Ernest Weinrib defends a duty of easy rescue, which would require help provided that (a) the situation is an emergency, and (b) the help would involve no risk and little other cost for the one who gives the help. Does this represent a viable alternative to more conventional forms of legal duties to rescue?

"The Talmud observes: 'How do we know that if someone sees his fellow drowning in the river or a wild beast dragging him off, or bandits coming upon him, that he is duty bound to save him? Because it is stated: 'Do not stand by your brother's blood.' (Sanhedrin 73a).

"Indeed, the common law appears on its surface to be revolting to every moral sense. Further inspection, however, demonstrates that the rule is founded on the very essence of a free society."

Katrina Turock capped her pen and sat up straighter. Ari Wiesenthal, not understanding the import of what the judge had just said, continued to slump beside her. His expensive suit looked rumpled, as if he had slept in it.

"Our society, contrary to many others and contrary to religiously based law, has as its first principle respect for the individual, and a belief that government and law exist to protect the individual and his or her rights. Whether we personally like it or not, the defendant has the legal right to refuse relinquishing the cord blood. Would the court also force his son to undergo a medical procedure, such as a bone marrow or liver transplant? Can the law rule that a part of an individual's body should be removed and given to another so that the other could live? To do so would defeat the sanctity of the individual. Forcible extraction of body parts in order to privilege the life of one over another causes revulsion to the judicial mind, and raises the specter of the swastika, the gulag, and other horrors."

Jay, the husband, threw a desperate look at the judge, but Nicole herself gazed past him, over his right shoulder, either not understanding or past caring what he was saying. A dark-haired woman the judge had never seen before sat next to Nicole, holding her other hand. At least the plaintiff was not alone.

"Ours is a court of equity," said the judge. "Equity follows the law but acts on the person. There is no question that this case acts not only on the person of Nicole Greene but on the very fiber of family relations and human decency. Every case involves people. The law is the energy of the living world, and it flows from and to the people.

"The defendant, Ari Wiesenthal, declares in effect that he can do wrong and not be liable to the person he has wronged. He thus urges a momentous exception to the accepted proposition that in law there can be no wrong without remedy. The remedy in this case rests entirely in his hands, and the court would urge him to consider this long and carefully.

He must take full responsibility for his decision. He dare not refuse lightly. But for our law to *compel* the Defendant forcibly would change every concept and principle upon which our society stands. Morally, the decision rests with the Defendant, and in the view of the court, the refusal of the Defendant is morally indefensible. He must live with the ramifications of a choice that dooms a family member, a choice made even against the will of his own young son. The power to change still resides with him."

The judge let his words rest a moment, as he let his gaze rest on Ari Wiesenthal. Ari's arms were folded tightly across his chest, his eyes were closed; his face was drawn and tight. This was easy for no one, Sol thought. He might as well get it over with.

"This court makes no comment on the law regarding the Plaintiff's rights in an action at law for damages, but has no choice but to deny the requested equitable relief. An Order will be entered denying the request for a mandatory injunction."

He banged the gavel down once. "Case dismissed."

Jay began to weep and gathered his wife into his arms as if she were a bundle of flowers, kissing her face and hair. She no longer looked frightened; if he didn't know better, in the glimpse Sol had through the husband's embrace, she seemed instead almost relieved. The resemblance to his own red-haired daughter made him weak at the knees. How had this happened, how? A beaming Katrina Turock stuck out her hand to shake Ari's, but he looked uncomprehendingly past it to the weeping man and his cousin, stunned. It looked for all the world as if he, and not she, had been handed a death sentence.

Ari had begun parking farther and farther away from the courthouse. At the start of the case he'd slipped his BMW into whatever spot was closest to the big, squat-looking building—not as impressive as you'd hope a Supreme Court might be. It looked like an ordinary dull office building. Even the Glen Cove City Central School offices near his house had a much finer edifice, complete with ivy-covered walls and a long, wide walkway leading up to marble stairs. If not for the official Supreme Court seals over the front entrance, you could have been walking into almost any public building— an airport, corporate headquarters, one of those large auto-supply centers he used to visit with his father on the Lower East Side.

But as the case went on, Ari came to regard the building with dread. He even dreamed about it, nightmares in which he wandered around the halls, lost, trying to make a phone call from one broken pay phone after another. It frightened him in real life. He hated the long dreary walk approaching the front stairs. He had learned to avoid glancing at the white-and-red Long Island News van parked near the curb. A burning rose in his stomach as the familiar statue of Columbus approached, as the American flag drew bigger and closer. That was how it felt to Ari—as if the building were striding toward him, not as if he walked toward the building.

So he'd begun to park a few blocks down, on a neighboring street. Then he parked a few blocks farther away, telling himself he needed the exercise. If it rained, he brought an umbrella. If the sun shone, he wore sunglasses. Lately he'd taken to parking in a strip mall a quarter of a mile away from the courthouse, a run-down open-air mall containing nothing but an empty storefront, a Dunkin' Donuts, a dry cleaner, and a real estate office that never seemed to get any business. His own office was thriving, despite the bad press.

"The only bad publicity is no publicity," his partner told him. "We're in people's minds now. They see the name, they remember it." But Ari noticed they'd pushed his large, framed, smiling photograph to one of the back offices, and replaced it with an oil painting of seagulls.

———————

On the morning of the judge's decision—a mild February day, warm enough to lull you into thinking spring had come—Ari had parked the BMW between the cleaner's and the real estate office, stopped, and bought himself a coffee and a bag of doughnut holes. He threw both away before he even left the strip mall. His mouth felt dry; he could not swallow. He squared his shoulders, in imitation of his father, and trudged toward his fate.

Two hours later, when he should have felt vindicated, when it was all over and he had run the final gauntlet of the cameras and reporters— there was no keeping them off this one last time—the walk back to his car seemed to stretch for miles. Jay's sobs echoed in his ears. His wife and son's betrayal still stung him, but what he pictured most vividly was his cousin Nicole, staring straight ahead, with that strange look of triumph and release on her face. She seemed to be gasping for air slightly, but that was not uncommon for her these days. She was drowning in her own death. He saw it. He might as well have said yes to the contract and walked away a hero, he thought. She'd never have lived past the filling out of the paperwork releasing the cord blood.

But then again, she might. He did not want to be both a villain and a fool. The nausea that had been with him all day worsened as he approached his car. It churned at the back of his throat. He feared he would actually be sick.

The sugary, powdery smell from the Dunkin' Donuts was so potent that he hurried into his car, put it into reverse, and drove straight back into a smiling woman standing behind his car. She appeared out of nowhere. He had a vivid image of her, smiling, falling straight down, and then there was a horrible crunching sound, as of bones splintering. No cry, no call for help.

He slammed on the brakes and leaped out of the car, expecting to see blood splattered all over the lot. His life was over. In ruins. He had managed to murder two women in a single day. With a macabre burst of memory he found himself thinking of the old fairy tale "Seven at One Blow." He tottered back behind his car, bracing himself for the worst, and found a life-size cardboard image of a female realtor mounted on a shattered piece of wood. The name of the real estate agency he'd parked near was emblazoned over her chest like a Miss America banner. Her image was cracked, split in two diagonally, but she was still smiling.

He dragged it upright and leaned it against the real estate office. No one had seen him, no one else had noticed. What kind of a moron puts something like that out in a parking lot, he thought, but he was already back in the car, his gloved hands shaking so badly he could not drive. He sat for several minutes, his heart still slamming, adrenaline coursing through his system like a poison. When he looked down at his gloves—they were high-quality Italian black leather gloves, decorated all over with tiny holes, like hundreds of puncture wounds—he saw the strange black-gloved hands of a killer.

SPRING 2012
The Hardest Thing

Of course Daisy knew that her mother was sick—she was not stupid, and besides it had now been in all the papers. Nicole could not prevent Daisy's friends from talking about that. She couldn't stop the teachers from cornering Daisy in the hall and murmuring their concern. Nor could she do anything to blunt Daisy's own powers of observation. If she had a doctor's appointment, Daisy seemed almost to smell it; if Nicole felt tired, or depressed, or frightened, or in pain, Daisy would offer to rub her shoulders or her back. She did not want her daughter to become her keeper, and Daisy was inclined that way, always had been. She bandaged Barbies, put them into their Barbie beds, and took their temperatures with a play thermometer. Daisy took the ones with half-chewed arms from the discards of her friends, and tried to nurse them back to health. As a result she had an odd assortment of dolls, to say the least. Jay and Nicole secretly called them One-Legged Barbie, Bite Victim Barbie (a friend's dog had left bite marks all over one arm), Amputee Ken, and so on. Nicole tried to be grateful for the times her daughter hung on her neck, and not to feel hurt when, as happened more and more these days, Daisy stayed away, tiptoeing out of the room to the safety of her father's robust good health and lively company.

With Jay she had the opposite problem. He was always on her, at her, he seemed to need to be touching her, as if to reassure himself that she was still there. They still hungered for each other, but she found herself exhausted and depleted afterward, as if she might never rise back up again into her body. He seemed to harbor the illusion that he could love her back to health. But she hurt a good deal of the time. Her chest ached, her stomach throbbed, all of her joints felt rusty. Her mouth and throat stung from sores.

These days she preferred to lie snuggled up against him, or simply holding his hand, that last bastion of strength and safety. She would will herself to stay up all night long, at least one night, gazing into his sleeping face. But then, sometime around four or five in the morning, close to dawn, she would give herself over to sleep, and when she woke again, Jay and Daisy were already gone for the day.

At least now she had Mimi to talk to again, or more important, to listen to—her beautiful corny jokes, the sound of her calm voice at the other end of a phone. An oasis in a desert. Her best friend was back in place, and that was serious comfort. Mimi, Jay, Daisy, Julian. But it was a lonely business, this dying. You had to leave the world unescorted—no matter how much the people around you loved you, no matter how hard they clung to you, or you to them. The clinging sometimes made it worse. Nicole turned to the company of acquaintances when the pain of leaving all this behind overwhelmed her, where there were no threads to disentangle, no ties to bind her. She stayed in touch with Ruby, Darnell's mother. Darnell and Daisy were as unalike as two third-graders could be, but ever since kindergarten they had gotten along—and they had always ended up in the same class. Darnell acted out a lot—"He doesn't always listen," Daisy would report disapprovingly—but he was sweet-tempered, and as Daisy said, "He's funny." The class clown, just as Ruby had predicted all those years ago.

If Ruby also remembered talking about the woman who had been diagnosed with cancer when her child was in kindergarten and died a few years later, she never mentioned it. Nor did she try to pretend that Nicole was healthy, or just "tuckered out," as many of the other mothers did. They'd invent some excuse for the way Nicole looked, or simply sidle away, avoiding her on the school playground where she came to pick Daisy up. She didn't have the energy to stand there for hours, like the other mothers, so she just sank down on the edge of the sandlot, watching Daisy run. Sometimes playing on the swings with her best friend, Claudia, sometimes chasing Darnell through the jungle gym. Nicole would lie in bed all day, reserving her strength so she could get up and do that one simple task, to be a human being for her daughter after school.

Aunt Patti visited, too. This took some self-sacrifice on her part, and self-sacrifice did not come easily to Aunt Patti. She was terrified of the expressway. So she took all the back roads from Little Neck to Huntington. She had shrunk so much over the years that she sat perched on a pillow and still could barely see over the top of the steering wheel of her Subaru. She was the kind of woman who took traffic jams personally; she could never get it through her head that this was simply how Long Island *was*, these days. It was a giant, slow-moving tangle, like a ball of gnarled yarn. There was no way around it. But Aunt Patti seemed to believe if she had left a half hour earlier, or taken Jericho instead of Hempstead Turnpike, or not stopped at that particular bakery, she would have simply glided through some imaginary open road that had not existed for fifty years.

Aunt Patti was more comfortable as host than as guest. She would arrive in her old Blackglama mink coat, bought in her heyday on TV, wearing a polka-dotted black-and-white scarf over her head and dark glasses—an ancient version of Marilyn Monroe. She had a key to Nicole's house, so after rapping twice to announce herself, she would sail inside, shed the coat and scarf, and make her way to whatever room Nicole was occupying—often the back room behind the kitchen overlooking the backyard, sometimes the bedroom, where Patti would knock again, more softly, waiting for Nicole's "Come in." She would make her way through the house, carrying a coffee cake wrapped in string, or a bag of chocolate and cinnamon *bobka*, a quart of strawberries. She never came empty-handed.

"Jesus, Nicole, why do you keep the house so *dark*?" she would say.

"The glasses." Nicole would gesture at Aunt Patti's face. Aunt Patti would remove the sunglasses, but to retain her dignity add, "It's still not very bright in here."

"*I'm* not very bright."

Aunt Patti pantomimed a laugh, then set about putting things away, serving Nicole tea and toast or pudding, watching her like a hawk till she ate a few bites. The sores in Nicole's mouth and throat made it difficult to swallow. Aunt Patti was constantly trying to rearrange the rooms, as if that itself would make the house larger. She shared theater gossip and told old stories, especially about her late husband and her sister, Nicole's mother.

"She was the pretty one, I was the smart one. Dark like a gypsy. I was always jealous of her, they made such a fuss over her. Sometimes I would give her a knip"—she pinched Nicole's arm lightly to demonstrate—"in the crib. Then when she cried, I pretended I knew nothing about it. My first acting job."

"You were a good big sister," Nicole protested.

"Well. Maybe. The night before her last surgery I slept in the hospital with her. Brought my pajamas, slippers, an old copy of Nancy Drew. I wouldn't let that bitchy night nurse throw me out. I just read from the Nancy Drew till your mother finally fell asleep. When the day-shift nurse came in, she tried to draw *my* blood. Your mother would have let her. Luckily, she was wearing the hospital bracelet, not me."

Aunt Patti always had to be on her way somewhere else, even at her age. Parties, lunches, meetings, classes—she was always flying off to the next event. Nicole supposed if she had been born later, she would have been considered ADD and given medication. Instead she had become an actress, an eccentric. Patti was the kind of aunt who had called twice, three times a year. She sent gifts when she felt like it, seldom for occasions, and often threatened to come for a visit, but seldom followed up. All you had to do to make sure she never came was urge or press her. She hated obligations.

Yet she had been a better aunt to Nicole and her sister than Nicole's mother had been to Aunt Patti's two boys. "They're boys, I never know what to say to them," her mother used to confide to Nicole. "That Al is a rotten apple, and the brother's not much better. They'll never amount to anything." She dutifully sent checks or gift certificates at Hanukkah and for birthdays and graduations—nothing personal.

Aunt Patti, on the other hand, hadn't even shown up for Nicole's high school graduation; she was rehearsing for some off-off-Broadway show. But when Nicole came down with pneumonia in college, Aunt Patti brought her a green-and-pink bead necklace that Nicole still treasured. Nicole let Daisy keep it in her jewelry box. Daisy was seldom around now for Aunt Patti's visits. Nicole suspected it was because Aunt Patti could not bear the sadness of looking at this soon-to-be-motherless child. She could bluff her way past Nicole—or so she thought—but she could never have fooled a child. Her acting was simply not that good.

In the interim hours, Nicole took up needlepoint. She no longer had the patience for books, and she could not bear watching television. The only TV shows she watched were Daisy's goofy sitcoms on the Disney channel, featuring improbably beautiful teenagers who were supposed to be "homely" or "fat" or "unpopular," who got themselves into one ridiculous scrape after another and then sang about them. But she didn't really watch the shows. She watched Daisy watching them. The needlepoint on which she was currently working was a large linen canvas—thirty-four inches by thirty-four. It featured a seascape: waves in the background, wild roses in the foreground. It was wool tapestry, and the stitches were tiny, one slant line after another.

Part of her knew she would never finish it. The other part, the stubbornly hopeful one, kept at it as an act of defiance against the inevitable. Slowly but surely it came to life under her hands, the bright threaded waves and flowers creeping up along the blank linen.

She sat with her needlepoint by the large bank of windows at the back of the house, where she could watch the same process of life spreading across the wintry waste of the yard. She refused to stop loving the world just because she had to leave it. Snowdrops and crocuses pushed through the blank snow, in white and yellow-gold and purple. Next came the daffodils, the dainty orange-eyed narcissi, and the large trumpet daffodils, yellow as rain slickers, creeping in clumps across the old snow. The forsythia began to bud, then the pussy willows, then even the pink tulip magnolia that had been a Mother's Day gift from Daisy the year she was only three.

Nicole thought a good deal about her past, as if she were watching a movie constantly playing in her mind. Childhood, adolescence, marriage, teaching, motherhood. Faces of people she had not thought about in years came to her, like the ones who appear in dreams. Some living, some dead. She'd remember scraps of long-forgotten conversations. Little romances. And moments came back to her as if they had been preserved in the back of her brain all along, just waiting for something to trigger them back to life. Skating around and around the community ice rink, holding mittened hands with Ari. Ancient vacations by the beach with her family. A nest of chicks, bright yellow, rescued by the dune buggy in which they were riding. It was one of her earliest memories, and she had lost it for years. I've had a good run, she would think. Short, but good.

————•————

Judge Solomon Richter could feel everyone walking on eggshells, eyeing him nervously as he set about emptying his chambers. He was closing up shop. The clerks and secretaries, the undersecretaries, recorders, security staff, and especially his own wife and daughter, appeared to be waiting for the other shoe to drop. He seemed altogether too calm, sorting through his law books, taking little with him, just a few boxes of books and memorabilia. In truth, now that the time had come, he was anxious to leave. And this shocked everyone, including himself.

He could not have said exactly what he was looking forward *to*. He had lost a principal clerk, a man he'd once considered his friend, and he had also finished his last case in a way that left a bitter taste in the mouth. He had always understood the limits of the law intellectually. But now he knew them intimately, as if the rending had happened in his own family. It was humbling.

After almost fifty years working in one office or another, he was about to enter the world. And it was spring. The weeping willows by the town pond in Roslyn had turned a tender golden green. The trees were beginning to bud in his own backyard. He looked with new interest at Joe Iccarino next door, planting vegetables and herbs in neat, tiered rows. Maybe he would learn to garden.

His final case had been, in his own private estimation, an utter failure from beginning to end. The press took his side, made him out to be a hero, which only proved how moronic the press was these days. He should have found the loophole that would have permitted justice and mercy to slip through the net of law. His great nemesis, the *Newsday* journalist, was the only man who agreed with him.

"If, as Justice Solomon Richter wrote in his final opinion, the case of *Greene vs. Wiesenthal* was 'morally indefensible,' why could he not come to a decision less 'revolting to every moral sense'? Where was the justice in Justice Richter's ruling?" It was a wail of wounded outrage. Clearly, Katrina Turock had already dumped the writer and moved on.

He had waited to begin missing Flannery, like an amputee waiting for the stump to ache. It simply did not come. He, the judge, had misjudged his right-hand man. *Et quod vides perisse, perditum ducas.* "What you see is over, accept that it's truly over."

Ari Wiesenthal, to the very last, showed no sign of remorse, no hint that he might change his mind. When interviewed by the press, he said, "This is a very sobering experience. There's nothing to rejoice about, but we feel that justice has been served."

Nicole, of course, did not speak to the press. Her husband stood guard in front of their house like the angel with the flaming sword outside Eden. He had protected her from the beginning; surely he would protect her to the end. Sol sometimes allowed himself to hope that Ari might at the eleventh hour have a change of heart. Such things were possible. He kept his ear to the ground, but no such rumors reached him. In the eyes of the press, the judge was something venerable. To himself, he was a man who had become ensnared by the law. He could not find a way out of it or through it so that this woman might live.

But Sol kept quiet about his own doubts and regrets, for once determined to spare those around him. He would go quietly and with dignity. He declined a glitzy retirement party, even when pressed. DeNunzio persisted. "It doesn't look good," DeNunzio said the third time he called. "It looks like you're turning your back on us. There is such a thing as collegiality."

"There is also such a thing as going when it's time to go."

"Not the tune you were singing last year," DeNunzio said. "When you came to me for help."

"I don't like big parties. Retirement parties least of all."

"Who does?" DeNunzio said. "Still, you do it."

"I don't," Sol said.

They did not part on good terms. Sol sensed he was burning bridges, but then, he was past worrying about all that, too. There were certain bridges he hoped never to cross again. Perhaps this is how dying people felt. One let go. The only melancholy he felt was over what must have seemed like the minutiae. Faces he would miss, morning banter with the staff. Simple pleasantries and human contacts. He would have to seek them out now, where for decades they had been given. The wisecracking mail clerk; the Chinese woman in the cafeteria who always slid him an extra helping of rice pudding—they had never been part of his home life. He never discussed these people, or even thought much about them beyond the walls of the courthouse. So there was no way to begin talking about them now. And no point in grieving over them in any case.

Instead of a formal gathering catered by the court, Sol's brother Arthur threw a small but elegant buffet luncheon at his two-bedroom apartment in Mineola. The chubby little man could cook. All those culinary classes had paid off. His wife Ruth dressed like a cross between a waitress and a hooker, in a short skirt with a frilly white apron, and went good-naturedly around the room, serving the tiny Manchego cheese tarts and tea sandwiches, the raspberry mousse desserts like jewels hidden in their ruffled, dark brown paper cups. This party was a casual affair to which Sol invited only the people he liked best from his days at court. For some reason his wife's rabbi was there, too, though mostly he stayed out of the way in the kitchen, helping Abigail and Sarah fill the trays.

"He's not going to pray over me, is he?" Sol muttered to his wife.

"I don't think so," she said.

"Then why is he here?"

She shrugged, smiling, her eyes mysterious.

When moving day came around, Sol refused all outside help. He cleared out the office himself. A young judge would be moving in the next week. Chambers like his were in high demand and short supply. The new judge looked like a kid to him, fresh out of law school, but he was in his midforties; he just appeared younger, with a short-cut Afro, a gleaming smile and shy manner. He was a protégée of Tom Lieu.

Sol waited till the end of the day to collect his few remaining boxes. It was still early enough in spring so that darkness had mostly fallen by six that evening. The sky was bluish black outside his window. The courthouse felt deserted, like an abandoned schoolhouse. Sol felt one quick, sharp pang of melancholy as he looked around his chambers. Already it felt like a stranger's office, no longer his.

As if to confirm his suspicion, a timid knock came at the door. Sol sighed and opened it, only to find his brother Arthur standing there, stamping his feet, his black wool overcoat buttoned up high around his throat.

"I came to see if my big brother needed help," he said. He was puffing from the exertion of walking down the hall.

Sol nodded, not wanting to show his relief. "Come in," he said. "There isn't much left."

Arthur whistled. "You cleaned the place out." He nodded. "Good."

"Suppose you take this box"—Sol gestured at the lighter of the two—"and I'll take that one."

Arthur slapped his gloves together. "That's it? Just two boxes?"

"That's it."

"Good for you," Arthur said again. He bent from the knees, the way he'd been taught, and lifted the box. "Not too terrible," he said. "Where do we go from here?"

"Out," Sol said. "Follow me."

Before he could get out the door, Arthur bumped him lightly with his left shoulder. His arms were full. This was the closest he could get to throwing an arm around his brother. "So...how you holding up?"

"Fine," Sol admitted. "I don't know. I feel—lighter. Maybe it will all blow up next week when reality sets in."

"I don't think so," Arthur said. "You've got little Iris in your life now. You'll have your hands full."

Sol nodded. He would never admit how he doted on this grand-daughter, barely a toddler now, with her long head and serious black eyes. Everything about her enraptured him, even the way she stored a mouthful of bread in her cheek an hour after he had given it to her. Apparently food hoarding was not uncommon among the orphans. He'd heard of children storing sandwiches in their toy cupboards, secreting candy bars under their beds. He would spend more time with her now that he was retired. He could take over on the nights when Sarah was going to her Jewish classes, he told Abigail, save her some babysitting money.

"Okay," she had agreed, surprised.

"I want to help out," he said.

"That's very nice of you, Pop."

"Don't expect me to do anything but spoil her."

"I don't." She laughed.

Sol paused at the threshold of his chambers. Empty rooms always looked smaller. His chambers seemed to have shrunk like something in *Alice in Wonderland.* There were holes left in the walls where he had hung his diplomas, patches of peeling paint. He had left behind everything he intended—office supplies, the coatrack he had used for thirty years, all of the filing cabinets cleared out and ready to be refilled by the next genera-tion. By Monday the room would be repainted and cleaned.

"Go ahead," he told his brother. "I'll get the light." And by pressing down with his elbow on the switch, he turned the lights out on his long, illustrious career.

A few days later his sister-in-law Ruth called, shrill on the answering machine. Sarah was out, Sol doing the dishes, so when he heard Ruth's voice he decided to ignore it, till he caught the pitch of hysteria. "Sol, please call me," she said. "Please, right away! Here, I'm going to give you the hospital number—" Sol rushed to the phone, his hands soapy, while she fumbled in the background. He snatched up the receiver.

"Hello?"

"Thank God!" she yelled, straight into his ear. Her volume actually increased once he picked up the phone.

"What's going on?" He could hear a commotion at the other end.

"It's Arthur," she said, sobbing. "He's had a stroke. We're at Long Island Jewish Emergency."

"I'm on my way," Sol said, and hung up. He drove straight to the hospital, his hands still soapy, shaking on the wheel.

By the time he got there, Arthur had been moved to the ICU. A white curtain separated him from the rest of the world. He was attached to a variety of machines and tubes, nearly all of them beeping or clicking. His eyes were closed, but he looked younger than he had in years. No lines marred the broad expanse of his white forehead. Ruth was weeping; she was dressed in an old coat and wore no makeup. She looked like an ordinary aging housewife, which endeared her to Sol with an unexpected lurch of his heart. As he came into the ICU room, she leaped for Sol's hand and clung to it.

"We were having lunch at that new French place in Roslyn," she explained. "La something. Arthur had been wanting to try it, and it's just a week"—she tried to stifle her sobs—"just a week to our anniversary. We were having a nice lunch, Arthur was enjoying himself, when all of a sudden he said, 'I feel funny,' and lurched over sideways. I thought he was kidding at first. I said, 'Arthur, quit kidding around. The French don't have no sense of humor.'

"Then he opened his mouth and nothing came out. I could see from the look in his eyes he was scared. So we called nine-one-one and they came right away and I told them—to take him here. I always heard it was a good place." She released his hand and blew her nose into a clutch of Kleenex. "If anything should happen to my Arthur! I should never have let him eat the goose liver pâté! Never!"

"Now, now," Sol said, awkwardly patting her on the arm. He had never been physically affectionate with Ruth—or with any women except his wife and daughter. He just didn't know how. "You're not even sure it's a stroke. Wait and see what the doctors say."

"But what if it *is* a stroke?" Ruth persisted. She had always been stubborn, a little bull terrier.

"Then we'll deal with it. People recover from strokes all the time," Sol said. "Arthur is tougher than he looks. You wait and see."

"They recover?"

"Sure they do. All the time." He was lying through his teeth. He had no idea about strokes. His own uncle Mortie had died of one. So had his cousin Sadie, when she was only in her fifties. In his experience, that's what happened. People had a stroke out of nowhere, maybe two, sometimes they eked along for a few weeks, and then they died. How old was Arthur? Sixty-eight. That was still considered young, these days.

"Have you called your son?" he asked Ruth.

"He's very concerned. But this is tax season. He told me to call the minute we have any news."

Schmuck, thought Sol. Aloud he said, "Look, I'm going to step out into the waiting room just for a minute and call Sarah, let her know where I am. Then I'll be right back. She can call Abigail. I'm sure they'll all want to see Arthur."

"You'll come right back?" Ruth asked. She seemed resigned to being deserted by the world. Her bulgy eyes were red and tear-filled.

"I'll be back."

"You're not leaving?"

"I'm not going anywhere," he told her.

She clawed at his hand again. Her fingernails were painted bright red. "You're a good guy," she said. "Some people say you're a mean bastard, but I was never one of those. I know you got a good heart, like your brother. I know you twos love each other."

"Can I get you anything?" he asked.

"How about a double martini straight up," she said. She opened her mouth to pantomime a laugh, but nothing came out.

LATE SPRING 2012
Flying High

The chains on the backyard swing creaked in and out, in and out. Jay kept promising to oil them, but lately he had let everything slide. The chains needed to be adjusted, too. Daisy's long legs barely skimmed above the ground as she swung. Julian wished, not for the first time, that he was handier, but his father had never taught him anything practical, as if Ari were afraid that if Julian learned how to use a hammer he was doomed to become a day laborer. Daisy seemed set on going up so high that the swing would flip right over the top pole. Every so often one of the frame poles lifted a little in its spot, and then thumped back down again, like an old man limping. What if it came apart?

Daisy twisted her lovely face around to look at Julian. "Push me harder!" she commanded. "I want to go really, really high."

"You *are* going high," he said, giving her a halfhearted push. "Aren't you getting a little too old for this swing?"

"No!" she said. "I'm only eight."

"Soon you'll be nine."

"You'll be twelve. You'll be a *teenager.*"

They both contemplated this a moment. Then Julian shrugged. "No biggie."

"Hang on," Daisy said. "I'm going to jump off."

This was Julian's least favorite part of her swinging. He was always sure his cousin, who looked as if she was made of twigs in the first place, was going to leap into the air and land in the dirt, snapping a few bones in the process. She never did, though. Instead she went flying again and landed graceful as a cat. Her dark brown eyes were flecked with gold, also like a cat's. She smiled at him through the swing, and his heart melted.

"Are you going to get bar-mitzvahed next year?" she asked.

He shrugged again. "I don't know. Things are sort of—up in the air."

"If you do, I won't be able to come, you know."

"Then I won't bother. It's a lot of work anyway."

"Don't be silly," Daisy said. "You'll be great. You're great at everything."

"So…" Julian stuck his hands into the pockets of his baggy khaki pants and looked around the yard. It looked sort of bare, especially compared to his. "What do you want to do now?"

Daisy squatted in the dirt, drawing something with a stick. She was a surprisingly good artist. She was always scribbling, painting, doodling. Her little desk was covered with dozens of little pieces of paper. Her artwork hung on all the walls of her house and completely obscured the Greenes' refrigerator. Julian even had a couple over his desk. She was drawing a mermaid in the dirt now, complete with tail and long, flowing hair. "I don't know," she said in a dull voice. "My mom's resting again. We probably should stay out here."

"Okay," Julian agreed, though he was thirsty.

"I don't know," she said again. Her shoulders slumped. She looked up again, her wide eyes catching the glint of gold from the afternoon. "I don't think she's very long for this world."

Something about the adultness of the expression made Julian shiver. It was partly to dissipate his own chill that he went over and put his arms around his cousin. She wasn't usually very demonstrative; for one thing it was hard for her to stand still in one place long enough. Like hugging a sunbeam. But now she rested her sharp little chin on his shoulder.

"I'll always be here for you," Julian said into her hair. "I'll always take care of you. That's a promise."

"I know," she said. His shoulder was getting damp; that was the only way he could tell she was crying. He patted her bony back.

"Thanks. Your shirts always smell nice," she said.

"They do?"

"Yeah," she said. "Like deodorant."

Julian laughed.

Daisy kept her face pressed against him. "I made my dad promise to live at least till you're twenty-one. Then you'd be old enough to be my guardian. He says he plans to live a lot longer than that, though."

"I'm sure he will," Julian said. He suddenly felt awkward, holding his cousin. A strand of her red hair fell over his wrist like a copper bracelet. That kind of thing came over him suddenly, these days. Feeling too clumsy to hold a pencil, much less a human being. Becoming formal all of a sudden, like a wooden soldier.

"So," he said, putting her at arm's length. "Seriously, what do you want to do? Ride bicycles?"

Daisy's bicycle was small and pink, covered with images of some cartoon character. She had just shed her training wheels that spring. But she was already more adept on her bike than Julian was on his. Her face lit up. "Yay!" she said, clapping her hands. "Let's ride. I want to show you my new basket and streamers."

"I'm sure they're very pretty," he said condescendingly. "Do you have a light?"

"What for? It's the middle of the afternoon."

"For riding at night, silly. You want one in front so you can see the road. Then you need a light in back, maybe with blinkers, so you can signal which way you're turning, like a car."

"Like a car," she breathed.

"Next time I come," he promised, "I'll bring you a set of lights. Cool ones. Blinking ones." He imitated the lights by opening and closing both hands. She smiled radiantly. It was worth making an idiot of himself, he thought, for that smile.

Arthur was able to sit up in bed. He had spent nine days in the ICU, suffering what the doctors feared was a second stroke, but now he'd been moved to a regular hospital room, which he shared with an old black man addicted to watching sports on TV. The room was never quiet for one minute. Shouts went up steadily, periodically, from the other side of the room, and the white curtain did nothing to muffle the sound.

Arthur had been in intensive care so long he had already lost weight. His face, no longer so chubby, had begun to sag with age. But he was perfectly cheerful. His speech was unimpaired, the muscles unaffected; he had escaped the worst effects of a stroke and knew enough to be grateful. They had him on all kinds of drugs, of course—something for high blood pressure, plus Coumadin to thin his blood and who knew what else. It seemed like every day they discovered a new condition for which there was a new medication. The result, he explained, was that his memory was all out of whack. He might not remember that Sol had visited him three days earlier, but he had a vivid and exact recollection of going blueberry picking in the Catskills with his brother when they were young children.

"You remember," he would prod his brother. "The hills were covered with blueberry bushes. Mama wore a red handkerchief, with little blue and yellow triangles on it. We brought tin pails along and the berries made the most wonderful *plunking* sound going into the pail. Like tree frogs."

Arthur's descriptions were so vivid that for an instant Sol would believe that he did indeed remember. A whole scene would flash before his eyes—but whether it was really memory, or just some picture that Arthur had created, he could not tell.

"You were so intense," Arthur went on. "You'd square up to the nearest bush and just pull whatever came into your hand and pop it into your mouth. Even the hard little green berries that weren't ripe. —I think you liked the sour ones best of all."

"Matched his disposition," said Ruth, calmly crocheting in the corner. She was making some rainbow-colored blanket for Iris, in garish colors— lime green, orange, fluorescent pink.

She seldom left her post in that hospital room, sitting on what was otherwise Arthur's commode and leaving the more comfortable armchair for guests. Day and night, she sat watching over Arthur, leaving only to bring him in decent takeout food. She drove all over Queens, looking for delicacies to tempt him. Ever the gourmand, he could not bear the sight, much less the smell or taste, of hospital food. The orderlies with their Styrofoam trays were banished from his side of the room, and often Arthur begged Ruth to bring some decent food for his roommate—partly out of pity, partly so he wouldn't have to smell the aroma of the hospital food six or seven feet away.

"I don't really remember," Sol said, regarding the unripe blueberries.

Sarah gave him a sharp look, as if his failure to remember were a kind of betrayal.

"They were so tart they made my mouth pucker. I could go for a handful of those green and red blueberries right now. You know," Arthur said, turning to Ruth, "the next time I make a blueberry compote I think I'm going to throw in a few of the little unripe berries, for extra flavoring. I'll bet it would be delicious. Like adding a squeeze of lemon or lime."

"Maybe," Ruth said dubiously.

The other side effect of the drugs, Arthur explained, was that he was having vivid and extended dreams. Almost like hallucinations.

"It's like living a second life at night," he said. "I wake up exhausted."

"Poor baby," Sarah said. She had always been fond of her brother-in-law; she saw what Sol regarded as his weaknesses as signs of his gentleness and good heart.

"Some good heart," Sol had grumbled. "Two heart attacks and two strokes."

"That's not what I meant," Sarah had rebuked him, "and you know it. Shah! Still jealous of your own brother."

"Take last night, for instance," Arthur said now. "I dreamed I was giving a luncheon party at our house. Everything very elegant—white linens, crystal, good wine. You were there, Sol, and Sarah, you, too."

"What about me?" Ruth demanded.

"You of course," Arthur said. "Looking like an angel, as usual. You know who else was there?" He looked at Sol, as if it would be easy for him to guess.

"Jesus Christ?" Sol said.

"Close. Mr. O'Hare. —Our elementary school principal," he explained to the others. "Nice man. Worked at that same job for forty years. He used to brag that you could eat off his playground. And you could." He shut his eyes, remembering. "So, we're in the middle of this elegant party when I suddenly realize— We are serving *canned salmon*." His throat wobbled with distress. "There it is, on each person's china plate."

"Oh, dear," Sarah said sympathetically.

"What's so terrible about canned salmon?" Ruth said. "It's not like we were serving canned tuna."

"Yes, but my dear," said Arthur tragically, "couldn't you at least have taken the salmon out of the can?"

———

Abigail and the rabbi—even now it was hard for her to think of him as simply Teddy—had seen each other six or seven times, but always just as friends. At the end of each event, the same warm friendly grasp of the hand, or at most, a kiss on the cheek. Yet he persisted in calling her. His gaze followed her wherever she went; when she stood across the room from him, no matter how crowded it was, she would find his dark eyes searching her out. He leaned close to her when they spoke; his voice was tender and warm. He had all the symptoms of a man in love except that he did not behave at all like a man in love. It was maddening. Especially since Abigail had no doubts about her own feelings for him. It was a textbook head-over-heels schoolgirl heart-hammering crush.

Even Iris seemed smitten—she reached for Teddy, flirted, batted her long eyelashes, cried when she was dragged away from him. "The child is the unspoken secret of the parent revealed," Jung wrote, and Abigail worried that everyone in the world would see her emotions on the open face of her child. They were closely watched whenever they went out in public. Her mother told her the gossip was incessant in the bat-mitzvah group.

"They're always nudgering me," Sarah complained. "Always trying to get me to drop some hint. Will you please let me know what's going on?"

"I don't *know* what's going on. We're just friends."

Her mother huffed. "Some friends."

"We're very good friends," Abigail said. "Mom, I promise you, as soon as I know anything different, you'll be the first to know."

"He's older than you are," her mother said.

"Not as much older as you think."

"He's had terrible tragedy in his life."

"He'll get over it."

"Hard-hearted Hannah," her mother groused.

"I would think you would approve," Abigail said. "A rabbi, for heaven's sake. What more could you possibly want?"

"I *do* approve," her mother said. "I just don't want to get my hopes up. And I don't want you to get *your* hopes up. I don't like it when things are so—indefinite."

Abigail held her tongue—she was learning this, too, from the rabbi. "You never regret the things you don't say," he had once told her. "We Jews are people of the mouth. And that's what gets us into ninety-nine percent of our trouble. Saying what's on our minds."

"You know I love you," Sarah said now, as if to prove the rabbi's point about the virtue of holding one's tongue. "I'll gladly dance at your wedding. —Which reminds me, isn't Tomas coming by to get the last of his things?"

"Next week, he says. He's moving out to New Mexico. Which is fine with me. —How's Uncle Arthur?" Abigail said, deftly changing the subject.

"Better," her mother said. "Much better. It's a miracle, really. The doctors are flabbergasted. He should be dead now."

"Well, don't tell him that," Abigail said. "He might die just to please the doctors."

Abigail didn't believe she would feel anything, one way or the other, when she saw Tomas again, and for the last time. Teddy told her otherwise. "It's going to hit you like a load of bricks," he told her. "I just want you to be prepared."

"It's different for me," Abigail told him. They were grabbing a quick lunch—he had a class to teach that afternoon, on Jewish kabbalah. That's all people wanted to hear about these days, he said. Ever since Madonna and the other movie stars started studying kabbalah.

"How is it different for you?" he asked her now. He was busy salting his eggs. He salted everything too much. Abigail wished she could cook for him. Keep him healthy and safe.

"Well, for one thing," she said, "we were never married. He was just a boyfriend."

"A boyfriend you lived with for almost four years."

Abigail forgot that she had told him that. She should have known better; the rabbi never forgot anything. "Still, it's not a surprise for me, the way it was for you. I saw this coming a long time ago. I don't know that Tomas and I were ever suited to each other, really. It's just not that big a deal."

"You wait and see," Teddy warned her. "Like a ton of bricks. Just call me when it happens. Will you promise me that?"

Laughing, she promised.

Only as it turned out it wasn't so funny after all. She did not anticipate the jolt she felt at the sight of Tomas standing among her things. He had helped pick out the dining room set; he had built the bookcase. It all came back in a rush. Tomas had already begun the move to New Mexico. He came to the apartment looking happy and fit. He'd even brought a little doll for Iris, with black hair and red smiling lips. He was wearing black pants and a white shirt, his olive skin beautiful above the open collar of his shirt. He talked about a new business venture with a female partner, and Abigail knew what that meant. His obvious happiness hurt her feelings. He kissed her good-bye, chastely, the way Teddy did. It took him two trips to the car to clear out everything he had left behind. And then, within fifteen minutes, he was gone forever and she was no longer anyone's anything.

She had left Iris to stay with the nanny, of course, pretty blonde Lauren. Lauren was athletic, kindly, tall, young, and surprisingly cynical about relationships. Abigail sent her home early that day. "I'll pay you, of course," Abigail said. "I just need to be alone with Iris."

"I understand," Lauren said, rising quickly to go. Her own parents had had a vicious divorce—it turned out her father had been cheating on her mother for years. She scurried out the door, head down, as if fleeing her own memories, but gave Abigail a rare hug before she went.

Iris provided a cushion against the blow of that day. They took out her new toy, a gift from Teddy: magnetized letters that clung to the white refrigerator. Each letter fit inside a white holder; the machine would sing them one by one: "A! A says A! Every letter makes a sound and A makes A!"

"Or sometimes aaa, like 'cat,'" Abigail would explain. She did this for all the vowels, not to mention C, G, K, and Y. The tune was always the same, and by the time they'd gone through all twenty-six letters three times she thought she would lose her mind.

They switched to stacking colored plastic cups of varying sizes—Iris's old standby, which could be stacked upside down, used as building blocks, knocked over, and used to play mini-basketball with rolled-up pieces of paper. At the end of the day, the same plastic cups floated in the bath and became water toys. Iris carefully filled them with water, sometimes drank from them, and used them as boats. This favorite of all toys had cost perhaps ninety-nine cents at the local drugstore. Abigail realized that the whole toy business was a hoax. What babies really liked to play with was wrapping paper, empty boxes, tags on clothing, and paper towels.

But after bathtime came bedtime, and then Abigail felt the weight of being alone hit her full force.

She was grateful when the phone rang at eight thirty and it was Teddy's voice on the other line, deep, masculine, with its own thrilling oddity and reverberations. A Jewish voice, a little nasal. Accenting words oddly, on unexpected syllables. Often his voice seemed on the verge of laughter, or of making a joke at his own expense. Often it was.

"So," he said. "How'd it go?"

She sank into a kitchen chair. "Awful," she said. "I feel like a hopeless old maid. You were absolutely right."

"That's why I get the big bucks," he said. "But I would rather have been wrong. And you are *not* an old maid." He changed the subject then, telling her about renovations scheduled for the synagogue that summer, asking her advice on architectural details. He had already arranged for her to be hired as a design consultant on the project. "I ask enough questions, at least you should be compensated for your time," he said. A new rug was being laid—what color should it be? he wondered. Someone had offered to make tapestry covers. Others had promised to donate paintings. They were putting in new pew cushions, should they match the carpet, or contrast? Abigail agreed to look at samples.

"I hate shopping," he said. "I can barely pick out my own shirts." Invariably he wore the same white button-downs, but Abigail didn't mention this.

"Look," he said in the middle of discussing the color of curtain swags. "What is it you like best in the world?"

"Iris," she answered promptly. *And*, she was thinking, *then you.*

"I mean activities," he said. "We're going to find something to cheer you up. Something to look forward to. Skiing, tennis, shopping, what?"

"Oh Lord," she said. "None of those. Music, I guess. Classical music or ballet."

"Thank G-d," he said. "Because I am extremely unathletic, and I hate shopping."

She was not surprised. He looked like the kind of big, lumbering guy who would have been handed the basketball—and dropped it.

"So how about we do this," he suggested. "I have a three-day conference in the Berkshires in July. How about you come with me and we go to Tanglewood and—there's some kind of a dance thing, too, nearby."

"Jacob's Pillow," she said.

"See!" he said. "Jacob's Pillow, amazing. One of my favorite Tenakah stories." This date sounded more serious than going to look at Judaic art at a synagogue in Hicksville. It was even more serious than his showing up at her father's retirement party.

Iris came along wherever they went, like a tiny chaperone: to the fish hatchery in Cold Spring Harbor, to Lollipop Farm, where on a chilly afternoon Iris stretched out her hand to patient sheep and baby goats. After that Teddy took them to Hamburger Chew-Chew, a kosher restaurant where vegetarian burgers were delivered on the back of toy trains that ran along a toy train track.

"Can you get off from work?" he asked now. "Do you think your parents would look after Iris?"

"Yes," she said. "Though I'll have to get back to you." Her heart was pounding in her throat. She had not been expecting anything like this quite so soon. Maybe it was too soon?

"I'll book your room for you," he said. "Do you have any special preferences? I'm such a big lunk I always need a king-size bed." The pounding got worse; she could hardly speak around it.

"You don't need to book a special room for me," she said.

"Of course I do," he interrupted. "You're my guest. I'm inviting you. In fact, I insist."

Had she been in her twenties, when she was reckless, almost sleepwalking through her life, she would simply have said, "We can sleep together. What's the big deal?" But she was in her thirties now. Now she looked and looked again before she leaped. The last thing she wanted to do was to offend this man—this *rabbi*, she reminded herself.

"No preferences," she said meekly.

"Okay, then," he said. "I'll ask them for the room with the best view."

She could have said something to *that*, too, but didn't.

———·——

Sol had been so young when he had first started working, packing groceries after school at age twelve—and then he just kept on working through all the years of steady schooling, into college, and then law school—he hadn't had this much free time since he was about six or seven years old and summer vacation opened out like an infinite vista.

Now he could pick and choose among many invitations. He agreed to a lecture tour to Asia in October; Sarah would be bat-mitzvahed by then. They would travel for three weeks, to the Philippines, to Malaysia, Singapore, and then to Thailand, home of Iris's birth. Sarah was eager to see it again and to bring back gifts and souvenirs to her little granddaughter.

He had begun tentative negotiations with one arbitration association he liked over in Glen Head. Consulting. He would have flexibility, they assured him, and the work need not begin till after his trip. He might or might not take them up on the offer. His last case had left a scar. He still occasionally dreamed about it, the usual courtroom dreams—he had come to the courtroom unprepared, had lost all his notes, and Flannery was nowhere to be found. Instead Sarah was his clerk and she chastised him for leaving his office messy. Or he came into his chambers only to discover a funeral for Nicole Greene already under way, with that new young rabbi, Teddy Lewin, leading the service and staring at him with burning eyes.

Thanks to Joe Iccarino's help, Sol started an herb garden. Nothing too fancy to begin with. He and Sarah spent two evenings a week sitting with Iris, and the other evenings were busy preparing for the lectures in October. Perhaps this was why, when he received the first letter from Brooklyn Federal Detention Center, from Naveen Abou, he did not respond with his usual speed. It was largely a note of sympathy. She had read about the case in the newspapers, she said, and her heart went out to him and to both the families. She would keep them all in her prayers. Her handwriting was fluid and ornate, in blue ink on coarse prison paper. He could hear her voice, even her lisp, behind the written words. She added in a postscript that she hoped he might find time to visit her soon, as she had news of her own to share.

Sol kept meaning to go, but then Arthur had his stroke, and some-how between lecture notes and his granddaughter and everything else— he had taken to playing chess with Arthur once a week, for instance, and was amazed to find his brother a formidable opponent—week after week slipped by.

Then came a second note from Naveen that read simply, "Come as soon as you can, please," and he was off to Brooklyn Federal the next day. It was the start of the Memorial Day weekend, and the traffic, as he feared, was horrendous. "Can't you go next week?" Sarah asked, but he waved the note at her, and she nodded.

"Bring a book," she advised.

"I always bring Naveen a book." This time it was Anne Morrow Lindbergh's *Gift from the Sea*.

"I meant a book for you," she said. "Trust me, you'll need it."

She was absolutely right, of course. It took him nearly an hour just to get *on* the expressway, and then he was more or less parked for the next two hours, inching forward—just often enough so that he could not, in fact, read the biography of Truman he'd brought along. Lucky he had a strong bladder, he thought. A horse and buggy could have made the trip in less time. He spent another hour negotiating the small highways and tortuous back streets that led to Brooklyn Federal. But he was lucky. Summer had come early, most cars had their windows rolled up tight and their air conditioning on, but a few poor souls sat panting like dogs with all their windows rolled down for a hint of a breeze, and others, unluckier still, had overheated and sat by the side of the road with smoke rising from the hoods of their stalled cars.

Sol felt only half-human by the time he got to the parking lot of Brooklyn Federal. The waiting room was cooled only by a standing fan. Technology fell back thirty years when you came to a prison. The computers were old and few and slow, Naveen had told him. The TV set in the women's wing of the prison was ancient and given to fits of static. There were only five or six working stations—no HBO, of course, no cable, no anything on-demand.

But it was only a few minutes before Naveen appeared, dressed in long sleeves as usual, over long pants. Sol was surprised that he had not been led to her cell. He had the rare privilege of being able to visit his inmates where they lived. Had this been revoked now that he was retired? Did word travel that fast? He felt a flash of annoyance, which disappeared as soon as she took her seat on the other side of the glass divide. Naveen said, "They won't allow me any guests, Tholomon."

"Why not? What's wrong?"

"In a moment. How are you? You look well. I think retirement is good for you."

"I'm fine," he said. "I want to know what's happening here with you. How long has this been going on?"

"A month." Yet she looked radiantly happy, as young as the first time she was brought before him in court, more than a decade earlier. "You thee, Tholomon," she said, "I've fallen in love. I am waiting for permission to marry."

"Marry!" Sol exclaimed. He had come to think of Naveen as a sort of Muslim nun.

"Yeth," she said. "He's one of the inmates here. We met in a thtudy group. He is younger than I am. But only by a few years. He hath an old soul, I think."

"What is the man's name?" Sol asked.

"Mohammad," she said. "It is quite complicated," she said. "It hath to go through a special board of appealth. We had to fill out many formth. Next week we also have our interviews. Individually. Firtht Mohammad, then me. But we are both very sincere. I have hope."

"I see," Sol said. "And who is on this committee?"

Her face brightened. "That is why I wrote to you, Tholomon," she said. "The man in charge is one of your colleagues at court."

He winced, waiting for her to pronounce the inevitable name of DeNunzio. The man had his fingers in so many pies. This is what comes of burning bridges, Sol thought glumly. You simply never know. "Be nice to everyone," his professor at law school had told them. First year. "Everyone, all the time." Why hadn't he listened?

He looked at her gravely, already shaking his head. But she seemed not to notice.

"Hith name is Tom Lieu," she said. "Do you know him?"

Sol smiled, a rare open smile, one that made his homely face almost handsome. "As a matter of fact, I do," he said. "Let me see. I would have a good deal of hope, if I were you."

She clapped her hands, leaned forward, bumped her head against the Plexiglas, and rubbed her head, laughing. Then, as if answering his unspoken question, she said simply, "It will make all the differenth in the world, Tholomon. I will no longer feel alone. I'm a new person already. I never expected this."

"Well, I don't know what kind of ceremony the prison will permit," he said. "But if I can, I will dance at your wedding."

JUNE 2012
June Is the Start of Summer

The children stood in a clump with Daisy toward the front, one of the smallest in her class. They sounded like gerbils, if gerbils could sing, Nicole thought. "June, June, hooray it's June! June is the start of summer," they all sang, more or less together. A few of them made hand motions to go with the song—Daisy did it enthusiastically. She was wearing a white cotton dress, much like the one Nicole had on, gauzy and lightweight, for it was a hot day, and the elementary school multipurpose room was not air-conditioned.

One yellow-haired boy kept wandering to the side of the stage, not even bothering to move his mouth along with the others. Occasionally he took aim with an imaginary bow and arrow and shot into the audience. Then he'd wander back to the others. Jay was laughing so hard Nicole had to nudge him to be quiet. The boy's grandmother sat right behind them. But she leaned forward to Jay and said, "He's quite a pip." She said it proudly.

After the school concert there was sugary punch and cookies, which the children served, glad to play at hosts. Then it was time for the children to return to their classrooms. Daisy wanted to go home right then and there, but it wasn't even noon yet, and Nicole ached to lie down.

"Just a couple hours more, Noodle Pie," Nicole said, using an old nickname. "Then I'll come back and get you."

Daisy's eyes filled. She had always been this way. Nicole dreaded coming to the school for any of her performances, the way her daughter carried on when it was time to go. "But all the other kids are going home!" she wailed.

This was not true. All of the other kids were lining up behind their teacher to begin the march back into the classroom. One lone girl was heading out the door with her mother, their two hands connected, swinging.

"Melissa's going home with *her* mother," Daisy insisted. "Why can't I?"

"Because you can't," Jay said. "Isn't Melissa the smart one?"

"She's very smart," Daisy admitted. "She's already reading at the middle-school level."

"Well, see, you need to stay here to *get* smart. That's what an education is for."

"We're not going to do anything but watch a dumb movie," Daisy said. "Mrs. Brown said."

"She said you were going to watch a dumb movie?" Jay raised his eyebrows. "Remarkably honest woman, Mrs. Brown. —I've got to be pushing off," he said. "My next practice starts at one o'clock."

"Okay," Daisy said. "But Mom doesn't do *anything.* She just lies there. Why can't she at least take me home?"

"You watch that mouth, young lady," Jay said, no longer kidding around. His eyes had a steely look.

"Never mind," Daisy said. "All right, all right. I'll watch the stupid movie!" She clenched her fists.

"I'll be back for you in just a couple of hours," Nicole said. "Then we can watch our own movie. Your pick."

"With kissing in it?" Daisy asked.

"Lots of kissing," Nicole promised.

"Not too much," Jay said.

Daisy rolled her eyes, but she leaned forward to hug her father good-bye. Mrs. Brown was already signaling from across the cafeteria/auditorium. She was a pretty woman, fashionably dressed, with brown hair, sharp features, and a warm smile. She was a relaxed teacher, gentle with everyone, which meant she got a lot of the "bad" kids—meaning the kids with ITPs, the autistic kids, the troubled kids, one boy who was deaf, one girl who was blind. "Quite a crowd," Jay commented, the first time he dropped Daisy off at school. "They just need the halt and the lame."

"Jeremy walks with a limp," Daisy said. "What's a halt?"

"Never mind," Nicole had said. "Mrs. Brown is a brilliant teacher. I wish I'd had half her patience."

Daisy reached out and threw both arms around her mother's waist now. She was surprisingly strong and wiry. She hung on for dear life. "I'm not going to let you go," she said. She burrowed her head into Nicole's thin chest.

But then the principal, Tom Corgel, blew his whistle. "Okay, parents!" he announced. "Time for your kids to get back to work!" He glanced at Nicole apologetically. Everyone in the school had read about her in the papers. But rules were rules. Daisy reluctantly let go.

"Don't be late, okay?" the little girl said. "I want you standing right outside the door when I get out. Right where I can see you."

"Bossy mossy," Jay said.

"I'll be there," Nicole said. "Count on it."

Nikki felt limp as a rag by the time Jay dropped her off at the house. "You sure you don't want me to call Claudia's mom, see if Daisy can go home with her today?" Jay asked.

"I'm sure," she said. "Besides, I promised."

"Want me to take the rest of the day off?"

"*No,*" she said. "Quit making me feel sicker than I am."

"Okay, okay," he said, holding up one hand in a don't-beat-me-up gesture. "You're sure you're okay with picking Daisy up from school? We can make other arrangements till school lets out."

"It's what I live for," Nicole said. This used to be said as a joke line, as in, doing the dishes, the laundry. But, she realized with a jolt, it was now actually true. This is what she was living for. The ordinary things other people take for granted, being able to do something, anything, for the people she loved. Making a bed. Picking up a few groceries. Opening a can of soup. Every time she rolled a pair of Jay's socks from the laundry, she told herself, This is one thing Jay Greene doesn't have to do.

They were at the house now, and she leaned forward for her good-bye kiss. He surprised her by kissing her long and passionately.

"Wow," she said.

She was looking into his round blue eyes, so clear and large and loving and troubled. Jay pretended to be more happy-go-lucky than he felt. "I'm shallow," he used to tell her. "That's why most things don't bother me." But that was far from true. All these years later, she still hadn't gotten to the bottom of her fathomless husband. He was still surprising her.

She climbed the steps to their little purple house, and managed to turn and wave jauntily before staggering out onto the back patio and falling into the chaise lounge, where she slept fitfully, but almost at once.

———————

Over the next few weeks her condition declined, precipitously once school was out for the year, as if her body had been hanging on till then, the way a car will go and go and then the engine dies as soon as it hits the home driveway. Before she had been losing ground bit by bit; now it was like sliding down the steep part of the chute. Mimi was away on one of her comedy conventions. She'd offered to cancel the trip, but Nicole insisted she go. Nicole was practically living on the back patio now—the bed was too uncomfortable, and she was up and down six or seven times a night. Sometimes she would wake to find Jay sleeping on a cheap plastic chaise lounge next to her, holding her hand. "We could get a better chaise lounge at least," she told him. "Maybe we can find a king-size."

"I wish," he said.

They were putting off the inevitable—moving a hospital bed into the house, or worse still, moving her into hospice. There seemed something prosthetic about the first, and something so final about the second. Selfishly, she thought, she wanted to die at home, if she could manage it. But she might not manage it. Her doctors had made that clear, even the nice oncologist who was half in love with her, and kept trying to stress the positives. For now, she was safely ensconced on the back patio. It felt like she was living outdoors, amid all the green leaves and flowers she loved, but the patio was air-conditioned and shady. A bottle of water lay close at hand. An untouched bowl of applesauce. Her cell phone.

Jay was out helping a colleague who was moving to Greenport, the next town over. Daisy was safely at camp for the day. The front doorbell woke her. It was an effort to put down the book she'd meant to be reading, facedown so she would not lose her place, to rise from the chair, push open the sliding doors, and walk through the small house to the other side. Mimi was standing there, back from her weeks away at a comedy conference. She looked like a mirage.

"Oh, Mimi," Nicole said. "I missed you, girl."

Mimi saw her through the screen door like a ghost. The screen made her figure blurrier, and so did the tears that swam in her eyes. Nicole was wearing something white and gauzy—maybe a nightgown, maybe a dress, it was hard to tell. Her body was no longer shaped like her own body. It was simultaneously too thin and bloated. Her head was wrapped in a large colorful scarf that for an instant looked like some kind of exotic crown, as if she had been made queen of a foreign country. Her eyes looked so dark they seemed like black holes in her head. Mimi opened her mouth but nothing came out.

"You look different," Nicole said. "You've cut your hair."

Mimi's hand went up automatically to touch it, as if she had to check and make sure that yes, she had chopped off her hair. It was as short as a boy's now, and curly in the back. She no longer had time or patience to fuss with it.

"It looks good," Nicole said. "*You* look good. You look great."

"So do you," Mimi said unconvincingly.

"I look like hell," Nicole said. "Never mind that. Come in. Can you stay awhile?"

"Sure, awhile. I don't want to tire you."

Nicole made a wry face. "If I fall asleep, just kick me."

She began to walk back through the house, turning her head to talk to Mimi. "I'm sitting out back, in the shade. A little bloated from the heat. Can't take the sun. Okay?" Her voice was deeper and scratchy, from all the painkillers.

"Fine," Mimi said.

Mimi saw with a kind of creeping horror that Nicole moved so slowly because her legs and feet were swollen to inhuman proportions. They looked like elephant legs. She did not know how Nicole could even stand on them. But by the time they got to the back patio she had managed to avert her eyes, and Nicole carefully arranged the long white gown over herself, knees up, so that not even her swollen toes peeked out. She leaned back in the chair and shut her eyes. "Better," she said. Then she opened them again. "All the better to see you with, my dear."

Mimi started to say something. She struggled to get the first word out.

Nicole held up one hand. Her hands were not swollen. In fact, her wedding ring hung loose, almost to the knuckle. "None of that," she said. "How's Julian?"

"Oh, Julian." Mimi smiled. "Julian is into magic these days. He likes making things appear and disappear."

"Not surprising," said Nicole. "You shouldn't keep him away from Daisy so much. You can't do that anymore."

"I won't," Mimi said. Tears sprang into her eyes again.

"A couple of times a week they pump the fluid out of my lungs," Nicole said. "So I won't drown."

Mimi nodded, her eyes wide.

"Tell me a joke," Nicole said.

"What kind of joke?"

"A new one," Nicole said. "Something with a kid in it. And a happy ending."

"Okay," Mimi said. She took a minute to think. "A child."

"Okay," she said again. "So little Shmuley is at the edge of the ocean with his grandma, playing."

"I love the name Shmuley," Nicole said. "Good."

"Suddenly a great wave comes along and sweeps him far out to sea. His grandmother drops to her knees and begins praying—'Lord, Lord, bring my Shmuley back! Please God, he's just a little boy and I was supposed to be watching him.'

"Bam! Another wave lifts little Shmuley up in the air and deposits him right at the grandmother's feet.

"She puts her hands on her hips and looks up at the sky.

"'He had a *hat*!' she calls."

"A hat," Nicole said, wiping her eyes. "It's true—he had a hat. That's great." She picked up a giant pair of sunglasses and put them on. "You want anything to drink?" she asked.

Mimi thought about it. "Maybe a glass of water?" she said.

Nicole startled, her arms and legs twitching. Obviously she had fallen asleep.

"Never mind," Mimi said. "I'll get it myself."

She walked into the kitchen where she had visited so many times, so many hours. They had repapered the walls. Gone were the old-fashioned horses and carriages that used to line the kitchen. Mimi could remember standing there a dozen times, trying to count them, and always losing track, watching Nicole cook, helping her get ready for a meal. Horses with plumes, she seemed to remember. It looked like a scene from "Over the River and Through the Woods" repeated countless times, stamped over and over and over. Mimi found the giant three-gallon tank of spring water sitting on its wooden cradle and poured water into a plastic cup sitting in the drainer by the sink.

When she softly slid the glass door open and shut, Nicole didn't move. Mimi wasn't sure if she was awake or asleep.

"I'm awake," Nicole said, as if reading her mind.

"How are you?" Mimi said. "Am I allowed to ask?"

Nicole considered. Her face got the thoughtful, schoolmarmish look she often wore before she pronounced on some book she was reading, some movie they had seen. She put one finger through the simple gold necklace she wore around her neck, with a Jewish star on it. "God's leash is on me," she said.

Mimi did not answer. Nicole would hate it if she started crying now. "Where's Daisy?" Mimi asked. "I brought her a little gift." She began rummaging around in her purse.

"Horse camp this week," Nicole said. "She's crazy about horses. Crazy about all animals. I think she likes them better than people. —That reminds me of the joke about Laddie. Can you tell it?"

"Which one?"

"The one about the dead father," Nicole said.

"I don't know it," Mimi said.

"Sure you do," said Nicole. "This little girl's father dies. The mother sits her down, and the daughter is inconsolable. Weeping and wailing, won't stop. Won't come out of her room. Finally, at dinnertime, her mother knocks on her door and says, 'Sweetie, I know you're upset, but Daddy would have wanted you to go on with your life.'

"The girl steps out, radiant. "Daddy died?' she says. 'Daddy? I thought you said *Laddie!*'"

"That is awful," Mimi said. "That is sick."

"Ah. Glad you like it." Nicole bowed her head modestly. She kept her head down. "If I call you very late one night," she said, out of the blue, "will you take me to the beach?"

"Sure." Mimi was startled. "Late at night?"

"At dawn really. I'd like to see the ocean with the sun rising over it. Jay thinks it will wear me out. Well, he's right. But it probably won't kill me." She wet her lips. "—You know, in the *Divine Comedy*, Dante and Virgil reach the wall of flame after Purgatory. It's like walking through molten glass, Virgil tells Dante, he'll feel his bones melting. But he's got to walk through to get to Beatrice. —You remember Beatrice?"

"Some girl he loves?" Mimi says.

"He fell in love with her when she was eight years old and he was nine. She was wearing a red dress. But she married some rich Italian dude. So now she's dead and in heaven. And Dante's got to walk through the wall of fire to reach her, and he asks Virgil if it will hurt." Nikki set down the glass of water inside its own wet circle, on the little metal table beside her. It seemed she was done talking.

"And?" Mimi asked, despite herself.

"Hang on," Nicole said. She picked up the glass and took a sip. "I have these sores all over my throat. One of the things they don't warn you about." She made a pained face.

"You don't have to talk," Mimi said. "I'll take you to the beach no matter what."

"So Virgil tells him, 'It will hurt, but it won't kill you.'"

Mimi laughed uncertainly.

"It *is* a kind of joke. But the beach won't kill me."

"The beach won't kill you." Mimi parroted, like a lesson she was trying to learn by heart.

"And if she dies, she dies." Nicole laughed without making a sound.

———

At four o'clock the siren went off at the fire station four blocks away, same as it did every afternoon. Nicole had dropped off to sleep and she woke with a start, kicking the book at her feet. Mimi bent down and handed it to her. "I'll go," Mimi said. "Can I come back tomorrow?"

Nicole flapped one hand. "Sure. Anytime."

Mimi got up. "You don't have to see me to the door."

"No," Nicole said. "How is Ari? Will you give him my love? Please. Tell him he can stop worrying."

"I can't," Mimi said.

Nicole raised her eyebrows. "Why not?"

"He's not there anymore," Mimi said. "I moved out."

"Oh, no," Nicole said. She shook her head. "Oh." She lifted her head, as if it weighed too much to lift very far. "Because of me?" she asked.

"You and—oh, lots of things," Mimi said. "It's never just one thing. You know that, Nikki. The court case was just the last straw. I asked Julian not to tell Daisy. It's been hard for him to keep it from her."

"I'm sorry," Nicole said.

"I'm not," Mimi said firmly.

"Who has Julian and Anna?"

Mimi's face hardened. "We share them," she said. "The baby's too young to know how she feels. But Julian definitely prefers being with me. We're trying to get Ari to agree to just one or two days a week."

"Poor Ari," Nicole said. "Ever since he was a kid, no one liked him best."

"He does all right," Mimi said.

"You wouldn't want to be Ari," Nicole said. "No one would. Including Ari." She shifted position, slowly and uncomfortably, fumbling at the small table beside her chair. She held something out to Mimi. "Hey," Nicole said. "Put your number back on speed dial on my cell phone."

Mimi looked at her quizzically.

"Jay erased it," Nicole said. "I didn't. I wouldn't."

Mimi put it back in, quickly, her fingers unexpectedly trembling.

"Now I can call you fast," Nicole said.

"Anytime."

"It'll be late," Nicole said. "And it might not be easy."

"That's all right."

"It will hurt, but it won't kill you," Nicole reminded her.

———

It was the start of July when Teddy and Abigail set off for New England, one of those perfect blue-skied days that people sing about. It felt as if summer had already come and gone. Memorial Day weekend the temperature shot up to over a hundred degrees. Today was breezy and cool by comparison, and they drove with the windows down once they got past the George Washington Bridge and were safely headed up Interstate 95, Teddy blithely, Abigail with a secret worry. She had done this ridiculous thing, and she did not know how to begin to discuss it.

Teddy—she still thought of him as Rabbi Lewin, but he had asked her not to call him that—was humming under his breath. His tie was loosened, his yarmulke flapped a little on the back of his head, in the breeze, as if performing an independent dance.

"You look happy," she said.

"I *am* happy," he said. "Whenever I escape the city, I feel as if I've triumphed over some great force. Like Jacob wrestling all night with the angel. 'I will not let Thee go except Thou bless me.'"

"He sounds like a tough guy," she said, thinking of her own cowardice.

"Jacob is powerful, all right. Maybe the greatest of all the patriarchs— and we're going to see his pillow tonight."

They had tickets that night at Jacob's Pillow. This reminded Abigail of what lay ahead. Just about two hours ahead. She took a deep breath.

"You know the hotel we're going to?" she said.

"Yes," he said. "Well, not personally."

"I canceled my room," she said.

"Canceled?" He turned his head sharply to look at her. "You're not spending the night? You decided to go back home?" He sounded distressed. This gave her hope.

"No," she said. "But I thought—" Be a big girl, she told herself. You got yourself into this. "I thought we could share a room. It would spare you the expense. Those places are expensive." She was babbling now. "I mean, we don't have to do anything. We could just, you know, cuddle or hold hands or something."

He laughed. "Or something." His big hand landed on her knee, as if he needed to reassure himself that she was really there. "Abigail, Abigail," he said in his gentle voice.

After another minute or two he said, "You already called them and canceled the room?"

"I'm sorry. I should have talked to you about it first."

He nodded. He still hadn't moved his hand. Now he patted her leg and moved his hand back to the steering wheel. He had olive-colored skin, and his hand looked even darker against the bright white cuff of his shirtsleeve. "I will not let Thee go except Thou bless me," he said.

They held hands all during the dance concert, the first extended physical contact between them. It could have been the effect of the summer night, the full moon, the hypnotic effect of the bright dreamlike dancers moving sinuously against the darkness, but his hand felt almost electric clasping hers. He was not one of those men whose hands grew clammy after a few minutes, nor was he the kind who felt he had to keep his hand moving to prove he was still there, rubbing her hand or constantly changing position. She felt almost faint.

Back at the room, their now-shared room—the hotel was fully booked by now—he kissed her before they had even gotten the door open. She had supposed he would be shy and abashed, the way she pictured all rabbis. He was neither one. He opened the door as if he was slicing it in half, with one swipe of the key card, and then he pulled her in after him. Even the way he did this made her go weak in the knees. He was so much taller than she was, smiling down at her, his brown eyes for once looking not at all tired.

"You have no idea how long I've wanted to be with you," he told her.

"Really?" she said. She hoped her voice had not just squeaked.

"Love at first sight," he said, tracing her lips with the tip of his finger. "I could hardly believe my luck when I saw you coming out of the syna-gogue apartment. You and that beautiful little baby in your arms. Your hair looked like it was burning against the snow. I said a quick *barucha* to thank God for his good taste in tenants. —But." He pulled her down gently so she was sitting next to him on the bed. "Here's the thing," he said.

Her heart sank.

"I don't fool around," he said.

"I'm sorry to hear that," she said, trying to smile.

"No, I mean it," he said. "I'm no good at being casual. And I don't want to be. I'm not going to sleep with you unless we're married."

"Married? You're kidding," she said.

"I'm dead serious." He turned sideways on the bed to face her, still clasping her hand. "And I'm not asking right this minute. Just tell me this: Would you even consider it?"

She looked at her hand, held between both of his. "I think I already have," she said.

He drew the hotel room coverlet over both of them. His black shoes stuck over the edge of the bed. He examined the shape their two clasped hands made, front and back. He looked around the room, as if seeing it for the first time. One bedside lamp was burning.

"God was in this place and I, I did not know it," he said.

She laughed. "Do you see God in absolutely everything?" she said.

"Yes. —But I was quoting Jacob again."

"Where was the place?" she asked.

"Do you know how beautiful you are?" he asked. "Seriously stunning. I have no idea why you're here with someone like me."

"Quit changing the subject," she said.

"This too is Torah, and I must learn," he said.

"What?"

"I'll tell you another time." He released her hand. "Jacob fell asleep on a stone pillow at Mount Moriah and saw a host of angels on a ladder. Some were climbing up and others climbing down. God was watching from above, and Jacob from below. Some say the ladder represents prayer—connecting us to God. Some say it's a vision of the twofold nature of the world."

"And you?" Abigail said. "What do you think?"

He reached out and touched her cheek. "I think the ladder is a bridge, connecting all the worlds. The world of action, the world of formation, the world of creation, and the world of intimacy. —Do you know that according to kabbalah, each time a man and woman make love, they create a child? It may only be in the spiritual realm, never the physical, but still— you want to be aware of the kind of offspring you are making."

"Do you really believe all that?" she asked.

"I do," he said. "Do you believe any of it?"

"Possibly," she said. "A little."

He spoke softly, as if he sensed she was falling asleep, which in fact she was. "When Jacob awoke, he said, 'God was in this place and I, I did not know it.'"

"That's beautiful," she said, her eyes slowly falling shut. With her eyes still closed, she asked, "Why did he say the word *I* twice?"

Teddy laughed. "You're a good student, like your mother. Well, there are lots of theories, and you need your rest."

"Okay," she said.

He reached over her and switched off the lamp on her side of the bed. She felt the darkness as a kind of coolness entering the room, since she did not bother to open her eyes. In the new dark, she felt the man at her side still looking at her.

"I'm not the self I was before Iris," she finally said. "So when Jacob wakes from the dream maybe he's become a new person. A new I. 'God was in this place and I, I did not know it.'"

He lifted her hand and kissed the inside of her wrist.

"Tell me the truth," she said. "Did you know we'd end up in the same room like this?"

"Like this?" he echoed. "No. Absolutely not. But I prayed to God, and was hopeful in my soul."

"Who said that?" she asked.

He squeezed her hand. "I did."

AUGUST 2012

The Last Time

The phone call came at 1:00 a.m. on a summer's night. The phone shrilled next to Mimi's sleeping head, in harmony with the deeper-toned phone downstairs in the kitchen. The whole house seemed to reverberate from the sound, as if from a fire alarm going off.

"Mimi?" the voice said. "You awake?"

It was Nicole's voice—her new, rougher, octave-deeper husky voice, slurred from the effects of the morphine.

"I am now," Mimi said. She shook her head hard to make it true. "I'm awake."

"It's time," Nicole said. "You sure?"

"Absolutely," Mimi said.

"It's perfect," said Nicole. "Full moon, stars, the works."

"I'll be over right away."

"Good," said Nicole. Then, "Thank you," and she hung up.

Mimi opened Rianna's door and peeked in. She left the door open a crack as she exited. Then she went into Julian's room and woke him. "Listen, honey, I'm going out for a little while." He blinked at her sleepily.

"How come?" he asked.

"Aunt Nicole needs me."

"Oh. Okay," he said, and closed his eyes again so that she wasn't absolutely sure he had heard her. But then he added, "Is she dying?"

"No," she said. "At least I hope not. Not right this minute."

"Okay," he said again.

"Keep an ear out for the baby," Mimi said. "She'll probably sleep through the night. But just in case, I'll leave a bottle of soy milk out, and you can always give her some of those little oyster crackers. But don't let her stay awake or she won't go back to sleep. I won't be gone long. You have my cell number. Call if you need me."

"Will do," he said. He reached out his long fingers and touched the back of her hand. "Mom?" he said.

"What?"

"Drive carefully, okay?"

"I will."

"And give Daisy a kiss for me if you can—and Aunt Nicole."

"Do you want me to wake you when I get back in?"

"No." He yawned hugely. "I'll be asleep."

———•———

Nicole was waiting out by the front door, a canvas beach bag in her hand. She wore a long caftan and, over that, a light cotton sweater. "Blanket, towels, morphine patch," she said. "Ideal midnight picnic at the beach."

"How about a flashlight?" Mimi asked.

"Good idea." Nicole went back into the kitchen, rummaged through a drawer, and was back after a few minutes. She moved very slowly these days.

"Do you want to leave a note for Jay?"

"Done," Nicole said, nodding toward the kitchen. "I left the light on so he'd find it before he could get scared. It's funny," she added. "I used to think nothing could frighten him. And I turn out to be the most terrifying thing."

Mimi helped her swing her swollen legs into the car. "Windows down?" she asked. Nicole nodded. How many times had they driven to the beach in summer, Nicole with her beautiful head thrown back, threads of red hair blowing in the wind, her feet out the window. Now she just sat slumped in the passenger seat, her head turned, smiling out at the night.

Mimi did not have to ask where they were going. Nicole's favorite beach was in Oyster Bay, a small private beach that closed at sundown and in any event was reserved for residents of Oyster Bay with the proper stickers on their car windows. But at this hour it wouldn't matter. The town beach was so far off the beaten path that no one bothered to fence it in, and the Oyster Bay cops had better things to do than chase down the few souls who ventured there at this hour. Yet strangely, when they finally got there—gliding over back roads as if they were made of black glass, no traffic this time of night, even the changing green and red streetlights seeming superfluous—the beach was roped off, like the entrance to a movie theater, blocked by a heavy metal chain. Mimi grabbed the flashlight and hopped out to investigate. The chain had a large lobster-claw clasp at one side. All she had to do was open it and drag the chain over to the other side. Then she drove through and refastened the chain. Theirs was the only car in the small parking lot.

"Come on," Nicole said. She got out of the car and hobbled straight down the hill toward the water. Mimi was suddenly afraid she might not stop when she got to the edge. What would she do if Nicole tried to drown herself? What if she loaded down her pockets with stones like Virginia Woolf and waded into the bay? Would Mimi have the courage—or the cruelty—to drag her back? But Nicole's voice came echoing back from the beach, and gravelly and hoarse as it was, it was a happy cry. "Hurry!" she called.

As soon as Mimi got fifty yards from the water, a fog rose around her. She could feel it swirling on her face. "Where are you?" she said. The flashlight was worse than useless. It bounced the light straight back into her eyes.

"Just follow my voice," Nicole said. Then she made her voice higher and squeaky. "Follow the yellow brick road. Follow the yellow brick road." Because of the roughness in her new voice she really sounded like a Munchkin.

Mimi slid and slipped down the sound. She nearly fell over Nicole. "Lions and tigers and bears, oh my," she said.

"Sit," ordered Nicole.

Mimi sat. Nicole had spread out the blanket and anchored it down with stones, with her slip-on shoes, with the edge of the canvas bag holding the rolled-up towels.

"Want to swim?" Nicole asked.

Mimi shivered. "Do you?"

"Absolutely not," said Nicole. "I may be dying, but I'm not crazy."

Mimi tilted her head back. "It's funny," she said. "I can't see the beach, and I can barely see you, but I can see the moon, and even some bright stars. Why is that?"

Nicole shrugged. "You'd have to ask someone smarter than we are, like Julian. But I know those are planets, not stars."

"How do you know?"

"One, hours spent in planetariums. Two, they're too big and bright, and they don't twinkle."

At that instant a streak of light arced across the sky and seemed to fall straight into the dark blur of the bay.

"Now *that*," said Nicole, "was a star."

"A shooting star."

"I don't know what to wish for."

"I do," Mimi said quickly.

"No. Don't waste your wishes on that," said Nicole.

They sat for a few minutes in silence. The fog seemed to grow patchier, seemed to lift slightly, though maybe it was just their eyes growing used to the dark. The waves slapped lightly against the shore, splashing one-two, one-two.

"This is so nice," Nicole said finally. "I'm happy. Thank you for bringing me."

Mimi had to speak around the lump in her throat. "You know," she said, "we'll never forget this—the beach at night, that shooting star, the waves. We will always remember this." She could not bring herself to use the pronoun *I*, even if that's what she meant.

"I am remembering it now," said Nicole.

That was the last good night. Nicole's condition went down from there, gone out of control. Despite all their efforts, she had to be moved to the hospital, where she saw less of Daisy, to her sorrow and relief. Jay had been furious when they came home from the beach that night; of course he had wakened, and then waited for them to show up.

He waved the torn piece of paper on which she had scrawled "Gone out. Don't worry." He waved it over his head, his eyes wild. "What kind of a note is that? You call that a note? I was going out of my mind. What if you'd gone out to kill yourself?"

"What if I had?" Nicole said calmly. "I'd have left you a better note than that. Besides, Mimi was with me."

"A fact that you forgot to mention!"

"You're right," she said. "I'm sorry." She sank down into a kitchen chair. Her face looked puffy. "It was so beautiful out."

He kneeled before her, instantly contrite. "Was it?" he said. He sounded wistful.

She realized that he was angry mostly because it wasn't him she'd chosen to take along. "My great darling." She put her palm flat on the top of his soft hair. "You I love," she said. It was a joke between them. The engraver had gotten it wrong on their wedding rings, and instead of writing I love you, had engraved *You I love*. The misengraving had become a secret code between them.

"You *I* love," he'd said. "Now let's get you back to bed."

Now she never moved from her bed, except to stagger to the toilet and back, and sometimes not even for that. For two weeks now the pain had raged out of control, a wild animal that could not be tamed. Her lungs kept filling with fluid. She'd blow up like a balloon, and then they would have to pump the fluids from her body and she'd be all right for a day, maybe two. Only she was never really all right. She went from morphine-laced stupor to an agony that seemed centered in the middle of her body, an iron anchor that held her to the bed. She had only felt this kind of pain once before, in labor, during the transition phase, and then at the end of it she'd had little Daisy to hold in her arms. Soon she must let go of all holding.

———

Jay climbed into the hospital bed and clasped her hand. The night nurses were always kinder than the strict day nurses; they allowed this kind of thing. Nicole felt like the Woggle Bug in one of the later Oz books, parts of her stick-thin, other parts swollen. She could no longer stand to look in a mirror; she could hardly bear to have Daisy look at her, for fear her daughter might only remember her this way. Jay was running his thumb softly up and down the back of her hand. In the old days, that touch had been a prelude to lovemaking. She tried to turn toward him, but the mere shift of her body brought a jolt of pain like a stroke of lightning, and she lay flat again, watching his hand on her hand. Tears spurted to her eyes. "No more!" she cried out in her new hoarse voice. "No more!"

The days got worse, and longer. Finally, late one night, Aunt Patti, Jay, and Mimi all gathered in the room. Jay brought her chips of ice to suck; Mimi brought flowers; Aunt Patti had provided a music player that was now playing old Sinatra songs.

"Why is this taking so long?" Nicole asked.

"I have to break up the ice with this plastic knife," Jay said.

"That's not what I mean." Her words came slow, broken up by pain or morphine, or both. "Why is *this* taking so long? I'm ready. I'm ready to go."

"No, you're not," Jay said. He came over to the bed and leaned over her as if to do—something. Some act of rescue. Mimi and Aunt Patti turned toward her.

Nicole raised her voice. She was actually yelling. "I *am* ready—but you won't let me! None of you. Why won't you just let me go?"

"Easy now," Jay said.

"It's not easy—it's too hard. Why can't you let me go?"

"Oh, Nicole," said Mimi.

"Why won't someone help me? Why are you holding me here?"

Aunt Patti turned away from the music player. "We can help you," she said. "If that's what you really want."

"It's what I really want," answered Nicole.

———

A day or two later the judge received his strangest invitation yet in the mail. It was not an invitation to give a lecture, or to visit a foreign country, to contribute to a charity, or to teach a class. He had received all those invitations and more. This was an invitation to a funeral. It was the funeral of Nicole Greene, but under date and time were written the words "To Be Announced—please watch the papers." And she had signed it herself, in a loose raggedy scrawl.

"That is absolutely heartbreaking," Sarah said. "A woman sending out invitations to her own funeral."

Sol turned it over in his hands, as if the blank back of the card contained some secret message. It certainly was peculiar. "I think—" He hesitated. "She wanted to take her life into her own hands. I think that's what the trial was all about for her. And this"—he turned the card yet again—"is very generous. It's an act of forgiveness." He wondered if her cousin Ari Wiesenthal had gotten the same card.

He had not. But it was not because Nicole had not made one out—she had. And she had even added the words. "Please come." But when Jay saw the envelope, he confided to Mimi, "I just can't do it. I hope she'll forgive me. But if I saw him, I might just kill him. And Nikki wouldn't want me to go to jail for murdering her cousin."

Mimi patted his arm. "It's all right, Jay. Really, it is. You're carrying enough."

He wasn't so sure, but nonetheless he shredded the envelope into pieces, and threw them into the cafeteria garbage can, under mounds of cottage cheese and discarded salad, apple cores and half-drunk cartons of milk.

Daisy was sleeping over at her friend Claudia's house. Nicole sat propped up on pillows, watching them quickly, nervously tearing open the morphine patches. The late afternoon sun shone outside the window. All she could see was the line of traffic, red taillights glowing on the expressway nearby.

They were unwrapping all of the patches they had on hand. Plus the ones they had managed to squirrel away. Aunt Patti had been especially good at arguing for more, alternately charming and bullying the nurses, playing one shift off against another, accusing the hospital of incompetence. Nicole called, in her new, deep, hoarse voice, "Jay!"

He turned around. His face was so full of sadness, so full of fear.

She licked her chapped lips. She said, "I want you to know what I'm thinking."

He nodded, waiting for her to continue. Everyone else stopped their preparations a moment. Aunt Patti's hands were full of the morphine patches.

"After I gave birth to Daisy, I sent you home for clothes, remember? I gave you a list. And you brought me this crazy stuff. The red-striped maternity pants and pink top. And the wrong boots. I said, 'I'm not going anywhere in this outfit.' Remember?"

He nodded again.

"You went home for me, and brought back the things I wanted, and you never complained. You never said a word." Nicole's eyes filled with tears. "I was such a—stupid—vain—ridiculous." She shook her head hard, as if to clear it. "I was always so lucky! So lucky." She shut her eyes and reached out. His hand entirely enclosed hers, square and broad and muscular. An athlete's hand, still. Jay's hand. "I want that on my gravestone, 'She was lucky in love.' That's what I'm thinking. I want you to know—"
She must have fallen asleep, because it was another minute or two before she said, "Jay. I'm just running back home to get something. This time I'm going ahead of you."

"Don't go yet," Jay said.

Nicole nodded and closed her eyes again. This time she did not reopen them. He thought, Never in this life will I see those eyes again. He could not bring himself to move, or to let go of her hand.

Aunt Patti said, "Are you ready, doll?"

Nicole moved her head up and down on the pillow to nod yes. "We'd better hurry," Aunt Patti said, "before the nurse comes back and we all get arrested for murder. —Mimi, keep an eye on the door. If someone starts to come in, go out there in the hall and tell a joke. Try to make it funny for a change."

Mimi made a noise between a sob and a laugh. She placed herself at the door while Jay and Aunt Patti set to work applying the patches. "Hurry!" Aunt Patti said every minute or so. "Hand me two more." Mimi hurried over with the patches in her hand, set them on her friend's chest, on the V where the white skin shone translucent above the green hospital gown. She could still feel Nicole's breathing——but it was shallow. She pressed her hands down as if she could speak through her palms, as if she could say good-bye with just the weight of her hands against her best friend's heart. Then she went to stand guard at the door.

Nicole's chest burned; every breath was an agony, as if she were drowning. Her lungs were filling, her body was exhausted; she'd gone too far from shore. She heard from far off a babble of voices, sped up, slowed down, a warped record. Among them she made out the sound of a familiar loved voice, very close to her ear, a boy's voice, one she had come to know as well as her own. All its inflections were familiar, yet she could not name him. He murmured, "I've got you," but perhaps it wasn't that at all, perhaps it was someone else now saying, "I've got to," or a woman's voice saying, "You've got to—"

She smelled the sting of salt air. A hint of pine and raspberries. There was a thrilling buoyancy in her body. She felt herself rocked in an embrace that bobbed up and down in waves. She felt sun on her face, the warmth of it, though it must have been the hospital lights glaring down. The pain writhed inside her like a snake. And then it all stopped. As sudden as that. She had come up for air. Her pain disappeared as if it had been wiped off a slate. Nothing intervened with the sounds of the hospital room. For the first time ever she heard with absolutely perfect clarity, without even the interference of her own heart beating, blood rushing through her body. The relief was incredible. In that crystal stillness and calm, came the sound of her machines, making a new, loud noise, a ringing sound, a rustle of bodies, footsteps, and outside her window a bird sang once, two times.

A minute later Jay said, "I think it's over." Then, "We can take them off now. My darling. My poor darling. Look at her resting." They shoved the used morphine patches into Aunt Patti's enormous tapestry bag.

The room was filled with the strangest silence, Mimi thought, like falling into a well, a deep, stern, eerie silence, and then she realized what was missing—it was the sound of Nicole's labored breathing. And in the midst of that absolute silence, heartless Aunt Patti began to cry.

August 21–22, 2012
You Shall Not Boil a Kid in Its Mother's Milk.

Arthur's wife Ruth had joined the bat-mitzvah group because everyone else in her mah-jongg group was joining, and what was she supposed to do in the afternoons, sit at home and play solitaire? Then she threw herself bravely into the fray the way she did everything else. She and Sarah practiced Hebrew together out loud in the kitchen, Ruth braying the unfamiliar sounds at the top of her lungs.

"Alef, bet," Sarah would chant softly.

Ruth would reply with something that sounded vaguely like "Oy vey!"

"Alef, bet," Sarah repeated, enunciating each sound.

"Alphabet!"

Sol escaped to the safety of their bedroom and closed the door.

The philosophical discussions about religion were even worse.

"I don't get it," he overheard Ruth say one night. "What's with the free will?"

"So we can choose. We can choose good or evil."

"That means God has no say in the matter? So we're stronger than God?"

"No, Ruth, that's not it." Sarah paused to grapple with the idea herself. "God is all-powerful. If He stopped caring even for an instant, the whole universe would cease. Remember Rabbi Teddy telling us that?"

"Sort of," Ruth grumbled. "So if he's all-powerful and in charge, what does he care if we have free will or not?"

"Because he wants us to choose Him," Sarah said.

"Wants, like I want an ice cream cone?"

"I don't know," Sarah said. "*Do* you want an ice cream cone, Ruth? We can go to Baskin-Robbins."

"A lot of people choose evil," Ruth said. "Hitler. My neighbor who hits his dog. Seems like a lousy plan."

Sometimes Sol thought that this Rabbi Teddy must be a saint. Either that, or a complete fool. Often, he reminded himself, the two went hand in hand.

———

Sol stood at the back of the synagogue, where he could feel most invisible. Women and men—but mostly women—milled around like elderly children at a birthday party. There was a gigantic kosher cake with "Mazel Tov" written in pink frosted script. All the old bat-mitzvah women wore white blouses and blue skirts, an unofficial uniform, the colors of the Israeli flag. Ruth wore a too-tight white T-shirt and a too-short denim skirt. But she seemed diminished these days. She was anxious being apart from Arthur for even a few hours, and she didn't give Sol such a hard time anymore. "When push came to shove, you came through," she told Sol. "You could have knocked me over with a feather, the way you came through."

Arthur had lost thirty pounds since his illness. His cheekbones had grown prominent; his face and body had lost some of its eternal baby fat; he no longer even wore the gaudy rings—perhaps they had grown too loose on his fingers. It was his younger brother's face Sol saw; the way it had looked when he went off to the Korean War. Handsome, vulnerable. Arthur was smiling, looking around at everything with interest, as usual, chatting and laughing. His new passion was heart-healthy cooking, and he now threw himself into making vegetable broths as enthusiastically as he'd once gushed over chocolate tortes. The man was unquenchable. He held Ruth's hand as tightly as she held his, their fingers interlaced. When she walked off to talk to one of the other women about some last-minute detail, he watched her, and she never left an invisible circle she paced around him, close enough to reach out and touch him at any time.

Sol thought of the lines of some remembered poem:

Weave a circle round him thrice
And close your eyes with holy dread
For he on honey-dew hath fed
And drunk the milk of Paradise.

Rabbi Lewin gathered all the bat mitzvahs around him. There must have been thirty or forty women, none of them a day younger than sixty, but all smiling and blushing like teenagers. They ranged themselves on the stairs, lined up as if for a class photograph, according to height—all but Ruth, who squeezed her way to the front and winked at Arthur sitting in the front row, his camera clicking away. Someone else was videotaping the whole thing from the back of the synagogue. Sol had not brought a camera; he might have forgotten even to bring flowers, but luckily his daughter Abigail called and reminded him. He hung on to his bunch of roses for dear life, the green of the tissue paper starting to stain his fingers. He took a seat toward the back, near the aisle, but Sarah spotted him and smiled, cool as a cucumber.

Sol knew the drill; Sarah had talked him through it beforehand. Each of the women would read a few lines of the day's *parsha*, that week's Torah portion. This week's reading was *Re'eh* (Behold), Deuteronomy 11:26–16:17. It worked out well, she explained, because it contained so many of the laws set down for the Jewish people, divided into small sections. The more advanced students took the longer sections, the less advanced undertook the shorter. Each would read first in Hebrew with the rabbi standing close by, holding his silver Torah *yad*, or pointer, to help the woman find and keep her place. Sol slunk down in his seat, ready for a few extraordinarily tiresome hours, like those he'd spent at Abigail's school concerts—all except when his daughter was actually performing, of course, her red hair catching the light. "A nap like this you can't buy," Arthur used to tell him, settling in for the long nights of junior orchestra.

Sol tried to relax. Perhaps he was getting old and foolish. The assembled crowd was large, filled with family and friends. Each of the bat-mitzvah women seemed so touchingly earnest. Many stumbled over their Hebrew, and he heard the steady murmur of the rabbi's voice, coaching them. Some of them sounded lost even reading the English. But when it came time to speak their minds, they put their heart into it. If not always their brains, Sol thought.

"Behold," the first woman had said, after butchering the Hebrew opening. She was a heavy woman, part of Sarah's swim group at the JCC. Rolls of fat hung down from under her short-sleeved white blouse. "Behold, or see, look. It means we should open our senses and choose God. 'Behold, I set before you today a blessing or curse.' This *parsha* is not about punishment or reward, but about purpose. We have a purpose in this life, and every minute we can make bad choices or good ones. Today I feel I've made a good one." She smiled at the rabbi, who smiled encouragingly back.

And so it went, on down the line.

Ruth had the shortest portion of all, but she trumpeted it at the top of her enormous voice, first in Hebrew, then in English. Arthur was on the edge of his front row seat, camera up, clicking away, as if he had captured a movie star stepping onto the red carpet. "You *shall* not boil a *kid* in its *mother's* milk!"

"So!" Ruth went on. "A lot of people use this why not to eat a cheeseburger, or even chicken à la king. I don't personally see how a chicken could be the mother of a cow, but the rule is don't eat a baby goat boiled in its mother's milk. It's not nice and it sounds disgusting." She sat down, beaming, to a spatter of laughter and applause.

Sarah's portion was one of the longest, and she got through it without a hitch. She was a natural student of languages. She was fluent in French, German, Russian. She had picked up quite a bit of Thai by listening to books on tape. Now she translated the Hebrew passage. Her voice was calm, her chin uplifted. Sol caught a glimpse of the young female student he'd fallen in love with so many years ago, her arms loaded down with books. Her eyes, sharp, brown, and eager, sought his now as they had then, and his heart soared.

"If, however, there is a needy person among you, one of your kinsmen in any of your settlements in the land that the Lord God is giving you, do not harden your heart and shut your hand against your needy kinsman." He listened to the notes of her voice, and let the words wash over him. "Later in this *parshat* of Re'eh, Elaine Newmark will read about the need to help 'the Levite, the stranger, the fatherless and the widow in your midst.' These two passages are connected, as we are all connected. Family can form between people of no blood relation. Family, very simply, are the people to whom we feel most closely bound. Family is where we hold nothing back."

She squared her small shoulders. "In the world to come, we will find that we are all related, to the poor, the needy, the stranger, the fatherless and the widow. In this holy month of Elul, God draws close to us. We draw closer to him when we turn toward each other, recognize our kinship, and act accordingly." She sat down to warm applause. Somewhat to Sol's horror, the stranger sitting next to him in the pew pressed his hand. Up front, Arthur blew his nose, and Ruth said in her ringing voice, "I meant that, too!"

———·———

For the second time in two late August days, Sol attended a religious ceremony, trying to place himself where he would be least conspicuous. Because of him, a woman had died. Because of him, he stood at her funeral, the sun beating down on his bare head, bare except for the black yarmulke a familiar-looking boy had handed him. "Thank you for coming," the boy said, and as soon as he heard the voice he remembered: this was Ari Wiesenthal's son Julian, the boy who had testified in court against his father. The boy who knew what he did and didn't want. Now, as then, his voice sounded adult, and Sol responded as he would have to a fellow adult. "I'm very sorry for your loss," he said. The boy nodded politely, somberly, and moved on, handing a yarmulke to the next man in the crowd.

Sol looked around, but he did not spot Ari Wiesenthal anywhere. This did not surprise him, of course. He caught the eye of Peter Allister, Nicole's lawyer, and they nodded to one another. Then he did his best to fade against the backdrop of trees. Jonathan Swift, that most cynical of cynics, had written, "Vision is the art of seeing things invisible." He hoped there were no visionaries at this event.

A large crowd stood in the cemetery. When someone this young died, there was often an outpouring of grief from the community. Sol recognized only a few of the many faces. He did not know the rabbi, thin and blond, not as solid as that Teddy Lewin fellow. The rabbinate seemed to be growing younger every year. Maybe they just grew quickly in the Long Island soil, cropping up in the place of potatoes. Of course the traffic had been horrendous— a Sunday morning in August, heading east to the beaches of the Hamptons. Traffic, like death and taxes, was inevitable. Things invisible, things inevitable.

Sol had sent a check to the charity listed in *Newsday* in Nicole's obituary. Blood money. A fund to help poor children get educational opportunities. He knew it wasn't enough—as much as it was, it wasn't close to enough. He decided to volunteer as a reading tutor at their local elementary school. These were tiny steps, but he must try to make amends. If you ever gave up trying to change and improve yourself, you were finished, kaput. He remembered the last conversation he'd had with Tom Lieu, before he left the Supreme Court for good. It was late in the day; Lieu was alone, for a change.

"I wish I had done better," Sol confided in Tom. "I wish I had done more, and I wish I'd followed your advice on this last case. It was a no-win situation."

Lieu tried to wave this last bit away. "Let it go," he said to Sol. "Do better next time."

"What next time? There is no next time."

"There is always a next time," Tom had said, stirring the sugar into his iced tea with a pleasant, chiming sound.

"I'm too much of a perfectionist," Sol had admitted.

"Everything is already perfect. Everything and everyone."

Sol wouldn't have expected such a Buddha-like statement from the practical Judge Lieu. "Really?" he said. "How about Pescatori?"

Lieu smiled. "Pescatori is a perfect asshole," he said.

Sol nearly laughed out loud at the memory, but quickly caught himself. You don't laugh at funerals unless you want to be thrown out on your behind.

But a few minutes later everyone in the somber-hued crowd was laughing at something the short, dark-haired woman was saying in eulogy to the dead. The young boy stood right next to her, and they looked enough alike that Sol realized they must be mother and son. The judge was standing too far away to hear anything more than the murmur of words, like the rise and fall of the sea. Maybe Sarah was right, he did need a hearing aid. He'd been told that years before, but thought it would look terrible on a Supreme Court judge. Justice was supposed to be blind, not deaf. Now he could relax, admit he couldn't hear as well as he used to.

The woman, with tears in her eyes, a face that the judge could see was constricted with pain, kept on making the crowd laugh. They were laughing and crying, but mostly laughing, a few people actually holding their stomachs. You'd have thought she was a professional comic.

When the boy, her son, stepped up to say a few words, everyone started sobbing again. If you were watching from another planet, you'd have thought these people were insane—laughing one minute, sobbing the next. There was a little girl hanging on to the boy's hand even as he spoke. She looked so much like Abigail as a child from the back, the judge caught his breath. He felt rooted to the spot, a man gazing at his own past. Her bright hair caught the light, like strands of brilliant copper wire. He was glad he could not see her face; he did not know how much more of this he could bear. But he would bear it for the sake of the woman who had borne more, and he vowed again to perfect himself—and not to become a perfect asshole.

Ari had found a place above the graveyard in which to hide. It was a cliff overgrown with trees and brambles and high grass. He'd had to climb up the far side and claw his way through dense vegetation and buzzing insects to reach this vantage point, but it was perfect. He could see but not be seen. He could hear without being heard. He had worn a black suit in case he had the courage to show up at the funeral itself, but of course he had not, and now it was soaked with sweat, stained green with grass, all but ruined. Its blackness seemed to draw the sunlight directly into the fibers of the cloth. He envied those below who stood beneath a white tent, in its cool shadow. Hanging on to the trunk of a tree, edging as close as he could to the edge of the cliff, he felt like one of those wild outcast characters from the Bible. Esau. Ishmael. Cain. Am I my brother's keeper?

The press had been relentless once Nicole died. They'd called his house a dozen times, till he seriously considered pulling the phone out of the wall. How do you feel about the death of your cousin? I feel terrible, I feel like throwing up, he told one reporter, till he'd decided to stop answering the phone altogether. How did they think he would feel—happy? Relieved? He was not a monster, even if he looked like one, in his ruined black suit, hunched over a cliff, gazing down on everyone he loved. His mother was there, in a ludicrous wide-brimmed black straw hat. His ex-wife, his son, even his daughter, since they had decided Arianna was too young to understand what was going on. He was not convinced. He had once read that by the age of four human beings have undergone every emotion they will ever feel for the rest of their lives—rage, joy, desire, abandonment, hope. He believed that was true. He had felt all these things and more. But no one consulted him. He had lost the only power he'd ever really cared about, the power to watch over the people he loved.

The rabbi was speaking in praise of the dead. A devoted wife and mother, a beloved teacher, valued member of her community. He did not especially recognize his cousin Nicole in any of these words. He remembered her best as Nikki, her childhood nickname. He remembered his red-haired cousin, beautiful, noisy, alive, skinny, unpredictable, brave. A child. His baby cousin. Not a grown woman. Never one of the dead.

The rabbi said, "In the words of Rabbi Menachem Mendel of Kotzk, 'There are few things as crooked as the straight face of a con-artist. There is nothing blacker than the white garments in which a corpse is dressed. And there is nothing more complete than a broken heart.'"

The rabbi began to recite kaddish in Hebrew, the prayer for the dead. Ari knew all the words. He had been at the top of his Hebrew School class;

he still had a sterling-silver-and-blue-enamel circle pin somewhere to prove it. The teacher had said, Maybe you'll grow up to be a rabbi, or at least a cantor, and even then Ari had thought, Yeah, sure. And live on less than nothing, and kiss the behind of every wealthy congregant. But he had nodded, as if he were giving it serious thought.

The words of the kaddish came to him automatically, words praising God. "Blessed, praised, glorified, exalted." If ever there was a moment he was in no mood to praise God, here it was, at his cousin Nikki's funeral. "Extolled, honored, elevated..." Ari wanted to throw rocks down at the rabbi, just to shut him up. He focused on the sound of the wind hissing through the leafy trees, blowing a burning breath through every desiccated blade of summer grass. He clung to the tree trunk and shut his eyes, listening. It sounded like waves, breaking and crashing on shore, the rhythm of a heartbeat. He saw his little red-haired cousin Nikki floating on one of those foam kickboards, at the edge of the vast ocean. It was decorated with hearts and dolphins. She was near enough to touch, and then she headed out, her slim legs vigorously kicking. None of the adults seemed to be paying any attention. Only Ari kept an eye on her. Nikki's mother lay with her eyes closed, behind one of those shiny three-paneled sun reflectors meant to intensify the sunlight—before anyone knew how deadly that was. The reflector lay fallen on her chest like the shield of a warrior. Ari's father was rubbing white sunscreen into his mother's back.

"Nikki, be careful!" Ari called.

She glanced back at him, her eyes darker than the water around her, and waved with one hand. As she did so, the board skidded out of her reach, and she started to swim after it, awkwardly. She had only really learned how to swim that summer. Before that she would just pretend to swim, setting her elbows down into the sand and poking her way along the shore like a crab.

"Let it go!" he called. He was nearly eight, she was not yet five. His bathing trunks were already dry from the wind, the water was cold, he didn't want to have to go back in there so soon.

She shook her head and kept swimming. "I'm fine!" she called back. And she did seem to be fine. The kickboard teased her, bobbing within an inch of her reaching fingers, then lurching forward again, swaying back and swinging away. She followed it out, her strokes surprisingly strong for such a little girl. She was already a better athlete than he was. She swam for quite a long time, and finally caught the board. He wanted to applaud. She was amazing, she was beautiful, and she was his cousin, his own flesh and blood. She turned the board around and began to head back for shore. He stood watching with his fists on his hips. Then the board escaped her again, darted up into the air and bounced away. Nikki looked at it, then straight at Ari. Her expression was unreadable at this distance. She treaded water for about a minute, and then went under. She came up sputtering, her arms flailing in panic, tried to swim forward, went under again.

Ari ran straight into the water. He was not a great swimmer, but he was strong. He kept his head out of the water while he did the crawl so he could watch her. He'd taken junior lifesaving classes at summer camp, and his head was surprisingly cool and clear. He called, "Hang on, I'm coming to get you!"

He seemed to be swimming in slow motion, as if in a dream, it took so long to reach Nikki. He watched her go under twice more, each time taking a little longer to bob back to the surface, a cork in a blue-and-purple-striped bathing suit. He headed straight for her, pulling his arms through the water with all his might, methodically slicing his way to her. His heart pumped so hard his chest hurt. When he reached her, he gasped, "I've got you!" and he caught her sharp little jaw in the crook of his arm and started to swim back to shore, the way he'd been taught. She did not struggle the way he'd been told drowning people do; she did not try to pull him under. She seemed to relax a little in his arm. He made sure her head was always above water, that she could breathe. He kept reassuring her, "I've got you, we're almost there. We're almost there."

When she was only a few days old, and he was not yet three, they had taken him to the hospital and laid her in his arms. She writhed like a snake. "Good muscle tone!" her father had laughed. She felt a bit like that now, so light, but so alive, every part of her body rippling, half in and half out of the water. As if she wanted to return to her liquid element. Well, he would not let her go. She was his flesh and blood. He claimed her. He would drag her back to earth. He swam all the way to shore, and even when he was sure her feet could touch the sand, he carried her in his arms. He expected to see crowds cheering on the beach, roaring approval and amazement at their safe return, but no one even looked up—just one heavyset woman who seemed to see nothing more than a big cousin carrying his little cousin. She smiled benignly. None of the parents had stopped what they were doing. There were no lifeguards at this end of the beach. What had just happened could not have taken more than five or six minutes, though it felt to Ari like a lifetime.

He hunkered down at the edge of the cliff now, a sweat-soaked adult, holding the tree trunk as if he still held his little cousin in his arms. The sound of the waves and wind rustled all around. The sun beat down on his head. "I'm not ever going to let you go." He pushed her wet hair out of her eyes, long coppery strands out of the way of her mouth and cheek. She was gasping for breath, but she was looking up into his face, smiling. He bent and kissed her salty cheek. He rocked her back and forth in his arms. "I've got you, I've got you," he said. "I'm not ever going to let anything terrible happen to you, ever." She nodded. He bent and kissed her wet bony forehead. "Never, ever." The wind sang in their ears, a promise.

ABOUT THE AUTHOR

Liz Rosenberg was born in Glen Cove, New York. She has written more than thirty books for adults and young readers, including novels, poetry, and nonfiction. For the past fifteen years she has been a book review columnist at *The Boston Globe*. Liz teaches at the State University of New York at Binghamton where she won the Chancellor's Award for Excellence in Teaching. Her first husband was the late novelist John Gardner, author of *Grendel*. She lives in Binghamton, New York, with her husband, David, her daughter, Lily, and two shih tzus. Her son, Eli, lives in New York City and works as an actor and magician.